ST. MARTIN'S PAPERBACKS TITLES
BY LESLIE LAFOY

THE
Duke's
Proposal

LESLIE LaFoy

St. Martin's Paperbacks

This is a work of fiction. All of the characters, organizations, and events portrayed in this novel are either products of the author's imagination or are used fictitiously.

THE DUKE'S PROPOSAL

Copyright © 2007 by Leslie LaFoy.

Cover photo © Shirley Green

ISBN: 0-312-34772-3
EAN: 978-0-312-34772-7

Printed in the United States of America

St. Martin's Paperbacks edition / May 2007

St. Martin's Paperbacks are published by St. Martin's Press, 175 Fifth Avenue, New York, NY 10010.

10 9 8 7 6 5 4 3 2 1

THE
Duke's
Proposal

Chapter One

D uty is such a bore."

The orchestra swept into a waltz and Harry lifted his glass of champagne to reply over the sounds of merriment, "Which is, I suppose, why they call it duty and not a grand old time."

Ian Cabott looked over the crowd, over the brilliantly lit ballroom, and couldn't see one person who appeared to be genuinely happy, or a single bit of decor that had been done for any reason other than to impress. A grand old time the London Season was not. It was serious business.

Business in which he was duty bound to engage with great fervor, a keen eye, and laudable success. He was a duke: an elevated member of the elevated class. The very foundations of the Empire rested on his ability to properly select an appropriately pedigreed wife and then successfully breed a new generation of Cabotts to shoulder the duties of wealth and privilege and political power.

He'd rather have a boil lanced. Or, more appropriately, be lancing boils. Or sewing back together a mangled soldier. The only casualties likely to be seen in tonight's gathering were a busted gut or two after dinner. The entire affair was an utter waste of his time, not to mention his medical skills.

But he'd promised his mother that he'd end the Season with an announcement of his pending marriage; and a promise, shortsighted and overly optimistic as it was, was a promise.

"Who are this evening's desperately hopeful?" he asked his cousin. *Other than myself.*

Harry sighed the sigh of saints and shook his head. "If you would make just half an effort to remember names, we wouldn't have to go through this at every social affair."

Ian snorted. "In the first place," he countered, "if any of these people were memorable, it wouldn't be a problem. But they're not. And in the second, if we didn't have to go through this, what would I need you for?"

"Good point," Harry allowed, grinning and saluting him with the champagne glass again. "Over by the center door leading to the balcony."

Ian looked. Dutifully. "I see three young ladies and a horse."

"The horse," Harry said dryly, "is Lady Edith, the daughter of Viscount Shaddock. This is her third Season."

"It won't be her last."

"Oh, I don't know," Harry drawled. "Her dowry is rumored to be huge."

It would have to be. "Just out of truly idle curiosity . . . how huge?"

"Staggeringly. Property *and* thousands of pounds."

Ian cocked a brow and sipped his champagne. "A purchased husband being better than none at all." His gaze skimmed the other corseted curves in Lady . . . whoever's group. "Who are the women with her?"

"The creature in the peacock headdress is Lady Sylvia, daughter of Viscount Wiston. This is her first season."

The *gigantic* peacock headdress. "Her attributes?" *Obviously not a demure fashion sense.*

"A reasonable dowry," his cousin supplied. "She is reportedly very good at making a pence do the work of a pound."

Which suggested that somewhere someone had a dazed and embarrassingly bald peacock running around their garden. "Negatives?"

"I believe that the expression has something to do with being able to eat an apple through a picket fence. She also seems to lack a sense of appropriateness when it comes to being frugal. In case you haven't been paying attention, which I sincerely doubt that you have, that's the third time she's worn that particular ball gown this Season. The feathers, however, are new this evening. I'm sure we'll see them another half dozen times before the week is out."

Not if the peacock tracked her down and exacted

revenge. "Who's the one beside her wearing the floral wreath across her torso?"

"Lady Sarah, daughter of Baron Heathwhite. In her second Season."

"Her positives?"

"I would have to say that it's largely optimism. Not much of a dowry to speak of. The barony was a grant from the Queen, reportedly for some minor miracle he performed in the Foreign Office while assigned to New South Wales. She's been sent back to snag a titled husband before the ink fades on the grant and her family goes back to the ignobility of being gentry. As I recall, she's under the sponsorship of Lady Atwell."

A brunette. Pleasingly tall, but not terribly big boned. "She's not unattractive." If she were to lose the silk floral wreath, she'd look considerably better. Not quite so much like the winning Arab at Ascot.

"True," Harry allowed after a sip of his drink. "But she's not a beauty, either. And, to be perfectly honest about it, having not been born to the peerage, she's lacking a natural social grace."

He could think of a good number of women who had been born to the peerage about whom the same thing could be said. Not that he could tell anyone their names. "And the other one?"

"Lady Anne, I believe," Harry said, squinting and leaning slightly forward—as though the few extra millimeters would make a difference in the clarity. "I think that one's father is the Marquis of Ditmoor."

Ah, yes. He remembered how his mother had always cringed when the Ditmoors' carriage had rolled up the drive for a house party. They were first to arrive and the very, very last to leave. In between they ate as though there were no tomorrow, imposed on everyone else's servants, and generally wallowed in the hospitality and luxury they couldn't afford for themselves. "Land rich, pocket poor," he murmured, quoting his father.

"That's what I've heard," his cousin replied. "She's looking to marry well so her papa has new pockets to rifle. Not that the odds of success are good. She's the second daughter and with a younger brother who'll actually inherit the title. Which is about all the poor blighter will get at the end of things."

And continue the family tradition of sponging off the social generosity required of others. Having exhausted the possibilities in that little feminine knot, he looked beyond it. "In the yellow dress over by the punch bowl."

Again Harry sighed. This time not sounding nearly as saintly as he had before. "You danced with her at Lady Atwell's ball. She's the one who is directly descended from Charlemagne. Remember?"

God, yes. How could he have forgotten? He'd been surprised that they'd finished their dance without her having hauled the ancient family patens out of her bodice. "Oh, yes. *And* William the Conquerer."

He took a drink and looked farther still. His gaze

skipped over a trio of women at the back of the ball-room and then arrowed back to the one in the vividly purple gown. "What about the redhead over by the stairs?" he asked his cousin. "I haven't seen her be-fore. A woman like that I would have remembered."

Harry chuckled. "I was wondering how long it would take you to find her. That would be the infa-mous Lady Baltrip. Twice widowed in nine years. Both of her late husbands reportedly died in great satisfaction. She's just this week come out of mourn-ing for the last one."

Great satisfaction? No doubt. He'd wager a hun-dred pounds that no man had ever left her bed unhappy. Ian slowly smiled. "Not exactly what my mother has in mind for a daughter-in-law, I'm sure."

"Oh," Harry drawled, "I think you could safely bet your personal kingdom on that."

"I assume she's of independent means?"

Harry nodded. "And temperament. At least as I hear it." His cousin slid his gaze over to him. "You aren't seriously considering her, are you?"

"Not as a wife, Harry," he assured him as his brain worked through the details of his immediate plan. "But I think she'd make a highly interesting diver-sion while I wade through the more appropriate, and considerably less appealing, matrimonial choices. Who are the women with her?"

"The older one is Her Grace, the Duchess of Ryland."

"Ryland," he said softly, searching the recesses

of his brain for memories. "We've been introduced, haven't we? As I recall it, His Grace was a distant relative of the old duke who inherited the title after Dinky cocked up his toes in Paris."

"You recall correctly."

"And he married the eldest of his wards."

"Reportedly after having already begun a torrid affair with her," Harry added. "It was the scandal of the Season that year. Of course it's been some ten or so years ago."

As Ian watched, Lady Ryland reached out and casually adjusted the diamond brooch that glittered in the center of Lady Baltrip's invitingly low décolletage. "She seems to be well acquainted with Lady Baltrip."

"The story, as I've heard it, anyway," Harry said, "is that she and Lady Baltrip have been friends forever and a day. Since before Her Grace was recognized, legitimized, and elevated by the Crown." He smiled and took another sip of his drink. "Lady Baltrip married up, as they say. Scandalously."

Of course. And laughing all the way. Just as she'd laugh all the way out to the garden with him this evening. His gaze slipped over to the third woman in the knot. "Is the younger blonde the duke's daughter?"

"No, Ryland's children are all very young. That's Lady Fiona Turnbridge there, Her Grace's half-sister and the youngest of the old duke's by-blow daughters."

She was turned, talking to her sister and Lady

Baltrip, and he couldn't see her face. She was a small thing, just barely a wisp. "We haven't been formally introduced, have we?"

"Not that I recall."

"Then obviously we haven't danced."

"I very much doubt it. She reportedly doesn't dance."

A woman who didn't dance? If only the hundreds of others who couldn't would have the sense to stay off the dance floor. "Any particular reason why?" Ian wondered aloud, smiling as it occurred to him that Lady Fiona's aversion could be used quite nicely to his benefit.

"I haven't the foggiest notion." Harry leaned closer to say confidentially, "The rumors are that she's a tad touched, if you know what I mean."

"I'm afraid that I don't," Ian countered, mildly irritated. "Touched in what respect? Mentally impaired? Or compromised?"

"Well, if she's at all like her older sisters, I wouldn't be the least surprised to learn that she's defied convention and taken a lover."

Oh, yes, the little wisp was such an obvious firebrand of rebellion, a bubbling cauldron of unrestrained passion. God, Harry could be such a lackwit at times. "But you haven't heard of any such thing," Ian pressed.

"No."

"Which leaves a mental impairment of some sort or another."

Harry nodded and again dropped his voice. "They say she looks through people. As if they weren't there, I presume. They also say that she can read minds."

"That would be rather unsettling," Ian allowed, wondering if it were even close to true.

"And she's renowned as an animal lover. Every stray in London is good for a free meal in the Ryland kitchen."

Well, once Lord Ditmoor and clan heard about that . . .

"This is, as I recall, her second Season," Harry went on. "Despite her dowry, which is reportedly a healthy one, no one regards her as a serious participant in the marriage market."

"Why's that?"

"Given her eccentricities," Harry said on a deep sigh. "I swear, I don't know why I bother to tell you a thing. You listen only half the time and hear only a quarter of what I'm saying."

True. Probably because half the time it was boring information and three-quarters of what was interesting was worthless. "You'd think her sister would have some pity and not drag her out for the gawkers."

Harry shrugged and finished off his champagne. "Perhaps Lady Fiona's unaware that people are gawking."

"All for the better," Ian said cheerfully, handing his champagne flute to his cousin. "Her feelings aren't likely to be hurt when I sweep Lady Baltrip away from the conversation and out for a private stroll in the gardens."

"Rather confident, aren't you?"

Ian shot his cuffs, studying the red-headed, purple-wrapped morsel on the other side of the ball-room. "Not exceedingly so. I can be quite charming when I want something that charm will get for me."

"She has been in mourning for the past year."

And sometimes, just mere seconds later, Harry could be remarkably astute. "And she is undoubt-edly well past ready to create happier carnal memo-ries. See you at dinner." He started away and then stopped, turning back to grin and add, "If I'm not there, please assume that I'm feasting elsewhere and *don't* come looking for me."

Harry saluted him with the glass and a wide smile. Properly encouraged, Ian set out to snare his quarry.

The happy torrent of Jane's words faded from Fiona's awareness as her senses prickled. She looked over at the mirror half tucked behind a pot-ted palm to be sure. Not that it was necessary, she al-lowed with a faint smile as she watched the Duke of Dunsford make his way toward them along the back edge of the ballroom.

It was such a silly-sounding title; as though someone had made it up to go with a cartoon charac-ter spoofed in the paper. Dr. Cabott was a much more fitting name for him since there wasn't anything the least bit cartoonish about him. Or about him being considered the top prize of the Season. His title and wealth aside, he was a terribly handsome man with a finely chiseled jaw and high cheekbones, thick dark hair, and hazel-colored eyes rimmed with long, lush lashes. All that and being tall and lean with broad shoulders . . . Fiona glanced down the reflection. Yes, of course his fingers would be long and slender; he was, after all, a surgeon.

Her attention shifted abruptly as Aunt Jane laid a hand on her shoulder. "What about that one over by the gaming room door, Fiona?" her sister's friend asked, leaning forward and looking pointedly off toward the other side of the ballroom. "The one with the red handker—"

"Jane," Caroline chided softly. "Fiona is not here this evening to serve as your personal . . . personal . . ."

"Medium," her aunt Jane supplied with a mischievous smile. "And yes, she is. Aren't you, Fiona, my darling?"

"Actually, yes." At Caroline's stunned blink, she added, "Aunt Jane said this was her coming out again evening and she asked me to help her discern the fortune hunters from the potential true loves of her life."

Caroline closed her eyes for a second and shook her head. Then, after a deep breath, she found a smile and said, "With all due respect to your aunt Jane, she views any male with a heartbeat—however faint it

may be—as a potential true love. *She's* the fortune
hunter. I'm astounded that you agreed to do this
for her."

"I'm supposed to be here," Fiona supplied with a
shrug. "I assume that it has something to do—"

"Quickly, Fiona," Aunt Jane said, deliberately
looking off toward the stairs. "The devil walking to-
wards us."

"Good God, Jane," Carrie muttered after a hasty
glance. "That's the Duke of Dunsford. He's nowhere
near putting a foot in the grave."

"Is he rich?"

"Obscenely."

"Then he can't be a fortune hunter, can he?"

They went on talking as the two of them did all
the time. Fiona watched their mouths move and the
lights in the eyes shift and shimmer in the course of
the exchange, but none of it mattered with the approach of the duke. Fiona cocked a brow as the realization drifted down over her.

Well, that was certainly interesting. *Why* she was
supposed to meet him this evening wasn't clear to
her yet, but then, that wasn't at all uncommon.
Knowledge of the full course of events seldom came
all at once. More often than not, understanding took
time and a willingness to patiently accept the fact
that one thing always led to another. Always. Nothing ever happened by pure chance.

"Good evening, Lady Ryland," he said, arriving

at last. He gave Carrie a slight bow and a smile as he added, "It is a pleasure to see you here."

"And you, Your Grace," Carrie politely replied. She went on talking, her hands fluttering gracefully as she went through the introductions His Grace had come over to get. Actually, Fiona amended as she watched him acknowledge Jane, the one introduction that he needed to have before he could move on with his plan for the evening.

His gaze touched hers and then he looked away. But not before Fiona had seen the startled spark in the depth of his eyes. A spark of something akin to recognition.

"Fiona," Carrie said, lightly touching her shoulder.

"Yes?" she asked, looking up at her sister. Carrie's gaze darted to the duke in silent instruction. "Oh." She turned her attention to the man who didn't care one whit whether they were introduced or not and with a little nod said, "Hello."

He started and again there was the flicker of recognition in his gaze. "Hello." He cleared his throat quickly and softly and found a pleasant enough smile. "Might you have a space free on your dance card, Lady Fiona?"

"No," she answered simply, knowing it was the answer he wanted to hear.

"Ah," he said on a sigh that was obviously far less disappointed than it was relieved. "I can only hope that my heart will eventually mend."

One. Two.

"Lady Baltrip," he said ever so predictably and cheerfully, "would you be willing to take pity on me?"

"Of course, you poor man."

He presented his arm, Jane took it with a lilting laugh, and together they walked off toward the dance floor.

"Fiona, dear . . ."

She smiled at her sister. "He didn't come over to ask me to dance, Carrie. He came over to secure an introduction so that he could initiate an interlude with Aunt Jane. I was simply an excuse, a device to allow him to engage Jane's sympathy."

Carrie thought about that for a half a second or so before smiling and arching a brow. "As if an introduction and a play on sympathy were necessary. He could just as well have stood by the terrace door and whistled for her. I hope she has a care for his heart and doesn't mangle it too badly."

"Not to worry, Carrie. His heart is well walled away. Where Aunt Jane is concerned, his intentions are just as intensely base and every bit as fleeting as hers. It's a perfect matching for the evening."

"He isn't going to batter Jane's heart, is he?"

Why everyone in the family thought she could see everything . . . "Aunt Jane has never once taken her heart along when she goes for a stroll in the garden. And you don't have to have a gift of sight to know that she's not taking it this time, either."

"True on both counts," Carrie had to allow. She

glanced over her shoulder and smiled broadly. "Simone and Tristan have finally arrived," she announced, turning away from the dancers. "Shall we abandon Jane to her fate and go say hello?"

Jane would prefer it, and it was unthinkable to ignore their sister and her husband. Fiona considered the couple making their way toward them. Well, there was yet another reason she was supposed to be here this evening. Good news was always better when shared with the people who loved you.

"Is it just me," Carrie murmured, "or do you think . . . ?"

Yes, Simone and Tristan were finally starting their family. They were both glowing with the joy of it. The pregnancy and birth would go well and easily for Simone. And it was about time for there to be another baby boy in the lineage.

"Let's try to act surprised when they tell us," Carrie suggested.

Fiona nodded and arched a brow as a vision of snow-dusted moors drifted across her awareness. No houses, no people. Just the gentle roll of ancient land. As she considered it, the sun warmed and the land gently greened with the first promise of spring.

Interesting. She didn't have the slightest idea of what it meant. But since understanding didn't have anything to do with accuracy or inevitability, she accepted that she would someday stand on the moors watching the passage of the seasons and remember this night. It didn't seem to be an unhappy vision. If

she were pressed to put an emotion to it, she'd have
to say that it was something akin to contentment, a
feeling that all was as it was supposed to be.

Yes, interesting indeed. And since there was no
point in speculating on what event or circumstances
would take her into the moors, or even when that
someday might be . . . Fiona put the vision away,
stepped into Simone's embrace, and focused her attention on living in the wonder and happiness of the
present moment.

Ian guided Lady Baltrip along the garden path and
away from the light and merriment spilling out the
terrace doors. She laughed and chatted pleasantly at
his side, the diamond brooch centered in her cleavage winking in the pale moonlight.

She'd told him in the middle of their brief dance
what her given name was. He'd repeated it to himself three times in the moments right afterward,
determined to commit it to his memory so that he
could murmur it appropriately while in the throes of
passion.

June? Anne? Or was she Sylvia? Damn. Bad form
to call her by the wrong name. He sorted back through
the recent memories of the evening. She's been standing with the Duchess of Ryland. Her Grace's given
name was . . . Hell, he doubted that he'd ever heard
it. Her Grace's sister's name was Fiona. Lady Fiona
Turnbridge. *That* he did remember. Why, of all things,

for that bit of information to be the stuff that stuck . . .

It had been her eyes, he allowed. A stunning shade of green. Not pale, not flecked, not changeable as his own were. A brilliant, new grass green. Clear and bright and . . . keenly, sharply intelligent. In a mere second . . .

Touched, his ass. That would be the last time he ever listened to Harry about anything. Lady Fiona wasn't the least bit impaired, and as for looking through people as though they weren't there . . . No. Lady Fiona looked *into* people and saw every shadow of their soul.

In the first instant it was disconcerting. He would allow Harry that observation. But once you thought about it a bit, it wasn't. Not at all. In fact, there was something rather deliciously dangerous about daring to—

"Are we going to walk to Scotland this evening, Ian?"

He blinked and focused his attention on the woman on his arm. Her eyes were dark, probably a pleasant shade of brown. Her hair was definitely red. And her smile was most certainly inviting.

"I suppose we've come far enough for the sake of privacy and discretion," he allowed with a smile of his own as he drew her to a most conveniently provided garden bench.

She settled herself on it gracefully and then skimmed her gaze slowly down the length of his body. Ian cocked a brow and waited for her to finish her perusal, thinking that Lady Baltrip's vision was every bit as focused as Lady Fiona's, just not at all concerned with anything beyond the simple surface of matters, beyond the immediate possibilities of attaining a quick but thorough physical satisfaction.

Which was fine with him, he told himself as she began to efficiently unbutton his trousers. Actually, sex with a beautiful, willing, just-met woman was his idea of the perfect mid-gala activity. Post-gala, too, if she was sufficiently good and genuinely disinterested in a more formal and permanent union.

He closed his eyes as she freed his stiffened member. God, what was her name? She leaned forward and he shuddered with the pleasure of her bold and artful advance. It didn't matter what her name was, he assured himself as he stepped closer for her ease. As long as he remembered that it *wasn't* Fiona.

Chapter Two

As Drayton and Carrie walked ahead toward their carriage, Fiona stepped off the shelled drive and paused to kick off her shoes. She wiggled her toes in the damp grass and sighed in relief. The worst part, physically anyway, of having to go to parties was the shoes. Hour after hour of standing about on marble floors in heels, hoping she didn't stagger from the boredom and fall off the thick-soled shoe that disguised her shorter leg . . .

She considered the distance to the carriage, how many steps it would take to get there, and how many people might see her. With another sigh, she slipped her feet back into her shoes and followed after her sister and brother-in-law.

"Is Jane not riding with us?" Drayton was asking, handing Carrie into the coach as Fiona arrived.

"I believe that she's found other transport," Caroline answered from inside.

Well, that was certainly one way to put it. Fiona smiled and let Drayton assist her up the steps.

Knowing from long experience precisely how the conversation about Aunt Jane would go, Fiona kicked off her shoes again and settled into the corner of the seat to enjoy it.

"God," Drayton groused, climbing in behind them and taking up the opposite seat. "She's utterly incorrigible."

"I prefer to think of her as being highly spirited."

"Highly is an understatement," Drayton countered as the coach rolled down the drive and toward home. "She just yesterday ended her mourning for Baltrip. Who's the poor old dupe this time?"

"He's not old. And I hardly think he's being duped. Jane is nothing if not straightforward."

"To the point of bluntness. Who is he?"

"The Duke of Dunsford."

"Well," Drayton drawled, "he's certainly younger and more healthy than her typical choice in men."

Carrie rolled her eyes. "She's not intending to marry him, Drayton. I suspect that she considers him something of a celebration of her return to Society."

"I'll refrain from comment on his likely perception of Jane." He snorted and added, "And what his mother would think of his carrying on with her."

"If she knew," Carrie countered. Then, as usual, she turned to smile at Fiona and explained, "The dowager duchess is known as something of a terror. It's no mystery at all why her son hasn't married yet."

Fiona shrugged. "He's been too committed to his profession to take the time to find a wife."

Drayton lowered his chin and cocked a brow. "Really?"

"His Grace is a surgeon," she supplied, wondering how they could be unaware of what all of London and Great Britain and half of the Continent knew. "By all reports, an excellent one. I've read several of his published papers and they're very interesting."

Carrie chuckled softly and reached over to gently pat her hand. "Fiona, sweetheart, a wife doesn't prevent a man from pursuing his interests. If Dunsford had wanted a wife, he could have easily had one and been a renowned surgeon, too."

"Absolutely," Drayton concurred. "And apparently his mother has reached the end of her patience about the matter. The word is that he's under some considerable pressure from the dowager to find himself a wife by the end of this Season and get on with his duty of preserving the title. There's a good deal of wagering going on in the clubs as to when and with whom he'll commit himself."

"Oh?" Carrie asked, grinning. "Is there money on Jane?"

"Not a pence that I've heard of," Drayton replied, sounding astounded that Carrie would even ask.

Carrie turned toward Fiona again. "Everyone knows that he won't choose anyone of whom the dowager would disapprove. She's unhappy enough at his defiance of convention in becoming a physician."

"Just a mere step up from being in *trade*, you know," Drayton added dryly.

"If he were to marry an unsuitable young woman," Carrie went on, "her life would be a living hell for as long as his mother draws breath."

"No one seems to think he's that callous."

Of course he isn't. Deep down, he has a very kind heart.

"And no one thinks the dowager's nice enough," Carrie added, "to do her son the favor of slipping this mortal coil any time soon."

Fiona started. "Carrie! How could you say something so awful?"

"Remember Lady Aubrey?"

That wasn't a kind comparison. "Yes. Not fondly, though."

"The Dowager Duchess Dunsford—say that fast three times—makes Lady Aubrey look like a sweet, doting grandmama."

"Thankfully," Drayton added, "she's following the Queen's example and has gone into perpetual mourning. Society events have been much happier affairs since she's been gone."

Well, that did explain a bit about the duke's cool detachment. She remembered the time in her life when pretending that she hadn't really been there had been the only defense against the unrelenting meanness.

"So, Drayton, who is the favorite in the betting pools?"

"Lady Edith Shreeves, Viscount Shaddock's eldest daughter," he supplied with a disbelieving shake of his head. "Shaddock's become a preening idiot over the whole thing. He's certain that Dunsford will be calling on him any day now to make the arrangements."

Caroline considered it all for a moment and then mulled aloud, "Not to be unkind, but . . . well, she's not a very attractive young woman."

"Yes, but Shaddock's plumped her dowry to the point of making it an impossible-to-ignore lure. Dunsford's wealthy enough already, but even he can't scoff at pedigree *and* money."

"Then he'd best be getting on with the negotiations for her," Caroline countered. "His cousin was paying serious court this evening."

Drayton stared at his wife a long moment, his jaw sagging a bit. "Harry? Viscount Bettles?"

"Yes, and do remember that Harry is the eldest and will be the marquis when his father passes."

"But he's incredibly shallow."

He's a perfect match for Edith. She's shallow, too.

"Please, Drayton," Carrie replied. "Calling Harry shallow is like calling a dwarf short. But he is charming and handsome, and Lady Edith is in her third Season. *And* Dunsford hasn't so much as cast a passing glance her way."

Drayton slowly smiled. "When did you become such an expert on peerage romance?"

"Good God, Drayton," Carrie replied, grinning. "Watching the goings-on is all there is to do at these affairs. There are only so many ways to prepare beef and fish and fowl and assorted vegetables for the table. The novelty of dining passed away years ago. The fashion sense of everyone can only be described as either rut-bound by convention or retarded by the absolute lack of creativity. Conversations outside of our family are . . . Well, they make Viscount Bettles seem deep and highly intellectual."

Fiona brightened. "I thought it was just me."

"No, it's not," her sister assured her. "I'm afraid that your prospects of finding an interesting man are abysmal, Fiona. I'm so sorry."

Well, she could find them, but there wasn't any reason for them to find her. And that was an important distinction. One that she didn't mind at all; it had saved her from having to risk hurting anyone's feelings in turning down their marriage proposals. "Then you won't mind if I sit out the rest of the Season?" she asked, hoping for the best and a moment of sisterly weakness.

"I certainly can't blame you for wanting to."

Well, that wasn't exactly permission to escape. But it wasn't an insistence on participation, either.

Drayton softly cleared his throat. "Lord Randolph asked after your health this evening while we were gaming."

Randolph is a walking disaster. And beneath that is a pervert. "One of his horses must have come up lame," Fiona ventured. "They're the only things in the world he genuinely cares about."

"Well, as a matter of fact, two of them have. Or at least so he says."

He's beside himself to help them. Two suggests that there's a problem in the training. Poor animals.

Carrie lowered her chin. "Fiona, don't you dare."

She would dare and they all knew it. But she wasn't stupid or foolish; she knew what people thought of Randolph. They were wrong, but they thought it anyway. "I'll just make sure he's nowhere around when I have a look at them."

"Make sure you take Alvin with you when you go," Drayton instructed as their carriage rolled to a stop in front of the townhouse.

"Ralph, too," Caroline added as the footman opened the door. "And Jim for good measure."

Fiona reined in her smile and followed them out of the carriage, up the walk, and into the house. Declining to join them for a sherry, she left them and went upstairs to her room. It really was amazing, she mused as she went, how everyone thought of her as thoroughly naive. For heaven's sake, she knew far more about the people around them than they did. Not that she shared the information unless there was a pressing need to do so. People were generally entitled to privacy, to keep their secrets secret. Up to the point where those secrets might endanger someone, of course.

Take Jim along to Randolph's stables. Oh, please. Randolph preferred young men and Jim was in

Drayton's employ in the hope that one of his friends would be old, generous, and looking for companionship. If she took Jim along, he was likely to latch on to Randolph and stay for as long as the old man's pockets had money in them. Or until Randolph put him in his will and then happily and conveniently died.

Fiona dropped her cloak on the end of the bed and then stopped as realization struck home. There was the familiar indentation in the feather comforter, but there wasn't a black-and-white cat in it. She leaned down and laid the palm of her hand in the spot where Beeps spent three-quarters of his daily existence. The cold shuddered up her arm and down the length of her back.

"Beeps?" she called, turning about, scanning the room. "Beeps, where are you?" Nothing. Not a sound, not a telltale movement. Her heart chilling, she opened the door and wandered down the upstairs hall, opening each of the guest room doors and calling for him.

Her stomach was leaden by the time she reached the kitchen. Polly looked up from her preparations for breakfast and arched a brow. "Is something amiss, Lady Fiona?"

She could barely nod, barely get her voice pushed past her sense of dread. "Have you seen Beeps this evening?"

"He was down here a hour or so ago, Lady Fiona. Cook gave him a bit of leftover fish and a saucer of milk before she went out to get a ham for tomorrow. I don't know where he went after that."

Went out . . . Fiona looked at the door leading into the rear yard. Beeps could have slipped out for an adventure. He could be sitting on the back step patiently waiting to be let back in. But he wasn't and she knew it. As her stomach heaved and then dropped, she took the lantern from the hearth mantel and went to look for him.

Ian checked the arrangement of his clothing one last time and climbed down out of the carriage. It was amazing, he decided as he made his way toward his front door, how a man could be both physically spent and invigorated at the same time. Lady Baltrip's husbands had, without a doubt, died happy men. Just as doubtlessly, she'd killed them.

Ian grinned. God Almighty, the woman didn't have a single inhibition or the slightest aversion to risk. Between the garden tryst, the cloakroom escapade, and the carriage ride to her townhouse, he couldn't remember the last time he'd had such a wonderful time at a Society event.

The prospects for the balance of the Season were considerably brighter now. Tomorrow night was Lady Miller-Sands' ball and Lady Baltrip—with a wink and a slow caress as she'd climbed off of him and dropped her skirts—had promised to see him there. He'd promised her that he'd make a trip by the apothecary shop beforehand to purchase an inexhaustible supply of French letters. She'd been delighted. He'd been hardening again as he walked her to her front door and reconsidering her invitation to try out the swing in her bedroom.

But duty and obligation had asserted themselves in the moment of final decision and he'd deferred on the swing until tomorrow night. Between now and then—well, between now and when he arrived at the Miller-Sands' mansion—he'd have to find out what the hell her given name was.

Calling her his wanton was certainly accurate as statements went. She was the very definition of wanton and, in the moments when they were physically joined, she was indeed his. But it tended to imply a possessiveness and an emotional attachment that he didn't feel in the least. She was a wonderful romp and he sincerely appreciated her easy willingness, but that was as far as it went. And as far as it was ever going to go. Terms of endearment, however tawdry, were likely to give her an entirely wrong impression of his intentions.

The door opened before him and he walked in past the footman to find the butler waiting for him in the foyer. Given the look on the man's face . . . Rowan was a sour-face even on the best of days. At the moment the corners of his mouth were practically under his chin. So much for basking in the delightful memories of Lady Baltrip.

"Welcome home, Your Grace."

"Hello, Rowan," he said, handing off his cloak,

hat and gloves and deciding to be optimistic. "I see
the house is still standing. I take it that it was a fairly
quiet evening?"

"Miss Charlotte refused three dinners, Your
Grace."

So much for optimism, too. "I assume it involved
the usual pitching of china and silver?"

"It did."

Ian sighed. "There's more, isn't there?"

"Unfortunately, yes, Your Grace. Sally has quit.
She packed her bags shortly after nine and departed
the house."

And that wasn't all of it, either. He cocked a brow
and asked dryly, "What role did Charlotte play in
her decision?"

"Miss Charlotte also flung the contents of her
chamber pot, Your Grace. Sally was not removing
the debris from the third dinner quickly enough to
suit her."

Good God. He was going to have to deal with this.
It was clearly over the line. "Has Charlotte retired for
the evening?"

"Yes, Your Grace."

"Without supper?"

"No, Your Grace. Cook was finally able to prepare something to her liking on the fourth attempt."

He could storm up the stairs and . . . and . . . Hell,
he didn't have the foggiest notion of what he ought
to do beyond crisply saying, *Bad, Charlotte! Bad!*
and slapping the end of her nose with a rolled up

newspaper. Since she wasn't a puppy and he'd been given a reprieve of sorts in her having retired, he took it. A crisis among the servants he could ably and confidently manage, though. "Do you know where Sally went?"

"I would imagine to her sister's store in Bloomsbury, Your Lordship."

Good, still in London. "Please send her a month's wages in the morning along with a note offering her a housekeeping position on the staff at Heathland. Please express my regrets for the incident this evening and advise her that, if she'll accept the Heathland position, she'll not be expected to provide service of any kind for my ward in the future."

"Very good, Your Grace."

"Thank you, Rowan. That will be all."

The butler bowed and Ian walked off toward his study. Yes, that would be all for this evening. Unfortunately, the sun would come up again in a few hours and they would all begin yet another day of Charlotte's tantrums. How long was one supposed to allow a person to behave badly in the name of grief and rage? he wondered as he got himself a brandy.

It had been just six months since Charlotte's world had come crashing down and all of her hopes for a normal life had been extinguished. Her parents were dead, her legs were useless, and she had been shipped across the world to be thrust like damaged freight upon the kindness of a complete stranger. It would be difficult for a grown woman to adjust to such radical and unexpected changes of circumstance. For a fourteen-year-old girl . . .

Her body was broken and would never be whole again. Because of that, her spirits were fragile and her emotions raw. In time, she would come to an acceptance of her limitations and life in a wheeled chair. Until then, though . . . he simply had to be patient and understanding. To demand that she accept on his schedule and for the ease and convenience of his household staff would be insensitive to the point of cruelty.

If only the London gossips were even slightly interested in learning the truth of the situation, the utter impossibility of a salacious relationship. But they weren't and he needed to make arrangements that would preserve both their reputations. If only his mother were the sort to have a bit of compassion. Or the sort to make accommodations for anyone. Sending Charlotte to her at Revel House simply wasn't possible; the girl had been through enough already.

He could buy her a London townhouse of her own. Or rent one for her. It would solve his problem with the rumormongers as long as he never went anywhere near the property or Charlotte. But doing so seemed a bit too much like warehousing her for him to be entirely comfortable with the solution.

The other alternative was to simply ride out the

whispers until he found a suitable woman and hauled her into the house as his wife. Not only would the gossips stop speculating, but he could hand the day-to-day management of Charlotte off to his bride. Women did tend to know how to handle the messier and more dramatic aspects of people.

As for picking the lucky woman, maybe he should just have Harry write all their names down on little slips of paper, put them into a hat, and then blindly draw one out. God knew he didn't care one way or the other for any of them. One would do just as well as the next. They were all daughters of privilege; they knew how to run households, could ably fulfill the expectations of society, and would do their duty in terms of providing the necessary heir and a spare or two.

Beyond those simple requirements, as long as he provided adequate financial support and was reasonably discreet with his lovers, she would be the picture of perfect wifely contentment and all would be well in the kingdom. Both his and the Queen's.

He sat back in his leather chair and considered a possible timetable. Harry would call as usual at ten. Ian checked the clock on the mantel. Eight hours from now. It would take only a few moments to fill a hat with names and pull one out. After that, he could trot out to inform the father of the bride-elect of his good fortune and make arrangements for an engagement announcement at Lady Miller-Sands' that evening. On the way home, he could stop by the apothecary shop for the letters.

Yes, quite doable. All of his problems would be solved. His mother would be pleased to hear that he was tending to his duties. The gossipmongers would cease their prattling over Charlotte's presence in his house. And somewhere in a dark corner of the Miller-Sandses' property, before the betrothal announcement was made, he would lift up Lady Baltrip's skirts, press her hard against a wall and assure her that his pending marriage was only going to add another very nice edge to their relationship. She would be delighted by the prospects, of course. Lady Baltrip liked edges every bit as much as he did.

Ian lifted his brandy glass in salute to himself and the sheer brilliance and perfect workability of his plan.

Certain of her course and determined to quickly see it through no matter the cost, Fiona shifted the bundle in her arm, freed her hand, and repeatedly slammed the knocker on the door. The sound pounded out into the silence of the sleeping neighborhood and succeeded, within only moments, of getting the door thrown open to her.

Dr. Ian Cabott literally rocked back on his heels at the sight of her. "Lady Fiona?" he choked out as he recovered his balance.

"Pardon my intrusion at this late hour, Your

Grace," she said hastily, the seconds ticking away in her mind, "but there is an emergency and I desperately need your help."

"What sort of emergency?" He looked past her and out to the empty street. "Has there been an accident?"

"This is Beeps," she said, pulling the edge of her bundled cloak aside just enough to reveal his head. "His right rear leg has been badly broken."

He blinked down at Beeps, then looked up at her, chewing his lower lip. "Lady Fiona," he said kindly, "I can appreciate your concern and sympathy for a suffering animal, but I don't know what you expect me to do about it. Unless," he added even more kindly, "you're hoping I will put it out of its misery for you."

Do and you'll be the one in misery. She swallowed down her anger and her fear. "I've read your papers on the experimental pinning of broken limbs. I want you to do that for Beeps."

He cocked a brow. "I operate on humans, Lady Fiona. Not animals. I'm sorry."

There was nothing to be done but force the issue. She reached under her arm, slipped her hand around the butt of Drayton's pistol and hauled it out, saying simply and honestly, "As am I, Your Grace," as she pointed the muzzle at his heart.

He stared at the maw for a long second and then, slowly lifting his hands, brought his gaze up to hers. "You can not be serious."

"I will assist you in the surgery," she countered

firmly, taking a deliberate step forward. "Kindly lead the way. And please keep your hands up where I can see them."

To the credit of his good judgment and sense of self-preservation, he stepped back, turned and slowly headed across the foyer, his hands up and saying, "I can't assure you of a positive outcome, you know."

"Better to try and fail than to not try at all," she said, following him and fighting back tears as Beeps shifted weakly against her. "He's my very best friend and I will not abandon him or hope."

One tiny little meow was all that broke the silence of their passage through the darkened house. They'd reached a room at the far end when Ian Cabott cleared his throat and said quietly, "While I light a lamp, place him on the examining table, please."

The outlines of the metal table glinted dully in the scant moonlight wafting through the room's windows. Fiona carefully, gently did as he instructed as a matchstick flared. The gun in one hand, she trailed the fingertips of her other reassuringly over the top of Beeps' head and watched the doctor put fire to a lamp wick. The match out, the wick adjusted, he turned with the lamp and met her gaze.

Yes, this moment was why she was supposed to have met him at the party. Fate had known that she'd need his medical skills before the night was done, had known that his sense of compassion would make it impossible for him to deny her request.

"Put the gun away, Lady Fiona," he said, setting

the lamp down on the table and gently opening the cloak in which she'd hastily wrapped Beeps. "It's not necessary and you need to scrub your hands. I'm going to need both of them in the effort."

She laid the gun on the desk in the corner on her way to the wash basin, absolutely certain that she'd made the right choices and that everything would turn out not just fine, but as it was supposed to.

Ian sat in the chair and watched Lady Fiona Turnbridge sleep, her beloved black-and-white cat bandaged and nestled in the blanket on her lap. She had been a remarkable assistant, her knowledge of general anatomy on par with any of the colleagues with whom he'd shared an operating theater. Not only that, she hadn't flinched once, nor turned pale or green. Her eyes had welled with tears when he'd announced that the bone was too badly crushed to be saved, but she'd pushed past her sadness, squared her shoulders, and ably assisted him with the necessary amputation.

Beeps was one very fortunate feline to have such a caring mistress. Beeps was also fortunate to have a world-renowned surgeon willing to risk his reputation in working on him. The cat would never walk on four paws again, of course, but then, as a pampered member of the Ryland household, it wasn't as though he were ever going to have to hunt for his own meals or go hungry. Three legs would serve him well enough to live a long and full life.

But now that the surgery was done and it was obvious that ol' Beeps had at least one more life allotted to him, there was the question of what to do about the fact that Lady Fiona had spent the night at the home of a single man. Odds were that no one was going to consider Beeps a proper chaperone.

Chapter Three

Ian checked the time on his pocket watch, slipped it back into his vest pocket, then took a thick medical periodical off the end table beside his chair. Holding it out in front of him, he looked over at the hearth to make sure that all was still well with the esteemed Beeps, and then over at Lady Fiona sweetly slumbering in the huge leather chair.

Time to begin. He opened his hand and let the periodical fall. It struck the wooden floor with a perfectly crisp *whap!* that, just as he'd intended, instantly awakened his cat-carrying, gun-wielding little guest.

"Good morning, Lady Fiona," he said as she blinked and blankly gazed around the room.

She looked at him, furrowed her brow in obvious puzzlement for a second or two, and then started in full realization. "How—?"

"Beeps is fine," he assured her. "Still a bit woozy for the trauma, of course, but he's managed to totter over to a food bowl and then lap up a bit of watered cream." He gestured toward the gently crackling hearth. "I made a nest for him by the fire and he's taking a comfortable nap."

She stretched and uncurled. Slowly, leisurely and in a stunningly, startlingly seductive way. "What time is it?"

To reappraise. He cleared his throat softly and took up his plan again. "Half past eight."

"Oh, dear. I have about ten minutes to get home before I'm missed." She pushed herself out of the chair, adding, "I truly appreciate all your help last night, Your Grace. If you'd care to send around a bill for your services, I'd be more than happy to see it paid."

He waited until she was swirling her cloak over her shoulders to rise to his feet and call her attention back to him. "Lady Fiona?"

"Yes?"

"It occurs to me," he said with calm control and a cocked brow, "that rushing home with your cat is not a particularly viable course of action at this point."

She stopped and considered him. "Are you suggesting that I leave him here to recover further?"

"Oh, he's perfectly capable of withstanding a reasonably gentle transport without ill effect."

"Then why are you—?"

"You have, my dear lady," he interrupted, "spent the night in my home, in my company."

She shrugged. "In your surgery, saving the life of my cat."

"The facts of the situation don't matter," he pointed

out. "Appearances do, however, and your reputation has been compromised."

"Assuming that anyone ever finds out that I was here. Which," she quickly added, as she moved forward to collect Beeps, "they won't if I say nothing, you say nothing, and I leave right this moment."

"No, Lady Fiona," he said, stepping between her and the hearth. "It's ridiculous to even consider the idea of you dashing across streets and yards and vaulting fences in an attempt to reach the family breakfast table before your night of adventure is discovered."

She looked up at him and slowly arched a pale brow. "I was planning to walk down the sidewalk at a brisk pace."

Lord, in the daylight her eyes were even more stunningly green than they had been last night. "To arrive in your brother-in-law's dining room still wearing your ball gown from the night before?"

She looked down at herself and then back up at him. "I'll have to walk a bit more briskly to allow for time to change my clothes." She moved to step around him, adding, "Now if you will excuse me, Your Grace."

Again he blocked her path. "Might I make a proposal?"

She sighed and the smile she gave him was polite but tight. "Quickly, please."

Actually, now that he considered the whole of her face, she was decidedly beautiful. Flawless skin.

Perfectly shaped lips. Their children would be the most handsome and gorgeous in England. "I will have my carriage readied, transport you and Beeps home, and explain the circumstances to His Grace."

"It would be easier on you," she retorted with a dry chuckle, "to simply get out of my way and let me go alone."

"Yes," he allowed, nodding, "but then I'd have to wait until calling time, present myself at the door, and then make some sort of preparatory speech before getting on with the asking for your hand in marriage."

She took a full step back. "Excuse me?"

Since there wasn't any point in dodging and dancing about the matter, he simply replied, "I need a wife. You've been compromised. It works out well for both of us."

She knitted her brows and stared at him for a few moments before saying, "With all due respect, Your Grace, you're out of your mind."

No, this wasn't how it was supposed to go. She was supposed to be concerned about her reputation and honored that he was willing to marry her to preserve it. In fact, she should have been honored by the proposal, period. He was the prize of the London Season. "Why would you say that?" he asked, truly mystified by her response. "I'm a duke. You're the daughter of a duke, the sister-in-law of his successor. I fail to see what's the least bit insane about our marrying. Actually, it's really quite appropriate in terms of our social ranks and family prestige."

She nodded and edged sideways away from him. Rather in the way, it occurred to him, that people tended to escape mentally defective beggars on the street.

"We barely know each other," she said as she inched toward her cat.

"That's what engagement periods are for," Ian countered, again blocking her way. He smiled broadly. "I'll start. My favorite color is blue and my favorite meal is roast beef, cooked rare, with pan-roasted potatoes and carrots on the side. Your turn."

She studied the floor, pursed her lips, and then drew a deep breath as she brought her gaze up to his. With a sigh, she lifted her chin a notch to crisply say, "My mother was a maid in the employ of the Duke of Ryland. He fathered me and tossed her out before I was born. She took up prostitution to feed us and then left me in the care of impoverished, ignorant, and not particularly kind or caring relatives when she was stricken with disease and dying."

"How horrible," he offered, thinking that that wasn't quite the sort of information he'd had in mind.

"I was rescued by Drayton after my father died," she went on as he was wondering if green might be her favorite color, "and the Queen's men had performed some sort of paper miracle to make me a legitimate child."

Yes, yes. Harry had told him all about that. "For which I am exceedingly grateful."

She sighed again and this time punctuated it by

putting her hands on her hips. "I was not born in the peerage, Your Grace. I am not and never will be a full member of acceptable Society. My pedigree is tarnished and I'm sure that you can understand how—"

"It makes no difference to me whatsoever," he assured her.

"Well, it does to me."

"Oh, how ridiculous. If the Queen says that you're good enough for Society, who would be stupid enough to quibble? I suggest that you put it in the past and move on with your life. No one will dare to challenge the suitability of the woman I choose to be my duchess."

She rolled her eyes, let her hands fall to her sides, and then very deliberately stepped past him saying, "You have been breathing far too many ether vapors for far too long, Your Grace."

I have not. "Please, call me Ian."

"No."

"Ian and Fiona," he said as she gently scooped up her cat. "Fiona and Ian. Either way, it has a pleasant ring to it, doesn't it?"

"It sounds as though we need to purchase a consonant or two."

"We'll buy each other one for a wedding present," he suggested, following her out of his infirmary. "Is there a particular one you've always wanted?"

"No."

"I don't believe in long engagements. I hope you don't, either."

"Oh, but I do," she answered blithely, not even bothering to look back at him. "Twenty years. At least. Twenty-five would be even better."

"Is your aversion to marriage a general, in principle sort of thing? Or is it . . . well, personal?"

"Your Grace, I—"

"Ian," he corrected.

"Your Grace, I plan to be in love with the man I marry," she went on, still without so much as sparing him a glance. "I regret that I must say that I don't love you. Not in the least."

Ian reined in his smile—just in case she decided to cast a quick look his way. "I'm crushed, you know. Devastated. How can you be so cruel?"

"It comes quite naturally," she told him as they entered the foyer. The footman, his eyes carefully averted, stepped forward to open the front door as she said, "Now, if you will again accept my thanks and forgive my haste, Your Grace, Beeps and I are going home."

He followed her as far as the doorway. Watching her march down the walk toward the public walkway, he called after her, "Lady Fiona?"

"I'm leaving, Your Grace."

What graceful determination! He chuckled. "Please tell your brother-in-law that I'll be calling on him later this morning!"

"Don't bother, Your Lordship," she called back. "Knock on someone else's door."

Ian turned to the footman. "Cooper, follow Lady

Fiona at a discreet distance and ensure that she arrives home safely."

The servant nodded and left, leaving Ian to close his own door. Laughing softly, he made his way to the breakfast room. How interesting, he mused as he buttered a hot muffin, that of all the possible brides in London Society, the obvious and easiest choice would be the one who didn't want to marry him.

Assuming, of course, that she was being honest about her feelings regarding his proposal. She might well have been all girlishly giddy on the inside and determined to hide it for the sake of dignity. Yes, she could be dancing about the Ryland breakfast table in just a few moments, gushing and giggling in anticipation of marrying the most eligible man in the kingdom. Yes, indeed. What woman in her right mind wouldn't want to marry him, to be a duchess?

And since her brother-in-law was a duke himself, it probably would be a good idea to see to the formal declarations and all the other necessary folderol without undo delay. Ian checked his pocket watch again and then, with time to burn before the acceptable calling hour, sat back in his chair to have a leisurely cup of coffee and to mentally craft something that approximated a heartfelt appeal.

Fiona shook her head as she hurried down the walkway. "Marry him, Beeps," she muttered to the cat in her arms. "Did you hear that whole conversation? Can you believe it?"

Beeps didn't reply, not that she gave him a chance to.

"God forbid that he simply tell anyone who asks what actually happened and defend my virtue. No. That would be too simple. Too honest. No, let's quake at the idea of people whispering lies. Let's shackle ourselves together so that we can spend all of eternity congratulating ourselves for giving the busybodies a sham marriage to wag their tongues about instead. Oh, what a fabulous solution."

Beeps blinked up at her in complete agreement.

"Marry a stranger. That's what he's proposing, Beeps. You know that, right? And he thinks that I should be delighted by the prospect. He actually seemed stunned by the fact that I didn't jump up and down and clap my hands in anticipation of being his duchess. The man is undoubtedly a fine surgeon, but he hasn't the foggiest understanding of how Society thinks. Either that or he doesn't care one whit."

The niggling realization wasn't a particularly welcome one, but she couldn't very well ignore it. Not and be fair. "All right," she allowed grumpily, "that he doesn't care what Society thinks might be a point in his favor. It would be nice to think that he's independent minded. But, honestly, Beeps, if he doesn't care, why would he offer to marry me to keep them from talking about us having spent the night at his house? Lord knows he couldn't possibly have any feelings for me.

"Oh, what a mess," she grumbled on a sigh as she

opened the gate and slipped into the rear yard. "I suppose the best thing to do is to tell Drayton and Carrie the whole story and hope that Dunsford doesn't actually show up to make a formal declaration of stupidity. If he does, though . . ."

Mercifully, she arrived at the kitchen door and didn't have the dubious luxury of thinking about what she'd do if the Duke of Dunsford persisted with his madness. The staff's eyes went wide at the sight of her coming in—at first it was the ball gown and the unspoken realization that she'd been out all night. Then they saw Beeps and the Dunsford Problem was swept away in the outpouring of their genuine concern for their favorite feline.

Seeing no point in slipping upstairs to change her clothes and delaying the inevitable revelation of her adventure, Fiona tried to smooth away the worst of the wrinkles in her skirt as she made her way from the kitchen to the breakfast room. Perhaps the thing to do, she mused along the way, was to pretend she was Simone and just plow her way through the conversation with flippant quips and brazen confidence. She didn't have to be particularly good at it; her sister and brother-in-law would be so startled by her manner that they'd reel for a week. With just a bit of luck, they'd never get around to taking her to task for having created the problem by her own actions. Yes, flippant was at least worth a try.

Caroline looked up from her newspaper, skimmed

her gaze down the length of her and arched a pale brow. "I assume there's a story to be told," she said softly as she sat back in her chair.

"It was a dark and storm-swept night," Fiona replied, stepping up to the sideboard and getting herself a much-needed cup of coffee. What a pity Simone wasn't here to see her brilliant performance!

"It was clear with a crescent moon," Drayton countered crisply over the rustle of folding his newspaper. "Where have you been?"

Bright and breezy, Fi. "Beeps required emergency surgery last night," she supplied, taking her seat at the table. "I took him straight to Lord Dunsford for treatment. Unfortunately, we weren't able to save Beep's leg, but he is alive and will eventually be just fine."

"You were with Dunsford?" Drayton asked, the words sounding a bit strangled. He cleared his throat, not bothering to be subtle about it. "Alone?"

Fiona reached for a slice of toast and the pot of strawberry jam. "If Aunt Jane was there, she didn't make herself known." As Carrie closed her eyes and shook her head, Fiona smiled and went on. "Beeps was most definitely there, though. He can vouch for my conduct. I was an excellent surgical assistant."

"Fiona," her sister said softly, "this is very serious."

As though she were the only one in the family who had ever risked scandal? Fiona shrugged. "Actually, it occurs to me, now that we're talking about it, that it's really rather typical of the Turnbridge women. You must admit that we seem to have a penchant for finding ourselves in situations that don't look good on the surface."

Carrie had nothing to say to that, of course, but Drayton wasn't as cowed by the truth. "Was Dunsford anything less than a complete gentleman?" he demanded.

She couldn't resist. Grinning, she replied, "He's an outstanding surgeon."

"You know what I mean," Drayton growled.

Yes, she did. Just as she knew that pretending to be Simone was becoming counterproductive. "His conduct was exemplary," she assured her sister and brother-in-law. "And if he shows up here in a bit, please assure him that there's absolutely no reason for him to sacrifice himself on the altar of matrimony on behalf of my reputation."

Drayton's mouth fell open. As he stared at her in mute silence, Carrie shot forward in her chair to grab the edge of the table with both hands and squeak out, "What?"

"He thinks we should marry," Fiona explained. "I've turned him down. Several times, actually." She shrugged, fastened her gaze on Drayton's and added firmly, "But he said he would call this morning and press you for a favorable answer. Please don't give him one."

Why the two of them seemed so deeply stunned . . . Well, all right, she could see that they had never expected *her* to present them with such a problem. She was the Perfect Sister, the shy and quiet one who went through life largely invisible. They'd never lain awake at night, bracing themselves to deal with disasters of her making. Simone's making, yes, but not hers.

So, all in all, she probably needed to allow them some time to come to terms with the fact that she wasn't quite as perfect or invisible as any of them had thought. Fiona sipped her coffee and prepared herself another slice of toast while she waited for their brains to stop staggering.

Whether it was the footman's mere arrival at the breakfast room door, or the fact that he softly cleared his throat to announce it, didn't matter. All three of them were looking at him by the time he bowed slightly and said, "Pardon the interruption, Lady Ryland. Lady St. Regis is in the parlor and says that she must speak with you on a matter of great urgency."

Carrie arched a brow and pulled her napkin off her lap. Rising to her feet, she laid the cloth on the seat of her chair, said, "I'll be back as soon as I can," and followed the footman toward the front of the house.

Drayton watched her go, then shrugged and turned his attention back to Fiona. "Dunsford's considered quite the catch, you know," he offered, reaching for his cup and saucer. Standing with them, he added, "It would be hard to do better than him," and headed for the sideboard.

"It wouldn't be difficult to do worse, either," she countered, passing him her cup.

"How so?"

"He's marrying because he has to, Drayton," she explained as she accepted her freshened cup. "Not for love. He has absolutely no intention of ever being a faithful husband."

"How do you know that?"

Fiona frowned and puzzled the notion as Drayton settled back in his chair. "I don't know how," she finally admitted. "I just do."

"Well, that is a negative," her brother-in-law allowed, as usual accepting her pronouncement as fact.

"A rather large negative."

He nodded slowly, then sighed and took a sip of his coffee. "So what happened to Beeps?"

The Dunsford Problem was done. Fiona leaned back in her chair and relaxed. "I don't know precisely. He slipped out the kitchen door at some point in the evening. I found him under the lilac bush shortly after we came home, his leg badly, badly broken. I scooped him up in my cloak and . . ." The memories rushed back in a torrent. "Oh," she whispered as the swift stream of them parted around a single detail.

"Oh, what?" Drayton asked warily.

"I borrowed your gun and forgot to bring it home with me," she supplied. "It's on the desk in Lord Dunsford's infirmary."

Again Drayton's mouth fell open. To his credit, though, it didn't take him nearly as long this time to recover. "You didn't use it, did you?"

Fiona chuckled. "I'm not Simone."

"True," he agreed. "*She* would have brandished a sword."

Not very well if she'd had a badly injured cat cradled in her other arm. But since that wasn't the point of the conversation, she kept the observation to herself. "You should probably know—just in case Lord Dunsford ever mentions it to you—I pointed the gun at him, but wasn't forced to fire it."

Poor Drayton. But he was getting better at recovering from the surprise every time. "Well, thank you, God."

"Save the thanks for later, Drayton," Carrie said from the doorway. Her skirt still swinging about her ankles and her hands gripping the doorjamb on each side, she added, "We have a little bit of a problem in the parlor."

A little bit of a problem was a little bit of an understatement, Fiona mused as they all sat in the formal drawing room and Dr. Ian Cabott, His Grace the Duke of Dunsford finished up his preliminary summary of the circumstances and moved smoothly into the request for her hand in marriage. As if the rest of her weren't attached to it.

Good God, she never would have guessed that their having met at the ball the night before would lead to this. Tending to Beeps' injury, yes, but beyond that? If only she'd had the presence of mind to scoot home right after the surgery instead of sitting down in the big leather chair to make sure that Beeps was going to emerge from the sedation without a problem. If only she hadn't fallen asleep. If only Dunsford had awakened her and sent her on her way.

But she had and he hadn't and the sun had risen with not only the two of them alone together in his townhouse, but also with half of Society's mavens rolling around town in their carriages desperately looking for an innocent situation to paint red and blow entirely out of proportion. And they'd found one. Sweet Mother of Pearl. The luck of the Turnbridge women was something truly, incredibly awful.

Carrie laid her hand on hers and gave it a gentle squeeze as she said softly, "We'll weather a scandal, Fiona. If you honestly don't want to accept the duke's proposal, we won't force you to."

Fiona nodded and stared at the carpet as she considered the situation. Yes, her family would endure anything for her. She knew that with absolute certainty. They loved her and her happiness mattered to them. Every bit as much as she loved them, every bit as much as their happiness mattered to her. She couldn't put them through the vicious gossip mill. It simply wouldn't be fair to them. She'd made the mistake all by herself, she alone should have to pay the price for it.

Surrender was the only reasonable course to take; she could see that, could understand it quite clearly. Still, the idea of going into a new life in passive acceptance of whatever terms the duke chose to lay down on a whim . . . No, there were limits to her willingness to make sacrifices. There were some things she wasn't willing to give up, some things she expected in return for graciously playing the part of the Duchess of Dunsford. There was nothing the least romantic about negotiating terms, but then, Lord Dunsford hadn't uttered a single word so far that could have been considered anything but purely pragmatic. And if he was approaching the matter rationally, then surely no one would fault her for doing the same.

Fiona dragged her teeth across her lower lip and drew a deep breath. Lifting her gaze from the carpet, she looked between Caroline's and Drayton's worried faces. "Might His Grace and I speak privately for a few moments?"

Caroline looked inclined to say no, but Drayton rose from his chair to cup her elbow and assist his reluctant wife to her feet. Saying, "We'll be waiting in my study," he led her out of the drawing room, leaving the doors open behind them as they went.

Ian Cabott stuffed his hands in his trouser pockets and began to pace. Fiona watched him, realizing that while she'd asked for the time to talk privately, she had no idea just what it was that she wanted to say to him. Simply declaring that he didn't own her and never would had a rather nice dramatic—if decidedly petulant—quality to it, but such a pronouncement didn't exactly leave the conversation with anywhere to go other than downhill. Which probably wasn't the best way to begin a marriage, forced or otherwise.

He made two trips across the room before he stopped and faced Fiona squarely. "As I assured your sister and brother-in-law," he began, "I had absolutely nothing to do with Lady St. Regis and Lady Phillips hieing themselves here to report seeing you leave my house this morning."

Of course he didn't; he hadn't had the time. But their busybody natures had undeniably helped his cause.

"I can't honestly say that I'm terribly distressed over them having inserted themselves in the situation," he offered. "I am sorry, though, that it's caused your family anguish in what should be an especially joyful time."

Joyful? What was there to be joyful about? This wasn't a proposed union of hearts. She'd seen Cook purchase onions in the market with more passion than Ian Cabott was displaying in the choice of a wife. "I can't believe this is happening," she muttered, closing her eyes and shaking her head.

"But it is, Lady Fiona," he said gently. "We can only accept that and make the best of the circumstances."

She sighed and lifted her chin. "And hope that it

somehow works out to be a happily ever after?" she posed, meeting his gaze. As she watched, his eyes went from soft blue to cool gray.

"It would certainly be wonderful if it did."

"And if it doesn't?" she pressed.

He drew a hand out of his pocket to rub the back of his neck. "No one ever enters a marriage with a guarantee of eternal bliss, Lady Fiona. Even those with stardust in their eyes as they head to the altar. We can only hope for the best and, if the reality should fall short of our greatest expectations, be prepared to make reasonable and caring accommodations for each other."

"Meaning that we would live largely separate lives."

He nodded. "Privately, yes." With a smallish smile, he added, "With a great deal of discretion so that it wouldn't become public knowledge, of course."

"What a lovely prospect," she observed, knowing she sounded shrewish and not caring that she did. Would it kill him to even pretend that he actually hoped they'd be happy together? Why his lack of blind optimism bothered her so much . . . Really, it wasn't as though *she* had any feelings for *him* beyond an honest respect for his abilities as a surgeon.

"Living separate lives is only one possibility among many," he added.

God. "And some of them are even more dismal."

"And some of them are considerably more happy and satisfying," he countered, apparently choosing to ignore her sour outlook. "I'd strive for the best possible outcome and see that you never have cause to accuse me of thoughtlessness or stinginess or callous disregard for your feelings."

Fiona nodded. What else was there for her to do? She couldn't very well demand that he promise her undying love and devoted companionship. Well, she could demand it, but she wasn't going to get it. Ian Cabott had a kind heart, yes. She'd seen it last night in his care for Beeps. But a kind heart didn't require that he also have an open and demonstrative nature. He'd promised to be respectful of her. He'd promised to be kind. He'd promised to hope that they could eventually become something more than businesslike strangers who shared a name and a lofty title. For him, the offers had been as effusive as he ever got.

There is no making the leopard's spots into stripes. Fiona tilted her head to consider the unexpected bit of philosophy. Undoubtedly true and quite appropriate, she concluded. Ian Cabott was as he was and there would be no changing him. Just as there would be no changing who she was. How a happy marriage could possibly work out between them, she couldn't even begin to imagine. And yet . . .

Everything in the world worked out as it should. Nothing happened without a reason. She knew that, had seen it happen time and time again. She and Carrie and Simone had been thrown away by their father only to be rescued by Drayton and given the

names they should have borne from birth. Carrie
had been forced to give up her dress shop and her
cherished independence to care for her and Simone,
and that sacrifice had been rewarded with Drayton's
abiding love and three beautiful, healthy children of
her own. Tristan had involved Simone in a twisted
murder plot they were both lucky to have survived
and their determination had resulted in one of the
best and happiest marriages in all of England.

"Lady Fiona? Are you all right?"

How nice of him to inquire. How sincerely concerned he sounded. Faith. It all boiled down to faith
and trust. If her sisters could live believing that
things would work out for the best, so could she. The
Turnbridge women were nothing if not survivors.
There was a great deal of comfort in that reality.
And, in fairness, there was an equal amount of consolation in the fact that Ian Cabott was no ugly ogre.

Fiona found a smile to give him. "Were you serious when you said that you didn't believe in long
engagements?"

"Yes," he assured her. "I hope to announce our
engagement this evening at Lady Miller-Sands' ball.
The banns will be published tomorrow with the wedding to take place on the first day following their
usual and appropriate run."

Oh, dear. Being resolved was one thing, being
rushed was entirely another. "Is there a particular reason for the haste?"

He cocked a dark brow in obvious surprise. "Is there a reason to delay?"

She could lie and avoid the awkwardness for a while. Or she could be honest and address her concerns squarely. For the sake of all their tomorrows, she opted for the latter. "Well, yes," she admitted. "Frankly, Your Grace, I'm not all that excited by the idea of bedding you."

He blinked several times, swallowed, and blinked some more before he finally said in a strained voice, "Really?"

"Really."

"Do . . ." He closed his mouth and swallowed before taking a deep breath and trying again. "Do you find me unattractive?"

Fiona caught the inside of her lower lip between her teeth to keep from smiling. How interesting to think that she might well be the first woman he'd ever come across who wasn't blithely willing to perform between his sheets. Even more interesting was the fact that he didn't seem to know quite what to do about it.

"It has nothing to do with your physical appearance, Your Lordship," she assured him. "You're a very handsome man."

He raked his hand through his hair, mussing the style in a boyish, unexpectedly endearing sort of way. "Would you please call me Ian?" he asked on a hard sigh as he considered her.

"I don't know you well enough to feel comfortable with calling you by your given name. Which, of course, should tell you that I most assuredly don't know you well enough to be at all comfortable with the notion of sharing your bed."

"Oh," he replied softly. He frowned for a second and then added, "Well, I suppose I can see your point."

"Thank you."

He lifted his chin and squared his shoulders, banishing the boyish confusion to firmly, manfully reply, "I promise that the consummation of our marriage will occur only when you decide that it's appropriate, when it's something you would be completely comfortable doing."

Why he thought she'd be more charmed and assured by the display of cool reserve . . . "Thank you again, Your Grace."

"Ian."

She smiled apologetically. "We'll have to work our way to familiarity by slow degrees."

"Of course." He cleared his throat. "Where would you like to go for a honeymoon?"

"Do we have to have one?"

"It's customary," he answered while blinking.

"I don't mind if we don't."

He knitted his brows and pursed his lips to study her. "Would you mind," he carefully ventured, "retiring to the country house after the wedding?"

"Not at all." In fact, it was perfect. Far enough away

from London to escape the watchful eyes and yet close enough that she could run home if she had to.

"Then that's what we'll do," he declared with a bow. "Would you prefer to tell your family that we've reached an accord, or would you like for me to relay the happy news?"

Of the two of them, he probably had the better chance of actually sounding happy. "I'll allow you to make the announcement, Your Grace. You can use the moment as practice for the grand announcement this evening at the Miller-Sands ball."

He bowed again, turned on his heel and marched out of the drawing room. Fiona arched a brow and watched him go, allowing that he certainly didn't lack in terms of being decisive and, at the same time, wondering if he had any idea at all where Drayton's study was.

Well, if nothing else, life with him was bound to be interesting from time to time.

Chapter Four

Ian glanced toward the rear door of the Ryland townhouse, then blew a stream of smoke toward the sky and thought back through the morning's events. His plan had been a good one. Nothing short of stellar, actually. He hadn't needed the assistance of the Ladies St. Regis and Phillips, but their outraged intrusion had weighted the situation nicely in his favor. If there really was such as thing as being smiled on by the gods, he most definitely had been.

He'd walked into the Ryland home, been greeted cordially, seated in the drawing room and encouraged to speak freely. He'd been served coffee and pastries and heard out graciously. Lord and Lady Ryland had both agreed on the wisdom of his proposal and, judging by their smiles, pleased with him for having made such an honorable gesture.

Admittedly it had been a bit of a surprise when Their Graces had handed the decision to accept his proposal or not to Lady Fiona instead of making it themselves, but he'd been confident in his persuasive abilities and the outcome. Looking back with the perfection of hindsight, he could see that that was the point where the plan had gone off the rails. Not at all like a speeding train, of course. If it had, he would have taken appropriate steps to head off the approaching disaster.

But he hadn't had the slightest inkling that he was heading for a derailment. In the moment that he and Lady Fiona were left alone . . . Ian blew another long stream of smoke and shook his head. Things would have gone quite differently if he'd remembered that she wasn't any persuasive slacker herself. Or if he'd had the presence of mind to recall her standing on his doorstep the night before, pointing a gun at him. But no, he'd blithely assumed that the demure little thing sitting on the settee wasn't any more complicated than she appeared. Ha! Beneath that calm exterior lay a rebellious and stunningly obstinate nature.

For heaven's sake, the woman had refused to call him by his given name. Then quite matter-of-factly declared her aversion to the idea of sharing his bed. She'd even refused to go on a honeymoon.

At the time, taken separately as her refusals had been presented, each point had seemed like such a minor issue on which to capitulate. At the end of it all, though . . . Well, the plain truth was that she'd taken him apart by small pieces. Yes, sweetly and gently, but nonetheless thoroughly.

He'd had two consolations as he'd gone off to
find the Duke and Duchess of Ryland to share with
them the happy news of the betrothal—that the
march to the altar was on the schedule of his choosing, and that his bride wasn't going to be the least
bit shocked if she ever found a stray feminine hair
on his jacket lapel.

As consolations went, they considerably out-
weighed the concessions he'd made. His original
plan obviously hadn't been flawless, but it had been
intact enough at that point that he'd been pleased
with the overall outcome.

Ian sat down on the garden seat and considered
the ground between his feet. It had taken the Rylands all of two seconds to pummel his sense of
satisfaction and control and then another second to
incinerate half of what was left of his grand and
stellar plan. No doubt there would be a day when he
would look back and appreciate the ease with which
they'd done it, but that day wasn't this one.

The way things were going . . . Jesus, the Queen's
army moved with less planning than it apparently
took to put together a marriage. It had taken serious
negotiation just to slip away long enough to smoke a
cheroot. How he was going to manage to escape for
the time it required to get to the apothecary shop was
beyond him at the moment. He couldn't very well be
honest about it.

Damnation, he didn't want to disappoint Lady
Baltrip this evening. And he certainly didn't want to

be disappointed, either. The only part the Rylands had left him of his grand plan was the traditional male freedom to bed whoever he pleased as long as he was discreet about it. But unless he put his foot down and insisted that Their Graces were perfectly capable of planning a string of gala affairs without his input on and approval of every piddling detail, he was going to lose that, too.

Lady Baltrip didn't strike him as either the forgiving sort of woman, or the sort to cool her heels and patiently wait for him to come around. And while there wasn't any doubt that he could find another woman to take her place, it would be difficult to find one as freely and openly willing as Lady Baltrip had proven to be.

"They say that misery loves company."

At the sound of her voice, Ian vaulted to his feet and turned to face his bride-to-be, his heart racing at the possibility that he might have been thinking out loud. Thankfully, she didn't look upset. Tired and strained, yes, but not wounded or angry.

"Or would you prefer that we wallow in it separately?" Lady Fiona asked.

"I don't consider myself miserable," he replied, gesturing to the seat he'd just vacated.

"Well, just as point of information, Your Grace, you're a miserable liar," she said, sitting down on the garden bench. "It doesn't take a sixth sense to see that you're just as unhappy as I am about being made the center of social attention."

He sat on the far end of the bench and stifled the urge to heave a huge sigh of frustration. "I thought all women lived to bask in the glow of public attention and congratulations."

"You thought wrongly."

About a great many things apparently. "You don't want an engagement ball?"

"It seems rather overblown since I don't dance."

"May I ask why you don't?"

To his surprise, she abruptly stood and stepped away from the bench, then turned back to face him, her skirts fisted in her hands. Surely she wasn't going to . . . Yes, she was. She lifted her hems quite deliberately, quite high, actually. High enough to give him a clear view of delicate feet and lovely ankles, as well as a tantalizing glimpse of silk-encased, perfectly shaped calves. A decidedly bold and provocative move for a woman who didn't know him well enough to call him by his given name.

Ian cocked a brow and forced himself to quickly look away. "I would think," he offered cautiously, "that you'd be a very graceful dancer."

"You're not looking close enough, Your Grace."

Well, since she'd invited him to stare . . . He looked again. "I see nothing but perfection, Lady Fiona."

She sighed and kicked off one of her mules, tossing it into the grass between them. Other than it being small, it was an ordinary-looking thing, the sort of shoe that a lot of women wore around the house during the day. Sometimes they even wore them to evening events as well, but those tended to be fancier, to have metal threads and pearls and . . .

She tossed her other shoe down beside the first one. The difference between them was immediately obvious, but he frowned and leaned forward for a better look anyway. If pressed for a judgment, he'd guess that the sole of the one shoe was a good five to seven centimeters thicker than the other.

He glanced at her feet. She stood there, her hems still raised, one foot planted firmly in the grass, the sole of the other barely brushing the tips of the green blades. He sat back, studying the shape of her foot. There being nothing wrong with it that he could determine by merely looking, he concluded that the problem was most likely in the length of either the lower or upper leg bones. Nodding and pinching his chin between his thumb and forefinger, he said, "I see."

She didn't reply, simply stepped forward on her shorter leg to slip her foot into the thin-soled shoe. Ian quickly looked up, noting that her expression wasn't the least bit pained by the movement.

"Is it the result of an accident?" he asked as she put on the thicker-soled mule.

"I've been told," she answered, sitting down beside him, "that I was born this way."

"I gather that it doesn't pain you in a physical sense."

"Not at all." She chuckled softly. "Which is not to say, of course, that the childhood tumbles I took as a result of it, didn't hurt. Looking back, I can see that

I was really lucky not to have broken my neck a time or two."

Given what she'd told him this morning of the circumstances of her birth and early years, it was a certainty that she hadn't been taken to a physician when a medical intervention might have corrected the problem. How long had she limped before someone had thought to differ the thickness of the soles of her shoes? he wondered.

"If you see the defect as cause for withdrawing your marriage proposal, I would understand completely."

He looked over at her, stunned. "I beg your pardon?"

"When I came to live with Drayton and Caroline, they took me to see a well-respected doctor. He said that there was nothing to be done to fix the length of my leg and that I should accept the possibility that any children I might have could be born with the same deformity."

"What a kind man."

"He was just being honest," she countered with a shrug. "But that aside, I can understand how you might be repulsed by the idea of our children being born deformed. If you want to rescind—"

"No," he declared, stunned anew. Did she really think that he could be that shallow? "My proposal stands."

"Well, if you should change your mind in the next few days, I—"

"I'm not going to change my mind, Lady Fiona."

She nodded—in what looked to him like sad resignation—and gazed off across the garden. "With the soles of my shoes being as they are, walking is easy enough. But dancing requires me to step backward, and despite the efforts of the best dancing masters in England . . ."

She shrugged her delicate shoulders. "I can't tell you the number of times I've toppled over, the number of times I've twisted my ankles in trying to learn. And there comes a point when you have to accept that the end result simply isn't worth suffering the process of achieving it."

"There's a great deal to be said for pragmatism," he allowed. "But considering the realities, I have to ask . . . Why are your sister and brother-in-law so delighted at the prospect of planning an engagement ball for us?"

"I don't have the foggiest idea."

He, too, gazed out over the garden. "We should," he muttered, "just run off to Gretna Green and be done with it."

"We'd have to keep running for some time," she countered. "All told, they're in there mapping out a plan for an engagement ball, a wedding, *and* a reception dinner ball."

"For some reason," he admitted, "I never considered how complicated this getting married business is. I always thought it was a simple matter of showing up at the church on time, not making a cake of yourself when it comes time to say your lines, and then letting people squeeze your hand into a soft pudding while they congratulate you on having decided to jump off a cliff."

She laughed. Not a soft little ladylike twitter, though. No, she tipped her head back and laughed outright and honestly. It was an amazingly delightful sound, full and rich and lively. Ian stared across the bench at her, captivated by the brightness of her smile and the sparkle in her eyes. He'd always known that she was pretty, of course. Any man would agree with him on that. But, Good God Almighty, when she was happy, she was nothing short of astoundingly beautiful.

She regained her composure by slow degrees, wiped a tear from her eye, and then moistened her lower lip with the tip of a pale pink tongue. He was marveling at how much she looked like a kitten when she said, "Better to be seen as jumping off a cliff than being asked if you're sure you haven't made a horrible mistake."

"You're kidding me." Surely people had more tact. "They actually say that to a bride?"

She nodded. "Oh, yes. Both my sisters were asked that time and time again. And there are any number of variations of it. Hug, hug. Kiss, kiss. Congratulations, my dear. I hope you've done the right thing. Although it is a little late to have second thoughts, isn't it?"

"How cruel."

With a shrug, she replied, "Yes, well, I think women tend to get vicious when they've lost out on snagging the bachelor of the season. It's their last chance to take a swipe at the victor."

Did men do such things to each other? Maybe they did and he'd just never noticed. It wasn't as though he'd ever paid much attention to the social pecking order in any respect. "One has to wonder why, given that tendency, one would deliberately have a party and invite them to it."

"I presume it would have something to do with the satisfaction of you being the bride and not them. Rather like rubbing their noses in their failure. Which," she quickly added, "doesn't strike me as being a particularly nice thing to do."

No, it wasn't. But from the sounds of it, that didn't prevent females from engaging in . . . well, a form of barely civilized warfare. And to realize that he hadn't had the slightest inkling that it was swirling all around him. Good God, he was lucky he hadn't bumbled into a cross fire at one point or another. He could have been seriously maimed.

"And of course all the details of the wedding and reception go to the same end," Lady Fiona went on, deepening and broadening his education. "What flowers and decorations you have. What food you serve. Which orchestra you hire. Who designs your wedding dress and trousseau. It's all terribly competitive, you know."

"I had no idea, actually. And I doubt that any other

man has the slightest clue, either. To us, a meal's a meal and music is music. The only competition we care about is the one around the gaming table."

"And who leaves on your arm at the end of the evening."

Well, there was a can of worms he wasn't going to open. "Only among those, Lady Fiona, who haven't had the wisdom and good fortune to marry a beautiful woman."

The look she slid his way said that she recognized ingratiation when she heard it. She slowly arched a brow, but instead of calling him on his too obvious dodge, asked, "Will we entertain a great deal after we're married?"

Relieved to have been let off the hook so kindly, he replied, "As a duke I'm rather expected to flaunt the wealth on a regular basis. I'm sure, being the sister-in-law of a duke, that you're more than familiar with the social expectations that go with the title."

"No, not really," she admitted. "Drayton entertains for political reasons. He doesn't much care for the social whirl outside of that."

Politics. Something else he had no real clue about, despite the fact that he held a seat in the House of Lords. "I've formed the impression that your brother-in-law is something of a reformer."

"Do you consider that a good thing?" she asked, looking out over the garden. "Or a bad thing?"

"I don't know much about His Grace's views on specific issues," Ian hedged. "I've been out of the country for the last few years. And to be perfectly honest about it, I haven't paid much attention to the business of Parliament since my return. It reflects poorly on me, I know, but I find the speeches and droning on to be incredibly . . ." He shrugged and, not wanting to risk insulting her guardian, left the matter there.

"Utterly, mind-numbingly boring," she finished for him with a smile and a twinkle in her eye. "Drayton says that if some of the members loved the people of England as much as they do the sound of their own voices, there wouldn't be nearly as much in need of reforming."

A statement that, if made publicly, would stir an ugly outcry, but one with which he could completely agree in private. "I'll have to pay attention in the next session," he offered as he contemplated the possibilities. "At least to what His Grace has to say. There's a great deal wrong in the world and I happen to believe that it's our duty to make life better in any way that we can. Since I've yet to see your brother-in-law's eyes spin or his mouth froth, I'm inclined to think that he's a sensible man with realistic goals I could support."

Lady Fiona nodded, too, and then, still gazing out over the garden, said, "You mentioned that you'd been out of the country in the years just past. Where have you been? Anywhere interesting?"

"Everywhere is more interesting than England," he groused before he could think better of it.

"Why is that?"

Since he'd broached the subject, he couldn't very well ignore her response to it. Not and be considered anything close to a gentleman. "The food is definitely different, for one," he offered, choosing his words carefully now. "Other countries tend to use spices freely. Spices other than salt and pepper. The cuisine of India is especially good. When I was summoned home to assume my father's title, I made sure to bring an Indian cook with me."

He smiled weakly and added, "I can only hope there will come a day when he and my English cook can reach some sort of compromise in the kitchen. At that point, I'll offer you a meal. In the meantime, though, dining in is a largely mishmash sort of experience."

"Our cook is very good," Lady Fiona said, grinning. "He was Drayton's regimental chef back in the day. When he was about to finish his service, he wrote Drayton and asked for a reference. Drayton took the carriage and went to hire him before anyone else could. He's making chicken biryani for luncheon today."

Chicken biryani? God, he could only hope that he wasn't drooling. "I know it's impolite to ask to be invited to a meal . . ." he began.

Chuckling softly, she assured him, "It's been assumed that you'll be dining with us. Chef Martin is preparing his specialty just for you."

And how would Chef Martin know what his

favorite dishes were? Maybe Harry was right and she could read minds. If she could, it was undoubtedly in his best interests to know just how extensive her abilities were. He summoned a casual smile. "How did you know that I enjoy spicy cuisine?"

"Everyone's heard that you were a surgeon in Her Majesty's Army medical corps," she replied brightly. "Drayton considered the likely garrisons and concluded that somewhere in the Near East was logical." She grinned and, her eyes sparkling, added, "After that it was purely a gamble."

So much for the possibly of marrying a woman with eerie, mind-reading powers. Harry had always been a gullible twit. After all the years, he really should have known better than to listen to him. That issue aside, the box had been rather neatly and conveniently opened on his immediate past. As his future bride, Lady Fiona had a right to know that it was going to create some difficulties for her.

"If you've heard of my service to the Crown," he said casually, "you must also have heard that my parents were appalled and embarrassed by it."

"Actually, I've been told that they weren't very happy with your decision to become a doctor."

"To put it mildly." *And the true start of the problem.*

"Why did you decide to train as a physician?" she asked, then hastily added, "If you don't mind me asking, of course."

Of course he didn't mind. He'd been asked the

question at least a thousand times over the years. "I was bored with being a child of extreme privilege."

She pursed her lips for a moment, then knitted her brows. "Perhaps that might have been part of it," she said slowly, "but I doubt it would have been a sufficient reason to endure their disapproval *and* the difficult training. I would expect that the reason would be more personal and closer to the heart."

How interesting. Of all the times he'd tossed out his ready answer, she was the very first to ever look past it and know there was more. That alone made her deserving of the truth. "My father owned a good number of properties, and when I was thirteen he decided that it was time that I surveyed the London part of what would someday be my personal kingdom. We rode around town in his outrageously appointed carriage, climbing out at each block so that I could meet the managers of the property."

Ian paused as the old memory rolled past his eyes, still every bit as vivid and disturbing as the day it had been made. With a deep breath for fortification, he went on, saying, "There was one stop, a tenement house where the Irish lived. On the walk in front of it lay a man with a badly mangled, badly bandaged leg. I knew looking at it that he had gangrene." Afraid that his voice would catch, he drew another breath and softly cleared his throat before adding, "My father stepped over him as though he wasn't even there."

And kept right on going, not even seeing the pain

and desperate hope in the man's eyes. The son of a bitch.

"He's not the only man to have ever done that," Lady Fiona offered gently.

"True," Ian allowed, pushing the anger away. "But I knew in that moment that I couldn't follow them."

"What did you do?"

Underestimated the quality of my father's character. "I demanded that the footmen help me load the man into the carriage and take him to a doctor. My father countermanded the order and had the footmen toss *me* into the carriage."

"And the man on the walkway?"

"He was dead by the time I found my way back there that night. It was as I watched them wrap him for burial that I decided that there was never again going to be a time when someone's life depended on my ability to get help for them. I was going to be able to help them myself. Right that moment, without having to ask or plead or hope for a flicker of compassion in others."

And, by God, he'd seen that promise to himself fulfilled. Despite all the nasty words and horrified outrage. Glaring at the ground between his feet, Ian lifted the cheroot to his lips and drew sharply. And got nothing.

As he considered the end of it and the rules about smoking in the presence of a lady, Lady Fiona said, "It's hard to imagine that a parent would oppose such a commendable ambition."

"You don't know my parents," he countered ruefully, flicking off the cold ash. "Well, as I've said, my father died last year. My mother still lives, though. In a way, he very much lives on through her. You'll see for yourself when you meet her. Probably next week sometime. Consider yourself warned."

She nodded in a thoughtful way and then smiled sweetly. "Well, however your parents feel about your choice, I'm sure there are a good many people who are grateful that you ignored their resistance and followed your calling."

"A few at least," he allowed, appreciating her determination to focus on the brighter side of things.

"Do you miss being in Her Majesty's service?"

"I certainly felt more useful there," he admitted. "And far more needed. No one in England is going to die if there should suddenly be one less duke."

"Fiona! Lord Dunsford!"

Together they looked up and toward the back door where Lady Ryland stood. Beside him, Lady Fiona sighed and then stood, saying, "Time to go happily plan the social campaign of the decade."

Ian, vaulting to his feet, quickly considered his options. "Please tell Her Grace that I'll be along in a moment or two. My cheroot went out as we talked and it would be a criminal offense to not finish it."

"Of course," she said with a demure nod and a knowing smile. "Take all the time you'd like."

She started away, her skirts fisted in her hands,

her hems raised slightly above her ankles. He watched her go, noting that her gait was even and certain, not the least affected by the different length of her legs. Perhaps, he mused, her inability to dance wasn't as much a matter of physical imperfection as it was the lack of the right dance partner. For women, dancing involved a great deal of trust.

Halfway to the door, she stopped and then slowly turned back. Her smile was soft and gentle. "Just so you know, Ian," she called to him, "I wouldn't be the least bit opposed to the idea of being a military wife."

He nodded, too stunned to form a coherent word before she resumed her way back to the house. What unexpectedly quick progress they'd made! One conversation on a garden bench and she'd called him by his name.

Maybe, if he made a concerted effort to be genuinely involved in the wedding planning, if he were a sparkling conversationalist during lunch, and if he pretended that he enjoyed the tedium of politics . . . She'd what? Give him a smile when he left the house? Let him kiss her hand in adieu? Be willing to talk to him when they met again that night at the Miller-Sandses' ball?

He cocked a brow and considered his choices: a perfectly polite conversation with a quiet young miss in the presence of God and all of London society, or a breathless, mind-staggering tryst in the garden and an alcove and the carriage with Lady

Baltrip. Ian sighed as his conscience clearly voted for the former and all the rest of him begged for the latter. Wondering how he could justify being a complete cad, he reached into his coat pocket for his tin of matches.

Chapter Five

Fiona sipped her punch and looked out over the edge of the Miller-Sandses' balcony. Something bad was going to happen. She could feel a kind of darkness gathering in the pit of her stomach. Nothing seemed to be amiss with the couples strolling in the gardens below. Heavy clouds were gathering to the west and a storm was certain before the night was over, but she sensed nothing unusual or particularly dangerous in it. From behind her, through the open French doors, drifted the notes of the orchestra and the sounds of a party well and happily attended. Nowhere was there the slightest hint of something about to go terribly wrong.

She sighed, took another sip, and wondered if she might simply be hungry. Or perhaps coming down with a bit of a cold. Not that either possibility was any more than a hope, she had to admit. God, she hated times like these, times when she could sense something coming, but couldn't say what it was or who it would happen to, couldn't prevent it.

The movement was at the very edge of her vision, quick and fluid and instantly familiar. *Simone,* she silently groaned. Lord, if ever there was a person who could create disaster out of nothing more than thin air, it was Simone.

"What are you doing out here?" her sister asked, closing the distance between them.

"Wishing I were at home, tending my animals or reading a good book."

"Trust me," Simone countered, laughing softly, "I know the feeling. Well," she hurriedly added, "the being at home part, anyway."

Fiona nodded, leaned down to plant her elbows on the balustrade, and gazed out over the shadowed garden again. "Why do we do these things to ourselves?" she mused aloud. "It's not as though our presence matters to anyone. Our absence, either."

Simone leaned her hip against the granite railing and replied, "Caroline just told me that Dunsford has asked to marry you and that you've accepted."

Leave it to Simone to get directly to the heart of any matter. Fiona nodded slowly. "You sound as though you don't believe it."

"I am surprised."

And not at all happily. The spark of irritation was just as instant as the words that tumbled off Fiona's tongue. "By which part? That someone would want to marry me? Or that I would accept a proposal?"

For a long moment the words hung between them in the night air, at obvious odds with the perfect notes drifting out from the ballroom. In the discordant clash, Fiona's irritation ebbed away, to be replaced by regret. She sighed and said, "I'm sor—"

"What I can't believe," Simone said, gently cutting her off, "is that you're willing to shackle yourself to a complete stranger. I'm assuming that there's one helluva reason for doing something so drastic."

"One woman's notion of drastic," Fiona countered, "is another woman's notion of reasonable. Lady St. Regis and Lady Phillips saw me leaving Lord Dunsford's home this morning and didn't waste a single second in getting to the house to tell Carrie all about it. Dunsford arrived about five minutes after they'd left, having done what they could to make a completely innocent situation just as scandalous as they possibly could."

"So?" Simone posed with a dismissive shrug. "It's not as if we've never been gossiped about or scandalized. Carrie and Drayton didn't twist your arm behind your back and make you say yes."

"Of course they didn't. But then, you and Carrie are made of sterner stuff than I am."

Simone snorted. "What a load of rubbish!"

It was the truth, but Fiona refused to waste the time and energy in arguing with her sister about it. "Weathering a scandal, however minor, is exhausting and painful and I refuse to be responsible for causing anyone grief. Dunsford offered to spare us all from the gossip. I certainly can't be any less considerate than he's being."

Simone sighed and, after a long moment, asked, "Were you at Dunsford's all night? Or did you just pop over at dawn to see if you could sell him some raffle tickets to the Orphan Canine Mission?"

"Half the night," Fiona explained, ignoring Simone's sarcasm. "While we were at the ball last night, Beeps got out of the house. Somehow he broke his leg and when I finally found him, I knew that if I didn't get him to a doctor, he was going to die. So I took him to the Duke of Dunsford for surgery."

"And?" Simone asked breathlessly.

"His Grace is a highly skilled surgeon and he honestly did the best he could. Beep's leg couldn't be saved, but he'll manage just fine on the three he has left."

Simone gently laid her hand on her shoulder, saying, "Oh, Fi. I'm glad he's going to be all right. I know he means the world to you."

"Thank you."

Her sister reached up and smoothed a curl off her shoulder. "I'd really like to think that the man you're going to marry means just as much to you as your cat does."

Yes, well . . . in a perfect world, in girlish fairy tales . . . "It will work out for the best," Fiona assured her.

Simone pursed her lips for a long moment and then slowly arched a raven brow. "Is that conclusion based on pure optimism, or is it one of those things you sometimes know?"

Optimism? No. Resignation maybe. Or perhaps it was more a stoic sort of guarded hope.

"Never mind," Simone said. "I can see the answer in your eyes. Carrie said that the engagement is going to be announced at her and Drayton's annual ball. Which gives you three weeks to make sure you really want to do this. Backing out after that would be possible too, of course, but a lot more difficult. Especially considering your aversion to scandal."

"Scandal or not," Fiona countered, "I've given Lord Dunsford my word, Simone. I'm not going to change my mind."

Simone's brow arched higher. "In that case," she drawled, "I'd like to meet my future brother-in-law. Is he here this evening?"

The chill that had been confined to Fiona's stomach suddenly spread into the marrow of her bones. Simone and Ian together? Simone who had never once in her life behaved in a manner even close to circumspect? Ian who was so keenly aware of appearances that he was willing to marry a physically deformed stranger to keep them from being tarnished?

"I promise to be nothing short of thoroughly proper and delightfully congratulatory," Simone cheerily offered, slipping an arm around Fiona's shoulders and giving her a quick hug. "Since he's obviously not out here," Fiona went on, turning her away from the balustrade, "he's probably in the ballroom. At least that would be my first guess. Shall we?"

Fighting the inclination to dig in her heels, Fiona allowed her sister to guide her toward the French doors. Maybe, she offered herself as she blinked into the bright light of the ongoing party, she might be lucky and Ian had already ducked into one of the males-only gaming rooms. If she were really lucky—and there was a truly benevolent God—Ian had decided to stay home this evening.

And if she wasn't lucky . . . "Perhaps we should freshen ourselves a bit before we start a serious search."

If a bird in hand was worth two in the the bush, what, Ian wondered, was a duke in the palms worth? "Not much" seemed to be the only answer, and it so disgusted him that he stepped out into full view of God and every professional gossip in London. He'd no more than made one passing glance around the ballroom and snagged a glass of champagne from the tray of a passing waiter than Harry was at his side.

"Where have you been all day?" his cousin asked. "I've looked high and low for you."

"You didn't look at Lord Ryland's townhouse."

Harry took a half step back, his eyes wide in horror. "Good God, you haven't taken up politics, have you?"

"I was getting myself engaged."

"No," Harry countered, laughing.

"Yes."

His cousin instantly sobered, blinked several times, and then quickly glanced over both of his shoulders before leaning close to ask, "To Lady Fiona Turnbridge?"

Fiona worried about having children that limped? He was far more concerned with the likelihood of producing a village of idiots. "Is there," he dryly asked, "another Ryland female who's unattached whom I don't know about?"

Again Harry looked over his shoulders before saying in a furtive whisper, "Good God, Ian. Why her?"

Ian shrugged. "She showed up on my doorstep in the wee hours of this morning, brandishing a loaded pistol and carrying an injured cat. I couldn't very well close the door in her face, and by the time the cat and I were both assured of seeing another day, that day had arrived. Given the appearances of her leaving my house in the early morning hours, there wasn't anything to be done but head off the scandal with a marriage proposal."

Harry shook his head, took a single step forward to impede a waiter long enough to get a glass of champagne for himself, and then came back to Ian's side saying tartly, "In other words, she trapped you."

Ian tamped down his flaring anger and looked over at his cousin. "She did no such thing. In fact, she initially refused to accept my proposal."

"They all do at first," Harry assured him in a

worldly tone. "It's part of the whole innocence facade. I can't believe that a man of your experience fell for it."

A man of his experience knew a genuine lady when he saw one. That Harry didn't was no great surprise, but his willingness to insult out of ignorance was disappointing. Ian turned to face his cousin and met his gaze squarely, saying, "Lady Fiona is a remarkably honest young woman, Harry. Please accept that assertion as fact and don't tread on her character again."

Harry, lackwit that he was, grinned. "You're actually smitten with her, aren't you?"

Smitten? Dim-witted and a romantic. "Hardly," Ian answered on a snort. "Let's just say, shall we, that from what I've seen so far, she possesses some unique qualities and that I realize that I could have done far worse for myself in the marriage mart."

"Her ability to look through people being one of those unique qualities. A rather dubious one, if you ask me."

He hadn't asked and quite frankly didn't care what his cousin thought. Despite those facts, Ian felt compelled to reply, "Harry, the only people she looks through are those with nothing to see when she searches inside them."

"Oh. That's even more disconcerting. That would suggest that she can see all the dirty little personal secrets."

An intriguing thought. What secrets did he have? He'd given John Albright two answers on their final chemistry exam. And he hadn't told anyone that Morris Preston had robbed a grave for his required dissection cadaver. There was the matter of the mysterious theft of quinine from the medical stores in New Delhi, but to his mind the fact that it had gone to treat local orphans rather balanced out the less-than-scrupulous means of attaining it. That children died in the process of compiling paperwork and making petitions for permission was unacceptable.

Of course there was the affair with Amanda Masters. If a person were to tally his sins without asking for explanations, cavorting with a fellow doctor's wife would undoubtedly count heavily against him. How much providing her a happy respite from her deeply unhappy marriage would be to his credit, though . . . At the time it had seemed not only a justifiable thing to do, but downright honorable.

And it wasn't as though he'd walked away without paying a price for the illicit relationship; without telling him, Amanda had named him as her daughter's guardian in the event of her death. Caring for Charlotte definitely qualified as penance. At least for the moment. Once he and Lady Fiona were—

"Your mother," Harry said from beside him, "is not going to be happy with this choice, you know. Lady Fiona's past isn't exactly sterling."

Through absolutely no fault of her own. "My

mother lives to be unhappy. It's her only satisfaction in life. And I long ago gave up any hope of changing her disposition."

"Well, let's cross our fingers that Lady Fiona can develop a similarly dismissive attitude about her."

Ian shrugged and took a sip of his champagne. "It won't be necessary," he assured his cousin. "My mother understands the basic reason why she has her residences, I have mine, and that there are several days' traveling distance between them."

"Except when you're both in London," Harry pointed out. "I assume you've already written to tell her that you're on the verge of taking the great matrimonial leap and invited her to be here for the occasion."

"The best thing about having respectable females in your life is that they liberate you from the details of social expectations. Lady Ryland wrote her this afternoon, asking her for her guest list for the engagement ball. I'm sure she also included the expected niceties about looking forward to meeting her in the near future."

"That should be interesting," Harry offered with a droll chuckle. "The Dressmaker Duchess Ryland does battle with the Dowager Dragon Dunsford. You could probably sell tickets to the contest, you know, and make a tidy little sum."

Tickets were a possibility only if the confrontations weren't done in full public view. "It might not be a battle at all," he posed hopefully. "They might well find themselves agreeable on everything."

Harry snorted before retorting, "Not once in all of my life have I seen your mother graciously cooperate with anyone about anything. Things are done her way or they're not done at all. She's contrary for the sake of being contrary."

True. "I'm sure Lady Ryland will be able to achieve some sort of harmony. If today was any sort of indication, she's very good at seizing control of situations."

"Well, I just hope that you've thought to warn Lady Fiona of what awaits her in terms of her future mother-in-law's proclivities and expectations. To let her wander into the maws of that beast without a warning would be unconscionably cruel."

"I've hinted at it."

"You better do more than hint. And the sooner the better."

"Agreed," Ian said before taking another sip of his drink.

"Have you hinted to her about Charlotte, as well?"

What did it say about his character that he found his irascible mother easier to talk about than his tempestuous, deeply grieving ward? "I'll explain fully as soon as the opportunity naturally presents itself."

Harry made a humming sound that held the un-mistakable notes of censure, then suddenly straightened his shoulders and stiffened his spine. "Speaking of opportunity . . ." He lifted his glass toward the ballroom entry. "Lady Baltrip has arrived."

Damn. So much for long odds and the hope that he wouldn't have to decide between being honorable and pleasured. He glanced back over his shoulder at the safe haven of the potted palms.

"Ah," Harry drawled around a grin. "Given the twinkle in her eye, I'd say that she has fond memories of your stroll in the garden last night."

Twinkle in her eye? So much for hiding in the greenery. Lady Baltrip would see any sort of seclusion as an opportunity for a—

"How long before you're clapped in manacles?" Harry asked as Lady Baltrip began making her way across the ballroom toward them.

"I beg your pardon?" Ian asked, his mind staggering through his rapidly dwindling options.

"When is the engagement announcement going to be made?"

"Lady Ryland had already scheduled a gala affair for three weeks from now. The betrothal will be announced that evening."

"And the wedding?"

"Three weeks after that."

"A crescendoing close of the Season." Harry lifted his glass in salute. "Perfect timing."

"Perfect for what?"

"Six weeks is just the right length for an affair. Either you're both bored by that point and ready to

mutually cry quits, or she's hoping for a more permanent relationship and you're suddenly looking for
a convenient escape. Marrying someone else tends
to send a very clear message that the tryst can only
evolve so much farther."

"That's true," he admitted. Of course he'd have to
tell her tonight that he was going to be engaged before the month was out. She deserved to know. Yes,
telling her immediately would be the only honorable
thing to do. That way there would be no deception
in their relationship. But what if Fiona were to find
out about the affair? he wondered.

"And who knows," Harry went on blithely. "It
could well be that by the time you march yourself to
the altar, Lady Baltrip might be quite happy with the
idea of being your mistress."

"Or not," Ian countered, unable to envision Lady
Baltrip patiently and faithfully waiting for stolen
moments.

"Well, in any event, enjoy every second that remains of your absolute freedom," Harry counseled
as he edged away. "Once there's a wife watching
your every move, having a good time becomes considerably more complicated."

Interesting. He didn't see Fiona as being the sort
who would expect a daily accounting for every
minute of her husband's life. She didn't strike him as
the sort of woman who would be enraged by her husband's infidelity, either. Deeply wounded, yes, but not
enraged. From what he'd seen of her temperament

so far, he'd wager that she was incapable of anything approaching anger. Yes, she'd pointed a pistol at his chest, but there was considerable difference between resolution and irrational fury. Lady Fiona clearly lacked for nothing in terms of determination.

"Oh!" Harry said, stopping and looking over his shoulder at him. "Did I offer my congratulations on the acceptance of your proposal?"

"No, you didn't."

He lifted his glass. Barely. "Congratulations."

"Thank you."

Harry winked and walked off, leaving Ian alone with his thoughts. They immediately arrowed back to his bride-to-be. Fiona also possessed an amazing sense of grace and uncommon good sense in difficult circumstances. She didn't want to marry him, but had accepted his proposal because it was the prudent and rational thing to do. And while she'd obviously been dismayed at the idea of their marriage being one of convenience, she'd accepted the possibility with great poise. And he had been honest with her about the likelihood of his having discreet affairs.

"Ian, darling."

Not that there was anything even remotely discreet about having an affair with Lady Baltrip. At any time.

She looked up at him, peering through her lashes, and purred, "You look as though the weight of the world is on your shoulders this evening. I'd be delighted to remove it for you."

His body instantly tingled at the prospect. His conscience squirmed. "I have a matter that I need to discuss with you."

"Shall we ever so nonchalantly wander off to someplace more private for it?"

He knew better. "It might be a good idea to—"

"Follow me, darling," she whispered, turning away with a seductive smile. "Discreetly, of course."

His conscience firmly told him that if he had a brain in his head and so much as a dram of good judgment, he'd stay right where he was. Ian threw the last of the champagne down his throat and went after her. By the time he reached the library, he'd disposed of the empty glass and acquired two full ones on the hastily-arrived-at theory that handing her one of them would slow her down a bit, that her taking a sip or two would give him time to tell her about his approaching engagement to her friend's youngest sister.

And if there was a God with even a modicum of benevolence, Lady Baltrip would instantly and clearly see the inappropriateness of their affair and put an end to it herself. Yes, it would ever so easily take the burden of decency off of him, but the end result was really all that mattered. If she didn't care one whit about a betrayal of Fiona, though . . . He'd simply have to find the inner strength to do the right thing without unduly hurting Lady Baltrip's feelings.

Resolved, he kicked the library door closed behind himself and carried the champagne flutes to the woman waiting for him in front of the flickering hearth. "Lady Baltrip," he said smoothly, offering her a glass.

"Jane," she corrected, ignoring the champagne and undoing the buttons on his jacket.

Jane. Now was a helluva time to come by that bit of information. He took a half step back and encountered the leather sofa. His calves pressed hard against the front edge of the massive piece of furniture, he extended the glass again, saying, "I'm afraid, Jane, that I must disappoint you this evening."

"Oh, that's impossible, Ian. You're simply not capable of a poor performance."

Well, yes, that was true, but . . . "I mean that I wasn't able to get to the apothecary shop," he replied, doggedly pursuing his objective. "Circumstances unexpectedly arose today and I—"

"Not to worry, my darling Ian," she said, dropping to her knees in front of him and deftly working open the first button on his trousers. "For the moment we don't need a letter."

"But—"

"And I brought a supply for us later, just in case."

God, he needed to stop her hands, but with both of his holding crystal flutes . . . He glanced at the mantel. Too far.

"Jane," he began as he tried to force the glasses between the hands artfully working their way down the line of buttons. She laughed and paused just long enough to brush his effort aside and slosh champagne over the rims and onto the carpet.

Ian quickly drained a glass and then blindly tossed the empty crystal onto the sofa behind him. With his free hand, he caught a slender wrist and stayed it, saying tautly, "Jane, stop. There's something I must tell you."

Only partially restrained, she smiled up at him and reached inside his trousers for his traitorous member. "You're so tense this evening, Ian. Not that it's entirely a bad thing, of course."

"Jane, please," he pleaded as he tightened his hold on her wrist. "I don't want to hurt you."

"You talk, I'll listen," she murmured as she leaned forward.

Desperate, his knees quivering, he tossed the other glass after the first, grabbed her shoulders, and pushed her away. "Jane," he said firmly as she gazed up at him in hurt and confusion. He cleared his throat and pasted a reassuring smile on his face. "I can't remember ever having a lover of your awesome skills and selfless desire to please, but we must break off our—"

The gasp startled him, and for a long second his brain worked with an odd, disconcertingly slow clarity. The sound of shocked outrage came from the doorway. Which of course meant that someone had walked in on them. A female someone. Making it a decidedly awkward situation. Unless, of course, there was a male with her, a male who would take her by the elbow and spirit her away before there was any chance of the shock deepening to the point of him having to stammer through an apology. Hoping for the best, he glanced toward the door in the same instant that Lady Baltrip did.

"Oh, dear," she whispered on a lilting giggle.

He withered in Lady Baltrip's hand and his stomach dropped to the soles of his feet. "Uh . . ." he managed to say as he looked into Fiona's tear-filled green eyes. And then she was gone, a blur of pale green silk and bobbing blond curls racing for God only knew where. Her dark-haired companion apparently wasn't inclined to follow her. Actually, if he had to hazard a guess, he'd have to say that she was more inclined to kill him on the spot. Slowly and brutally. And he couldn't say that she was overreacting all that much.

Lady Baltrip laughed softly from her position at his feet. "There's no reason to be so angry, Simone. If Fiona doesn't know the most basic facts of life by this point, it's high time that she did."

The woman's eyes sparked with cold fire as she looked between the two of them. "Fiona is well aware of the facts of life, Aunt Jane," she said crisply. "Her shock and my outrage comes from walking in to find you with the man who just this morning asked her to marry him."

Lady Baltrip started and cried, "What!" as she looked up at him, horrified.

"That's what I've been trying—"

The rest of his explanation evaporated in an excruciating bolt of white hot pain that shot from the apex of his thighs to his brain only half an instant before it set every fiber of his being on fire, buckled his knees, and obliterated the rest of the world.

A flash of lightning turned night into day even as the thunder rattled the rain-streaked panes of her bedroom window. As darkness returned, Fiona pulled the bed coverings to her chin and glared up at the ceiling. She'd known the instant she'd walked into the Miller-Sandses' ballroom that something bad was going to happen, but to walk in on Aunt Jane and Ian Cabott in the midst of a tryst . . . God, she hadn't even considered the possibility of something like that.

And then, in the horrible moment of discovery and realization, she'd turned into an utter ninny and run away in tears, her heart wailing that he didn't love her. Of all the ridiculous, absolutely groundless fantasies . . . He'd told her in the parlor that morning that they'd likely have a marriage in name only, that he had no real intention of putting any genuine effort into developing a loving relationship with her.

She'd told herself after that conversation that she would find a way to be content with whatever kind of marriage they managed to build together. Apparently she'd been lying to herself. Obviously, given her hurt at finding him with Aunt Jane, she, in her heart of hearts, believed in fairy tale happily ever afters. In love being able to conquer all. She was nothing more than a stupid, dreaming fool.

Another flash of lightning illuminated the room. The window panes rattled again as the tree limbs outside groaned in the fierce wind. God, in hindsight, she should have let Simone run him through. But no, she'd lifted her chin, claimed that she didn't care enough about Dr. Ian Cabott, the Duke of Dunsford, to be bothered with retribution. And Aunt Jane . . . sobbing and begging for forgiveness, claiming she hadn't known about the proposal . . .

Fiona closed her eyes and clenched her teeth. *Always nice Fiona. The Good Sister who overlooks slights and shortcomings and always forgives. Fiona who believes that people are, at their core, kind and don't intentionally hurt others. Quiet Fiona who never says a word when others disappoint, abuse, or wound her. Fiona who rolls her shoulders and disappears within herself so they can't hurt her anymore.*

Tears rolled out of the corners of her eyes and down into her ears. Sniffling, angry with herself, she sat up and used the corner of the sheet to mop away the evidence of her pointless self-pity. Why she couldn't be angry with other people when it might actually have a positive effect . . .

Shock and anger had propelled her out of the Miller-Sandses' library. Pride and anger had been at the root of her forgiveness of Aunt Jane and her refusal to let Simone exact justice on her behalf. Indignation and anger had carried her away from the ball and all the way home. Anger alone had gotten her upstairs to her room and into bed. But had she bothered to turn so much as a scrap of her outrage and anger at Ian? At the cause and source of her turmoil and anguish? Her abiding embarrassment?

Her heart pounding and her breathing quick and shallow, Fiona flung herself back down into the feather mattress as the mantel clock quietly chimed the arrival of the fourth hour of the new day. A new day. Perhaps, she mulled, it was the day for a new Lady Fiona Turnbridge to be born. A Fiona who wasn't quite so nice, quite so innocently and freely giving. Maybe it was time for her to put her own happiness before that of everyone else on earth.

And in the spirit of her newly adopted selfishness she ought to announce first thing at breakfast tomorrow morning that not only had she changed her mind about marrying the Duke of Dunsford, but that he could take a flying leap under the nearest set of speeding carriage wheels for all she cared. Caroline and Drayton, interested only in her happiness, would be understanding and respectful of her decision. And they'd most definitely appreciate that she'd called off the engagement before they'd spent a fortune on an announcement ball that wasn't going to be one.

Although, come to think of it, Carrie and Drayton weren't planning an engagement ball from scratch; they were simply modifying the purpose of a gala event they'd long ago scheduled. They could easily make it *not* an engagement ball again.

Fiona arched a brow as a bolt of lightning lit up the world and thunder shook the foundation of the house. A not-so-nice Fiona wouldn't let a cad like Ian Cabott off the hook quite so neatly and easily. No, she'd delay rescinding her acceptance of the duke's proposal until the very last possible moment. And then do everything within her feminine power to make sure that, between this moment and that final one, he came to truly appreciate the wonder and joy he was going to lose.

And if that didn't work . . . Well, then she'd have to see how Simone felt about running him through.

Chapter Six

The next morning arrived clear and bright, all traces of the storm gone and the world washed clean. Fiona sat at her dressing table, staring at her reflection in the mirror and pondering the course of the resolution she'd made in the midst of the tempest. Just exactly how did a woman go about weaving her feminine wiles? she wondered. She considered each of the women in her life and how they had . . . well, for the lack of a better word, *captured* their husbands.

Caroline had been thoroughly competent and efficient, making over Drayton's country house from top to bottom in record time and then graciously entertaining all of Lady Aubrey's idiot friends. Simone had thrown a knife into Tristan's back. Yes, there'd been considerable intrigue in their relationship leading up to that moment, but as defining moments went, it was quintessentially Simone. As for Aunt Jane . . . Sex. Freely given. It really wasn't any more complicated than that.

Wondering just what skills she might have, Fiona glanced around the room, her gaze coming to rest on Beeps lying in the center of the feather comforter, diligently cleaning his face and ears. Her heart filled at the sight of him so contentedly going on with his life after having come so close to losing it. If it hadn't been for Ian's compassion . . .

Clenching her teeth, Fiona struggled against a tide of guilt and second thoughts, reminding herself that the esteemed Dr. Ian Cabott hadn't been willing to help Beeps until she'd pointed a gun at his chest and given him only one other choice. Then he'd let her fall asleep in his surgery so that she was in a compromised position when she finally woke. The ever so businesslike marriage proposal counted against him, too. And the affair with Aunt Jane . . . a good meter of icing on the huge cake of his short-comings.

No, all things considered, Ian Cabott, the Duke of Dunsford, deserved to be taken down by at least a dozen pegs. How to do it, though . . .

She didn't have any particular skills. She couldn't design and sew as Carrie could. Despite having pointed the gun at the duke, her skills at creating mayhem and physical injury weren't anywhere near those Simone possessed. She'd been absolutely desperate; Simone did such things as a matter of instinct and usual course. As for freely giving her body à la Aunt Jane . . . Well, that was a bad idea for any number of reasons, not the least of which was that as a virgin she didn't have a well of expertise from which to draw, and since the whole goal was to make the duke regret losing her . . . No, better to let him imagine what could have been rather than risk having him utterly relieved at being shed of an awkward, novice lover.

Skills . . . She could read and write in three languages and do advanced mathematics. Hardly the sort of activities that made men fall to their knees in gushing worship. Beyond those dubious abilities, the only other skills she truly had were those necessary for taking care of injured animals. Of course her family were the only ones who considered those abilities laudable. Everyone else considered them to be proof positive of a simple mind and a wildly eccentric character. The latter view being the one she'd already amply proven for the duke.

With no answers and weary of futile thinking, Fiona sighed and rose from her seat. She checked Beeps' food and water bowls, the bandage on his leg, and then gave him several long reassuring strokes before heading down to breakfast and the looming inquisition.

Well, perhaps *inquisition* was too strong of a word, she allowed as she glided down the stairs. Caroline and Drayton were concerned about her, about her feelings, and wanted only to help her cope with the nightmare she'd inadvertently walked into. She'd evaded the issue last night by promising that she'd be prepared to fully discuss the ramifications of the "unfortunate Aunt Jane incident" over the morning meal. It was hard to imagine that they'd approve of her plan to be an Evil Fiona, so maybe the best thing to do was to let them do the talking and just nod a lot while looking contemplative.

Fiona barely had a foot over the dining room threshold when Caroline looked up from her plate, smiled, and said softly, "Good morning, Fiona, dear. How are you feeling?"

Confused, angry, and uncertain. "Fine, thank you," she replied as she stepped to the buffet and picked up a warm plate.

Drayton didn't bother with either the pleasantries or a preamble. "Do you want me to call on Dunsford this morning and rescind your acceptance of his marriage proposal?"

And punch him in the nose while I'm at it, she silently finished for him. Smiling as she helped herself to sausages, she chose her words carefully as she replied, "It's kind of you to offer, Drayton, but I think not. At least not today. It seems to me that such important decisions are best mulled on for a while. I'd rather not act rashly out of shock and pure emotion."

"A very mature point of view," he allowed, sounding, to Fiona's ears anyway, both suspicious and amused.

She turned to carry her plate to the table and saw a quiet, knowing approval in her sister's smile, a surprisingly appreciative twinkle in her eye.

"So," Carrie asked sweetly, reaching for her cup and saucer, "how long do you intend to let him stew, as they say, in his own juices?"

She should have known that Carrie would see right through her. And since she had, there was no point in pretending otherwise. "I haven't decided."

"But," Drayton responded, his brow cocked, "you *do* intend to break the engagement in the end."

Well, there was no doubt as to the course Drayton thought she should take. "I'm willing to give His Grace a bit of time to make an attempt to redeem himself. If he does so in a spectacular sort of way, then we'll go forward. If he doesn't . . ." She shrugged. "My heart isn't going to be broken."

Carrie nodded, sipped her coffee, and then said, "Well, as scandals go, having been seen leaving his house yesterday morning has decidedly paled against last night's fiasco. Don't feel obligated to go through with the marriage simply for the sake of appearances."

Everyone in London knew about the unfortunate Aunt Jane incident? It wasn't bad enough that she'd been mortified at walking in on the two of them together, but now she got to see the pitying looks from everyone she met? Wonderful. Just wonderful. The only reason she was going to leave the house in the next week was if it were on fire. And then it was going to have to be a huge fire.

"Pardon the intrusion, Your Graces."

"Yes?" Drayton said as Fiona looked up from her

plate to see the footman standing in the doorway, a paper packet in his gloved hand.

"This has just arrived via a courier, Your Grace," the man replied, advancing to the table, "and to your immediate attention."

"Thank you."

The footman bowed and left as Drayton cocked a brow, broke the seal, and opened the folds. Reading, his brow inched ever higher.

"So?" Caroline prompted. "Are you going to tell us what it is? Or make us guess?"

"It's from Dunsford," Drayton answered, still reading. "The settlement offer for Fiona's hand that he and I discussed yesterday. At least it bears a vague resemblance to what we decided."

"Oh?" Carrie prodded diplomatically.

"I can conclude one of two things," Drayton said as he refolded the document. "Either he's consumed with guilt and remorse for his conduct last evening and is attempting to make amends, or he's in such physical pain that he's drunk himself to the point of wild generosity."

Carrie chucked and Drayton grinned. Fiona looked back and forth between them and then finally asked, "Physical pain?"

Her sister cleared her throat softly and then replied ever so sweetly, "Jane made a concerted effort to unman him. In his shock, he toppled backward into the sofa, sitting down rather hard on a pair of champagne flutes. Apparently that pain moved him forward, but not quite to his feet. He toppled off the sofa and face-first into the carpet where he was left alone to contemplate his poor judgment and then collect what he could of himself to get home."

"How horrible," Fiona murmured. He'd been a cad, yes, but—

"He'd have been in worse shape," Drayton growled, "if he'd still been lying there by the time I heard what had happened." He held up the packet. "Do you want to see what His Grace is offering? Bearing in mind, of course, that the settlement should have no impact one way or the other on your ultimate decision to marry him or not."

Without a word she took the packet from him, opened it and began to read. There was a clause pertaining to the soundness of mind of the signatories—her and Ian respectively—and another clause regarding the freedom of their individual wills. Following that was a rather lengthy and surprising provision transferring the titles of two houses—one in London's Mayfair district and one in Scotland—into a trust for perpetuity, regardless of the length of their marriage and whether or not she produced any children for him.

The most shocking discovery Fiona made, though, concerned the amounts of money the Duke of Dunsford was delegating as annual stipends for her and their eventual children. She read the passage twice, but even then found the figures hard to grasp. To call such a staggering amount an allowance would have been ludicrous.

After the section detailing the yearly income, there was a clause concerning the disbursement of the estate in the event of Ian Cabott's death. She read that passage three times, unable to imagine sums that large, but understanding that the funds and property he intended to leave her would likely make her one of the wealthiest women in England. The provisions for any children they might have were just as large, just as generous. Clearly, as the Duchess of Dunsford, she would never want for money or the things it could buy.

If only it could buy her love and happiness.

She knew full good and well that Ian Cabott hadn't offered to marry her out of the demands of his heart. Given the incident in the Miller-Sandses' library, he obviously had no great and abiding aversion to scandal, either. No, he'd made it clear in his initial proposal that he was motivated primarily by the need to fulfill his obligations to the peerage, to produce the expected male heir and a spare so that the title would continue on. His secondary motives were no more complicated or personal; he needed someone to manage his home and a respectable, reasonably attractive female to take to Society events.

Undoubtedly, to his way of thinking, any single female would do just as well as another. If she hadn't shown up with Beeps and inadvertently put herself in a compromising position, he'd likely have written the names of single females on slips of paper and tossed them into a hat, drawn one out and considered the matter neatly resolved.

Given all of those realities, the settlement offer was far more generous than he had cause to offer. Drayton could be right as to Ian Cabott's motives, but which possible scenario it might be made a considerable difference. Genuine regret was one thing, a drunken, pain-clouded mistake was entirely another. She had absolutely no intention of letting the promise of wealth and material comfort affect her judgment, but she truly wanted to know the reason for Ian Cabott's exceptional—and completely unnecessary—kindness and generosity.

Fiona put down the settlement papers asking, "How long do I have to think about signing this?"

"Good manners," Caroline explained, "suggests no more than a day or two."

"Good manners being a reciprocal thing," Drayton added firmly, "I'd say you can take however long you damn well please."

She nodded, considering her course, and then announced, "I think that I'd like to call on His Grace this morning." At Drayton's glower and Caroline's arched brow, she added, "If he was kind enough to offer a huge settlement, I can be kind enough to check to see if his brain was scrambled when he fell to the floor last night."

Drayton muttered about Ian Cabott's brain being

located in another region of his anatomy. Caroline shot him a warning look and then laid her napkin beside her plate. Rising, she said, "I'll be glad to accompany you. Let me change my clothes and we'll be on our way."

Fiona offered Drayton a reassuring smile as Caroline left the dining room.

"Be careful," he admonished with another glower as he picked up his morning newspaper. "Words are cheap. A man is best judged by his deeds."

With that pronouncement, he snapped open his paper and ended the conversation. Fiona nodded anyway and dutifully made a note of his advice.

What a difference daylight made. Daylight and not being preoccupied with getting home before she was missed and the scandal mill began to churn. Fiona followed the butler across the cold marble foyer of the duke's home and willed herself not to shudder. Carrie trailed behind her by a pace or two, but Fiona didn't dare look back at her sister. One glance, no matter how quick, and Carrie would know that her confidence was crumbling by the second.

Fiona's first real opinion of Ian's residence had been formed as they'd climbed down from the carriage and made their way up the front walkway. Massive dark gray granite stones stacked one atop the other to the height of three stories and looking so much like a fortress that she'd craned her neck and searched the roof line for archers' slits. There

were windows, of course. On all three floors, all of
them exactly alike and very precisely spaced. All the
curtain linings were of the same fabric.

The front door that had seemed only old and thick
in the darkness was, in the light of day, also huge and
clearly designed to keep the Huns from battering
their way in for tea and biscuits. The poor little pair
of carefully manicured boxwood topiaries potted up
on either side of it were undoubtedly supposed to
whisper a refined and stately welcome. Unfortunately, the rest of the house was bellowing *Go Away!*

A swift visual survey of the house's interior from
the front door had only deepened her initial impressions. Obviously Ian had spared no expense in either the construction or the furnishing of his city
residence. The rugs were from the Orient, thick and
obviously finely woven. Only the sheerest silks and
finest damasks—with luxurious fringes trimming
the edges—draped the windows. The floors were
tiled in dark gray tending to black marble and the
walls and banisters were paneled in dark woods that
spoke just as much of far off forests as they did the
impressive skills of the English craftsmen who had
transformed them into works of art.

The furnishings throughout were clearly expensive and—were she to hazard a guess—culled from
the finest estate collections from all across Britain
and the Continent. The linen covering the tables was
brilliantly white and probably Irish. Everywhere—
on the table tops, on the bookshelves, in the wall

niches—were the very best appointments money could buy anywhere in the world. There were crystal figures of elephants and giraffes, gold boxes of every size, and silver . . . well, silver everything: trays and candlesticks, picture frames and bowls, and even floral arrangements.

And despite all the money with which Ian Cabott's home had been furnished, it was a gloomy, dark, forbidding place with all the homeyness of a two-hundred-year-old mausoleum. There wasn't a doubt in her mind that a formal tour of the whole thing would reveal a grand structure with wide staircases, countless rooms—all of them perfectly decorated and meticulously maintained.

Yes, if Ian's home were being described by the architects and doyens of home fashion, the homage would be to every nook and cranny speaking eloquently of great wealth and refined taste. It wouldn't occur to them to mention that there was nothing in this house that said anything about the owner other than his ability to spend whatever he wanted to acquire whatever he wanted.

There were no portraits of his family—living or dead—on the walls, no obviously personal items scattered here and there. There wasn't even a scrap of mail on the foyer table or a newspaper lying on the parlor settee—a monstrous thing upholstered in the current fashion rage of dark plum brocade. In fact, she'd seen absolutely nothing in the house so far that suggested that anyone actually lived there. It most certainly wasn't a home as she knew them.

Fiona nodded to the departing butler and then deliberately turned about to study the parlor in detail. Yes, just as she expected; it was perfection. She hated it. And from that realization came firm resolution: There was no way on God's green earth she was ever going to agree to be the resident docent of this Museum of Privilege and Extreme Wealth.

Ian looked up from the architect's drawings to stare at his butler. "I beg your pardon, Rowan. I don't believe I heard you correctly."

"Her Grace, the Duchess of Ryland has called with her sister, Lady Fiona Turnbridge. They are awaiting you in the parlor."

Well, at least there was nothing wrong with his hearing. "Thank you, Rowan. I'll be there directly."

"Very good, Your Grace. Shall I have refreshments served?"

"It depends. Are they armed?"

"They both appear to possess two of each, Your Grace. Perfectly normal in appearance."

Ian rubbed his fingertips over his rapidly tightening brow and rephrased the question, asking, "Did you happen to catch sight of what might be considered a lethal gleam in either of their eyes?"

"No, Your Grace."

"Well, if it's all the same to you, I'd rather not be

found dead, draped over a tea cart with my head stuffed into a teapot and fussy little sandwiches mashed into my shirtfront. We'll see how it goes before we order tea. But as a courtesy, please inform Mrs. Pittman that we have guests and warn her of the possibility of me having to be a gracious host."

"At once, Your Grace."

Ian waited until Rowan had closed the heavy infirmary door behind himself before he walked stiffly to the sideboard, poured himself a generous amount of whiskey, and swallowed it down. He didn't normally drink this early in the day and certainly not at home, but if ever there was a looming conversation that required high-proof alcoholic fortitude, it was the one awaiting him in the parlor. He tried to remember the last time he'd so badly mangled a relationship. And couldn't. No, last night he had managed to stumble and bumble his way to an all new high level of achievement. Or depth, depending on how he looked at it.

The aftermath was nothing short of an unmitigated disaster. To his mind, Lady Baltrip's vengeance had been considerably over the top, especially considering the ruthless degree to which she'd been pursuing her objective just prior to the door being flung open. He was going to spend the next week or so in acute physical discomfort and then at least another two after that fully healing.

He'd earned his pain, though. Fiona hadn't. Which meant that healing her hurt was going to be a far more difficult task to accomplish. For as long as he lived he'd remember the wounded shadows darkening her beautiful green eyes, remember the sight of the tears welling along her lashes and how she'd run away before they could spill down her cheeks. To know that he was responsible for her anguish . . .

And God, her embarrassment. Personally *and* socially. A gently raised young woman, a complete innocent, so sweet, hopeful and trusting . . . If she had a mean bone in her body, he'd hand her a pistol and invite her to shoot him. Lord knew he deserved it.

If only he'd listened to his conscience and not followed Lady Baltrip off to the library. If only he'd been more forceful with her at the outset, said to hell with finesse, and bluntly announced his pending engagement. The entire mess could have been so easily avoided.

But he hadn't done one sensible thing and now he was going to have to pay the piper. Dramatically increasing the marriage settlement had been the first thing he'd thought of to address the wrong he'd done her. Not that he expected her opinion of him to be swayed by the offering. He didn't know much about Lady Fiona Turnbridge in a personal sense, but of one thing he was absolutely certain: money wasn't the reason she'd agreed to marry him. In fact, he wouldn't be at all surprised to learn that she and her sister were waiting in the parlor to fling the settlement papers in his face and tell him, ever so succinctly, to go to hell.

And if they did, he'd have two choices: either gracefully accept being discarded as bad rubbish and go about selecting someone else to be his duchess, or figure out a way to get back into Lady Fiona's good graces. The first of his options wasn't without its difficulties. All of London was talking about his escapade with Lady Baltrip, and scandals did tend to make fathers a bit leery of handing off their precious daughters to a male of dubious judgment and no sense of fidelity. A few weeks would see the worst of the whispering past, though. And what paternal qualms remained after that could be soothed with a sizable marriage settlement. Yes, he could find himself another duchess easily enough and without an unreasonable delay.

But he really didn't want to. It was odd how settled his mind was on making Lady Fiona his wife. He'd only met her a scarce day and a half ago and yet there'd been precious few minutes between then and now that she hadn't been in his thoughts.

What was it about her that so consumed his thinking, his feelings? No one else had ever had that kind of power over him. Was she worth groveling for? Even as he wondered, he knew the answer: yes, she was. She was the most decent, honest and kindhearted person he'd ever known and his world would be infinitely brighter for having her in it. Ian poured himself a second glass of whiskey, downed it as quickly as he had the first, and then set off to do whatever he could to salvage hope from the mess he'd made.

Six long strides took Ian across the foyer and to the open parlor doors. Not bothering to announce himself with a knock, he simply stepped across the threshold. A slim, golden angel stood gazing silently into the fire, her gloved hands clasped demurely before her. She started and turned as he entered, but said nothing as her gaze quickly swept the length of him in critical appraisal. The firelight at her back, illuminating her pale curls and burnishing her silhouette in golden bronze light ... Ian swallowed and dragged a breath into lungs that had suddenly become painfully tight. Jesus, she became more beautiful every time he saw her. Her eyes were such a bright and clear shade of green and her pretty pink lips ... They'd be a delight to kiss. So soft and yielding.

Ian willed his awareness away from temptation and along necessary paths. Remaining where he stood by the doors, he softly cleared his throat, and began by saying, "Thank you for calling today, Lady Fiona." He glanced over at her sister, dipped his chin in acknowledgment and added, "And you, Lady Ryland."

Fiona squared her shoulders. "It remains to be seen as to whether we can truthfully call the occasion a pleasure."

The cool distance, the reserve of her response didn't deter him; in fact, given the circumstances, it seemed only right. Ian nodded and faced the situation squarely. "I sincerely apologize for my conduct last night, Lady Fiona. I won't attempt to offer an explanation or an excuse. There are none sufficient to absolve me of my lack of good judgment."

"True. But I'd like to hear an explanation anyway. However paltry and flimsy it may be."

Her words, though calmly and evenly spoken, struck him with the force of a well-aimed, well-thrown brick. He blinked in shock, slowly realizing that her eyes were bright with fiery indignation. The resolute angle of her chin, her tightly laced fingers . . . Good God Almighty. He'd never guessed that she possessed such strength.

He managed a shallow breath on which to reply, "As I said, there are no adequate explanations to excuse my behavior last night. The fault is entirely mine."

At the edge of his awareness he saw Lady Ryland roll her eyes, heard her mutter something about stupidity and gallantry. Lady Fiona didn't give him the time to ponder it.

"Your Grace," she said, taking a step toward him, "I have never in my life met a man as presumptive, insensitive and self-centered as you are. And to put it bluntly, despite your misguided attempt to shield Aunt Jane from any sort of culpability, what I've seen of your behavior so far doesn't speak well of either your honor or your character. Which in turn leads me to believe that we would *not* be the least bit suitable for a life together."

Ian stood in silent, awed amazement before the quiet fierceness of her anger.

"Know this, Ian Cabott," she added. "Write it in blood and carve it in stone. I refuse to be nothing more than a glorified housekeeper and a brood mare for any man. I won't tolerate a husband who cavorts with any and every woman willing to lift her skirts for him. And if you think that offering me houses and obscenely huge annual allowances is going to make me deaf, dumb, blind, and sweetly accepting, you can very well think again."

To be honest, he'd thought that perfectly possible at one point. Just yesterday, in fact. But today was a new day that clearly required him to adjust his thinking on a great number of things. He cocked a brow, wondering just how much ground he could afford to give. There was a fine line between agreeing to a marital partnership of relative equals and surrendering control of his entire life to the whims of a female.

"I can understand that you need time to ponder your decision," she said, stepping to the side and obviously preparing to leave.

Ian stepped as well, blocking her path as he said, "No more time than I've already had, Lady Fiona. If you'll accept my apology for last night and give me a chance to prove that I'm not nearly the faithless, mean-spirited beast you believe me to be, I'll promise that you'll never again have cause to doubt either my fidelity to you or my devotion to your happiness."

She met his gaze and for a long moment considered him in silence. Finally, slowly and warily, she nodded. Knowing that his victory was a small one and that it could well fade to nothing if she had time to reflect in solitude, Ian smiled, bowed, and said, "Thank you, Lady Fiona. Would you like to see the rest of what I hope will be our London home together?"

Her eyes went wide and he watched her struggle to swallow. Her delicate lips parted and her breasts rose and fell in quick cadence.

"We'd love to," Lady Ryland chirped from over in her corner of the parlor.

Chapter Seven

The only joy she'd found, fleeting as it was, had been in the faces of the household staff who'd been quickly assembled in the foyer. She'd been mortified when Ian had introduced her as the woman he hoped to be the new duchess, but the gasps from his servants had been ones of delight. Their smiles had been wide, and she'd felt truly welcomed as Mrs. Pittman, the tiny, grandmotherly-looking house-keeper, had introduced each member of the sizable staff in turn, detailing their length of service and giving her a quick summary of their respective responsibilities to Ian and his estate. By the time the introductions were done and everyone had either bobbed a curtsy or bowed to her, her mind was mush, capable only of whispering, over and over again, that they were all kind people and they would help her.

She'd cast a quick plea at Carrie as Ian had begun the tour of the public rooms of his monstrous dwelling, but Carrie's analytical, designing mind was so immersed in the new surroundings that she was absolutely oblivious to anything and anyone else. Initially, she'd felt betrayed by Carrie's absorption, but as the tour had progressed, she'd found herself more and more grateful for it. Carrie had asked a thousand questions and *oohed* and *aahed* every time they'd turned a corner or opened a door. Her sister's obvious interest and lively conversation with Ian had made her own silence both less noticeable and considerably less awkward.

"I hope that you'll feel free to make any changes you'd like," Ian said as they passed side by side through the open double doors of the drawing room, Carrie gliding silently—for once—in their wake.

"There are all kinds of fine rugs and furnishings in storage. Mostly things my grandfather and father collected over the course of their lives. If you'd like to see them, Mrs. Pittman will show you where they're kept and have them brought out for inspection. All you have to do is ask," he continued as they came to a halt in the center of the large, chilly room. Carrie moved past them toward a pair of leaded glass French doors that led out into the gardens.

"If there's anything you don't like at all," Ian went on, "just send it out to auction and replace it with whatever it is that you do want. There's nothing in this house that I have any particular feelings about one way or the other. Well, except for my surgery and office," he added with a grin. "I would appreciate it if you'd ask me about things in there before you have them hauled off."

"Of course," she said, with a nod of acknowledgment. How could she tell him that she was completely overwhelmed? That she thought it would be impossible to turn this cold, uninviting mansion into a warm and welcoming home? There was absolutely no way to kindly or gently say that the only hope she saw was in selling every stick of furniture, every piece of bric-a-brac, before knocking the whole thing down and building a new house.

"I'm sure I'll eventually think of some changes I'd like to make," she added diplomatically. "Assuming, of course, that I eventually become the mistress of all I survey. And even then, I'll take time to see how your household functions and discuss any changes with you first."

"It's *our* household," Ian corrected. "You don't have to ask for my approval for anything. I trust your good judgment and good taste."

While she smiled and nodded in acceptance, Ian was keenly aware that the expression didn't reach her eyes. As he had been several times in the course of their tour, he was again struck by how terribly out of place she seemed in the house. At first he'd thought it was simply a matter of the masculine colors of his inherited decor being at complete odds with her feminine grace and elegance and the huge rooms making her seem even smaller than she was. But while those possibilities might well have been part of it, he sensed that there was considerably more. What it could be, though . . .

"Forgive the intrusion, Your Grace."

He turned from Fiona and his musings to find Rowan standing in the open doorway of the drawing room. Ian cocked a brow in silent inquiry.

"Mr. O'Connor has arrived, Your Grace. He says the matter is urgent and requires your immediate attention. I have placed him in your study."

O'Connor wasn't a man given to either exaggeration or panic. If he required Ian's time, then the matter was important enough to stop what he was doing and take care of it. "Please tell him I'll join him directly, Rowan. And when you've delivered that message, please instruct Cook to prepare some tea for Lady Ryland and Lady Fiona."

"A messenger has arrived for Lady Ryland, as well," Rowan replied.

"Oh?" Carrie said, turning from her inspection of the gardens.

Rowan bowed slightly. "From His Grace, your husband. He asked that you be reminded that the interviews for the nursery maid were scheduled for this afternoon, Your Grace."

"I had completely forgotten," Carrie exclaimed, her surprise sounding something less than completely genuine to Fiona's ears. "Thank you, Rowan," she added as she came to Fiona's side. "And thank you, Ian, for the tour of your home. I've very much enjoyed it."

"It's been my pleasure, Lady Ryland. Please feel free to return any time you'd like."

Fiona didn't have to work up a smile; her relief was completely real. "Yes, thank you, Your Grace. Perhaps we can stay for tea next time."

Carrie put an arm around Fiona's shoulder and gave her a quick hug, saying, "Just because I'm going, doesn't mean you have to, Fiona, dear. In broad daylight with a bustling household staff and a formal engagement just weeks away, the requirements of propriety can be stretched a bit."

A protest was on the tip of her tongue when she saw the resolution in her sister's eyes. She and Simone called it The Look. Part flint, part love, all determination, it wordlessly said that Carrie had set her mind on a course and no amount of pleading, negotiating or arguing was going to alter it. Fiona had no idea why Caroline had decided she should stay, but she knew better than to make a scene about it. Later, when she finally escaped and made her way home, though . . .

Carrie smiled sweetly in silent victory, kissed her cheek, said, "Enjoy your afternoon," and then breezed toward the door without so much as a backward glance of regret or reassurance.

Rowan cleared his throat. "Would Your Ladyship prefer to take your refreshment in the drawing room or the dining room?"

Trapped, abandoned, Fiona mentally compared the distance of the two rooms from the kitchen and opted to inconvenience the staff as little as possible. "The dining room, if you would please," she replied.

"As you wish, Lady Fiona." He bowed again and departed.

Ian turned to her. "I'm sorry to have to leave you so abruptly and in the middle of our tour. I'll try to make quick work of whatever concerns and questions O'Connor has."

"It's quite all right," she hurried to assure him. "I understand how matters can arise unexpectedly and demand attention. Please take all the time you need and don't be concerned about me. I'll contemplate possible renovations until you return." *Either that or arson,* she silently added.

He seemed to want to say something, but after a moment he simply nodded, turned and left her alone in the opulently furnished and cheerless drawing room to contemplate how her day had gone so utterly and completely wrong.

Staring down at the black-and-gold Persian carpet, Fiona shook her head in dismay. She'd come here intending to play the part of a demure, deeply wounded maid, to let him see what a genteel and gentle lady she was and make him feel like a worm for being unfaithful. But, as was the way with most lies and false pretenses, it had all fallen apart. He'd walked into the parlor looking as though he were prepared to take yet another beating and her heart had twisted and melted. Angry at herself for being so weak, she'd been anything but demure, genteel, or gentle.

And then, despite having all but picked up the fireplace poker and lopped off his head, he'd not only apologized, but groveled. All right, he'd groveled in a dignified way, but it was still a surrender. And in acceding to every single one of her demands, he'd left her with no choice except to be gracious in victory and allow him a chance to redeem himself.

From there . . . Once her plan had begun to ravel, it had just kept on unwinding. Carrie had accepted his invitation to tour the house, ending any possibility of a quick retreat. The staff assumed she'd accepted the duke's proposal and would soon be their mistress. In encouraging her to make any changes she wanted to in his house, Ian had repeatedly presumed that she would eventually accept. Hell and damnation. Carrie assumed it, too, or she wouldn't have left her here alone.

Fiona lifted her head and squared her shoulders. Everyone could make all the assumptions they wanted to. She wasn't of a mind to do the same. She might have verbally accepted Ian's proposal but, until she signed the settlement papers, nothing was official and she wasn't legally bound to go through with marrying him. And she wasn't going to sign anything until Ian Cabott had proven himself capable of being a decent and genuinely caring husband.

Fiona sat alone in what amounted to a hallway, sipped her tea, and looked down the length of the dining room table made of what she thought might be rosewood. Whatever the wood was, it had been polished to a mirror finish. There were twenty-four chairs—thirty-six if she counted the ones that were pushed up against the walls. Good Lord, if she and Ian ever dined in this cave alone, the only way they could have a conversation would be by having servants running back and forth between them with written messages.

Why they'd choose to dine in here, though . . . The outside wall was of a line of tall windows spaced every few meters. The inside wall had no fewer than three huge marble fireplaces spaced down the length. With ornately carved mantels, brightly polished brass tools and gorgeously worked fire screens, they were nothing short of beautiful. But the flames dancing in the grates didn't touch the chill in the room. The tea she'd poured steaming into her cup had gone stone cold within seconds. Food, no matter how hot when brought from the kitchen, wouldn't stay warm in here any longer than a minute or two.

With chilled fingers, Fiona smoothed the forest green silk of her sleeve and pulled the black velvet cuff down over her hand. God, given how cold the room was, either Ian never had parties or he didn't believe in his guests being comfortable long enough to linger for a meal. If he thought otherwise, he would have lowered the ceiling by putting in a false one. No one would ever know, not with the skills of a good carpenter and a talented plasterer. Not only would the dining room be more inviting, the heat from the hearths would actually have a chance of keeping both the diners and their food warm. She shook her head and drank the rest of her cold tea thinking that since he could well have afforded to make the change long ago, it must mean that he hadn't seen the necessity of it.

It was this way throughout the house, Fiona mused darkly. Not one single room invited a person to come in, to linger, to enjoy living life in it. The dimensions were huge, the ceilings high, the carpets and drapes dark and heavy. And while the furnishings were nice and obviously expensive, they were placed for display rather than to encourage either quiet conversation or happy gatherings.

Ian had said that he wasn't particularly attached to anything in the house. She could certainly believe that. In many respects, Fiona decided, the house was very much an extension of Ian Cabott's manner and physical presence. One could see the wealth and gentility, feel the imposing size and power. It was all very impressive on the surface. But beneath that there was nothing but a hollowness, a lack of warmth that said that comfort and personal relationships weren't the least bit important.

The sound of jingling keys brought her from her less-than-charitable thoughts. She looked up to see Mrs. Pittman standing in the doorway that led into the foyer. In her hands was a small square silver picture frame.

"If you prefer to be alone, Your Ladyship," she said, "I can come back another time."

"No, please," Fiona quickly assured her, motioning her to come forward. "I'd love the company. There's an extra cup since His Grace hasn't finished his meeting yet. The tea might even still be warm enough. I've been very careful about keeping the cozy tucked around the pot."

"It does tend to be a bit chilly in here in the early afternoons," the housekeeper said, settling herself onto the chair at Fiona's right. She placed the picture facedown on the table as she added, "It's somewhat better in the early evening, once the sun's warmed the outside walls and the heat from fires has had a chance to settle into the lower part of the room."

Fiona nodded and, as she poured out, shared her idea of lowering the ceiling with Ian's housekeeper.

Mrs. Pittman smiled broadly and happily as she accepted the cup of tea. "Oh, Your Ladyship, it's just such wondrous things that we've always hoped for when His Grace finally decided to settle down and marry. I can't tell you how happy the staff is with the coming nuptials, how very pleased and reassured we are by His Grace's choice for his bride and our mistress."

It wasn't kind to let the woman assume. "Thank you, Mrs. Pittman. It's nice to know that I'd be so warmly welcomed here, but I haven't formally accepted His Grace's proposal."

The other woman opened her mouth as though to reply, then closed it and studied her tea. Determined that there be only honesty and plain speech between them, Fiona said, "Please say whatever you want,

Mrs. Pittman. I don't stand overly much on formality, and if I do decide to marry the duke, I'll consider you my most valuable partner in running this household.

"Frankly," she added on a sigh, "I can't even begin to do it without you. I don't have the foggiest notion of how it's supposed to be done. I've never paid the least bit of attention to how my sister goes about it."

Again the older woman's smile was broad and genuine. "I appreciate your openness, Your Ladyship. I'd be delighted to assist you in any and every way I possibly can. I had thought to say that I've been in His Grace's family's service for many years and that I deeply respect him as both a man and, since his father's passing, as an employer. I know that he often has a distant manner, but he truly is a decent man; not at all mean-spirited as are some members of his . . ."

Before Fiona could prompt her to finish the thought, Mrs. Pittman set aside her tea cup and picked up the picture. "I thought you might like to see this," the housekeeper said, handing it to her. "It's a picture of His Grace, drawn by my late husband years and years ago. When we first came into the family's employ."

Fiona looked down at the ink drawing and felt an invisible hand close gently around her heart. The face was Ian's, as a child of no more than five. Despite all the years since, his basic features—the well-defined line of his nose and cheekbones, the firmness of his jaw and the arch of his brows—were still the same. But that was all the similarity between the boy and the man he'd become. The boy in the picture had an impish smile and a light in his eyes that spoke not only of a joy in living, but also of an openness and willingness to love. This boy wasn't anything like the self-possessed, reserved and commanding man he had become.

"Sometimes," Mrs. Pittman said, softly intruding on her thoughts, "I catch a glimpse of that little boy in His Grace. It's usually in the oddest moments, when I least expect it, but always when something surprises him and he forgets for a moment that he's a duke and that he bears a world of obligation on his shoulders." She sighed and added wistfully, "No matter how hard and cold he seems, that little boy is still inside. So eager to please, so happy when he does. He'd have become a much different man if he'd been born to different parents."

Yes, his parents, Fiona mused. He'd mentioned them yesterday when they'd shared the bench in the garden. While he'd provided little in terms of detail, the impression he'd given of them spoke of an unhappy home and uncompromising expectations. She had only a vague recollection of the shadows of her own childhood; the years since Caroline and Drayton had rescued her had replaced them with happy memories of a home and family in which she was loved without condition and allowed to follow her heart and her dreams. To not have that . . .

"Thank you for showing me this," Fiona managed to say, handing the picture back to the housekeeper. *And for reminding me not to judge a man I don't really know,* she silently added.

"I knew the moment I saw you that you were the kind of woman who would appreciate it," Mrs. Pittman said with a soft smile while rising from her chair. "Is there anything I can do for you? Perhaps have Cook prepare another pot of tea?"

"It's most kind of you to offer," Fiona answered. "But I'm fine."

When Mrs. Pittman had gone, she sat alone in the dining room, lost in silent reflection. For the first time since she'd met Ian, she let herself consider the feelings he stirred in her. There was no denying that she found him physically appealing. He was not only a breathtakingly handsome man, but powerfully, magnificently built. How such a large man could move with the easy, lethal grace of a cat . . . He could easily break her in two. Not that he would. No, she knew to the center of her bones that he would never intentionally hurt her.

He was an excellent surgeon and his motives for becoming a physician spoke of a man with a strong conscience and a keen sense of public service. There was absolutely no fault she could find in him for having defied his parents to take up the study of medicine. In fact, she had nothing but extreme admiration for him in that regard.

But something about him made her uneasy, made her wary of . . . Of what? she silently posed, frustrated. She couldn't even define what she was reluctant to do. She picked up a crustless sandwich from the tray and nibbled as she sorted through her impressions of Ian Cabott. Handsome. Independently minded. Highly educated and intelligent. Wealthy and generous. Definitely persistent.

Kind? Well, yes. He'd saved Beeps' life and offered to marry her to save her reputation. The whole thing with Aunt Jane hadn't been so much an unkindness as it had been an incredibly bad moment of poor judgment compounded by really horrible timing.

Maybe, she mused, absently picking up another sandwich, her wariness had nothing to do with Ian and everything to do with herself. What it could be . . . She shook her head and thought back to the last time she could remember feeling as though all was right in the world. Her life had been so serene, so predictable and comfortable until . . . Until Aunt Jane had asked her to go the ball and peruse romantic possibilities for her. In that instant she'd sensed the hand of Fate propelling her forward. She'd gone without resistance, blithely accepting, never suspecting that the order of her world was going to be so quickly turned upside down and so slowly turned inside out.

Fiona sighed and closed her eyes. It was all so very complicated. And, yet, at the same time so very simple—if one were being honest. She didn't know precisely what lay ahead in her life, but she was certain that if she agreed to marry Ian Cabott she'd no longer have complete control of her world. Yes, there would still be moments of serenity and predictability, but there would also be feelings wilder and more powerful than any she had ever known. What, precisely they were, she couldn't say, but she could clearly sense them gathering out on the edge of her tomorrows. And she knew—to the very center of her soul—that if she married Ian they'd consume her and change her both profoundly and forever. It was the possibility that she might not be able to control those changes that made her uneasy. Maybe even a little frightened.

Ian walked beside Fiona down the garden path, his hands clasped firmly behind his back, his gaze carefully fastened on the paving stones ahead of him. Wisdom said that being alone with her wasn't a good idea. Ian smiled ruefully and silently admitted that his injuries, the sleepless night before, and the day of unexpected decisions had worn what was left of his good judgment to a weary nubbin. He was to the point, he had to admit, of being too tired to think straight, too dizzy by the unexpected turns his life had taken in the past two days to care all that much about propriety.

Silence hung between them, heavy and taut. Clouds scudded across the afternoon sky and Fiona drew her black velvet cape more closely around her neck. Ian, walking at her side, noted the cool breeze that blew through the gardens and wished that she hadn't thought to bring her cape along so that he could have given her his coat. At least offering it would have given them something to talk about.

"I'm sure," Fiona said gently, apparently as aware of the awkward silence as he was, "that Caroline could tell you the Latin names and the growing habits of every one of these plants. She has the most amazing mind when it comes to designing things."

Ian paused to examine a leaf bud. "Do you like to garden, too?"

"I'm afraid that my approach to it's considerably less informed and a lot less precise than Carrie's. She plans and plans, draws pictures and stands forever, squinting and imagining. I garden because I like the feel and smell of freshly turned earth. My planning amounts to mixing packets of seeds and scattering them everywhere. When they come up . . . I like the surprise."

He nodded. "So Lady Ryland sees gardening as an exercise for the mind, while you see it as a respite for the soul."

The fullness and depth of his understanding stunned her. Fiona smiled, her spirits buoyed. "Perfectly stated," she replied. "I gather that you like to garden, too?"

"Like your sister, I enjoy the planning and the initial planting. There's a unique satisfaction in transforming bare ground into something ordered and beautiful."

"You planned these gardens then?"

He nodded. "Oh, I thought I was the grand planner at the time, but in hindsight I can see that George, Mrs. Pittman's husband, was very good at guiding. He had a gentle hand and an easy way. We worked for the better part of three seasons to lay out and establish the basic design." His smile shaded to sad as he added, "And then I was sent off to school and became too important to spend time with the gardener."

"You must have very fond memories of your days with him," Fiona ventured.

"Sometimes," he said quietly, gazing into the distance, "it's the smallest gifts that mean the most. Time. Kindness and patience. It's a shame that we often don't realize how special people are until years later." His attention came back to her as he added, "I hope you'll feel free to make any changes you'd like out here, Fiona. Plant whatever you want, wherever you want. Make surprises to your heart's content."

"I wouldn't want to alter your and George's design. It's lovely and has good memories for you." As though heaven wanted to second her observation, a cloud rolled on its way, allowing sunshine to spill softly over the garden. The golden light touched the chiseled planes of Ian's face just as he lifted it to gaze into the distance. Fiona felt her breath catch. So handsome, so sad. So very, very alone.

"Actually," he said, "George wouldn't mind at all. He always said that gardens that didn't change were the sign of a dead imagination and a stagnant soul. I've been thinking that were I to do it over again, I'd do several things differently. For instance . . ." he said, placing his hand on her shoulder and leaning close to point at a distant object. "Do you see that pear tree over there? The one crowded into the corner? It hasn't had the room to spread its limbs to grow as it should and really needs to be moved to a more open spot."

She murmured something, but her awareness was focused not on the tree in the distant corner, but on Ian standing beside her, on the warmth and gentle power of his touch. She caught the scent of shirt starch and warm skin, felt the deep timbre of his voice pass through her, felt the protective strength of his presence. How had she never noticed that his dark hair curled at the nape of his neck and softly encircled the pulse beat at his temples? Had her heartbeat always raced like this when he was near?

"A lilac or a forsythia would do nicely there," Fiona suggested, trying to distract her attention. "Or perhaps a flowering vine of one sort or another."

"Excellent ideas." He removed his hand from her shoulder and, half turning, indicated a garden bench with a sweep of his arm. "Why don't we have a seat and discuss other changes we'd like to make?"

Her first thought was that he was again presuming that they were going to be married. It was quickly

brushed aside as she remembered Caroline's account of Aunt Jane's anger and the aftermath. "Can
you sit comfortably?" she asked before she could
think better of it.

His eyes sparkled and his grin went lopsided in
the most charming, disarming way. "I gather that
someone told you of Lady Baltrip's retribution."

"Carrie did. Are you in great pain?"

"Well, if pressed, I'd have to say that I've had
better days. But I've also seen men mangled far
worse soldier on, so I'll do the same without complaint or self-pity."

Fiona nodded her assent and settled herself onto
the bench. She held her breath and stared out over
the boxwood hedges as Ian eased down beside her
and leaned back. At his quiet sigh, she glanced over
at him, noting that the sunlight revealed the lines of
fatigue etching the corners of his mouth and creas-
ing the space between his dark brows.

As they sat, side-by-side, the silence settled between them again. This time, though, it wasn't at all
tense. Why the difference, Fiona couldn't say, but
she found their companionship enjoyable.

Ian settled his shoulders against the back of the
bench. "A rich silence," he murmured, his words
soft and dreamy.

Fiona looked over at him and watched as he
drifted into a light sleep. The tightness eased from
his lips and the furrow of his brow smoothed. And
suddenly he wasn't a duke of great importance or a

surgeon of brilliant mind and highly skilled hands, but a man exhausted, vulnerable and in need of protection. Her heart swelled and tears gathered at the base of her throat. It took every measure of her self-control to keep her hands in her lap, to caress the line of his cheek with only her gaze.

A bird trilled in the pear tree, calling to his mate. The sound must have penetrated Ian's awareness, because he opened his eyes and looked about in confusion for a second. His gaze came to her and stopped. Again his smile was lopsided and boyish. "I didn't mean to drift away," he said. "I promise that it had nothing to do with the quality of your company."

"You're very tired, Ian," Fiona answered softly. "And it's flattering to know that you're comfortable enough with me to relax."

There was a light in her eyes that Ian had never seen before. Soft and gentle and caring. It touched his spirit, soothing something deep inside him. "You are an incredibly beautiful woman, Fiona Turnbridge."

Her cheeks blushed the softest shade of pink as she looked down at her hands. Ian reached out and gently took them into his own. As he lifted them, her gaze came up to meet his, and in their green depths he saw a flicker of uncertainty.

"I couldn't have chosen a better woman to be my bride, Fiona," he declared. "I promise that you'll never regret agreeing to marry me."

Her lips parted and although she said nothing, he

felt the quickening of her pulse. He slowly turned her left hand palm up and bent his head to press a feathery kiss to her soft skin.

When he straightened, his gaze returned to hers and he was rewarded by the return of that gentle light to her eyes. A timid smile touched the corners of her mouth and he sensed that he might have not only a decent chance of mending the fences he'd so badly damaged the night before, but also a real chance to have a happy, satisfying marriage.

The moment between them was shattered as glass rained down on the garden and a chamber pot splashed into the fountain. Fiona looked up at him wide-eyed. With no other choice, he smiled tightly, cleared his throat, squeezed her hands reassuringly and began, "I should probably tell you about Charlotte."

Chapter Eight

As he and Fiona made their way inside and toward the rear room on the third floor, he quickly explained the basic facts of how he'd known Charlotte's mother and father, how he'd come to be named her guardian, and how she'd been crippled in escaping the fire that had killed her parents. He refrained from detailing her daily conduct, saying only that it had become something of a problem for the staff. On the landing between the second and third floor he paused to look down at the green-eyed beauty who had been following silently in his wake.

"Is there anything else you'd like to know? Need to know?" he asked.

She arched a pale brow. "Just out of purely idle and prurient curiosity, am I the only woman in the Empire with whom you *haven't* had an affair?"

"I know that it must seem as though I have no control," he allowed, "but I'm really quite discriminating."

She rolled her eyes and gestured to the stairs.

Deciding that the subject was best dropped, he led the way up and then down the corridor without further attempt to defend himself, but mentally ticking back through the years and the women, even the ones whose names he hadn't known or couldn't now recall, who had drifted through his life in any sort of a romantic way. He kept count until he reached a number that shocked even him.

Good God. There had to be something wrong with a man who went through life making love at every opportunity but without feeling the slightest bit of anything beyond a cursory appreciation for his partner's willingness. It had to say something about his emotional health that a truly personal relationship with any of them had never once crossed his mind. Not even fleetingly. He'd charmed and cajoled for a single purpose, performed admirably— and to their pleasure, too—then put his clothes on, thanked them and walked away without so much as a second thought.

Arriving at the open door of Charlotte's room, he paused and gestured for Fiona to precede him inside. She glided past and he stepped in behind her, thinking that if he were in her dainty little mules, he'd have second thoughts about marrying him, too. And third and fourth ones.

"Who are you?"

Ian blinked and tore himself from his thoughts to take in the details of his surroundings. And instantly wished he were anywhere but there. Charlotte sat in her chair beside her bed, her hair matted close against her head, her dark tresses hanging in greasy wads over her shoulders. Her dress was, as usual, soiled and, as always, her black eyes burned with fury as her gaze settled on him. Ruth, one of the kitchen maids, knelt on the floor in front of the hearth, frozen in the act of gathering onto a badly dented silver tray the shattered bits of china and mounds of flung food.

"I'm so sorry, Your Grace," she murmured, her voice shaky as she stared down at the floor.

"It's quite all right, Ruth," he assured her. "It's no fault of yours. Please go on downstairs and calm yourself. Leave all that right where it is. We'll worry about Miss Charlotte's luncheon later."

She dropped the tray and vaulted to her feet, saying "Yes, Your Grace," and then dashed out of the room in a flurry of black skirts and white petticoats, somehow giving him a quick curtsy as she ran past him without so much as a hitch in her stride.

As he watched the maid leave, his gaze passed over Fiona. It arrowed back to her, stunned by the smile tipping up the corners of her mouth. What the hell she had to smile about . . . Probably, he mused darkly, it was the certainty that if she didn't marry him, the young gorgon in the wheeled chair wasn't going to be her problem. At least not beyond being polite through a brief conversation that wasn't likely to be terribly polite on Charlotte's side.

"Lady Fiona Turnbridge," he said, beginning the

necessary introductions, "I would like to present my ward, Miss Charlotte Masters, late of New Delhi." He met the young woman's gaze squarely and cocked a brow in warning as he continued, "Charlotte, may I present Lady Fiona, the woman I hope will someday soon become my wife."

Charlotte's gaze remained fixed on his, the fury still dancing in their dark depths, the muscle in her jaw flexing as she clenched and unclenched her teeth.

"Hello, Charlotte," Fiona said softly, easing toward her without so much as a rustle of fabric. "It's a pleasure to meet you."

Finally, Charlotte tore her gaze away from him to fix it on Fiona. She opened her mouth as though to speak, but apparently thought better of whatever she'd intended to say. She closed it and then, a moment later, said dryly, "I'm sure you've heard all about me."

"A bit," Fiona replied, unruffled by the girl's rudeness, "and only enough to know that we need to become better acquainted." She gestured toward the unmade bed with the dirty sheets. "May I have a seat?"

Ian bit his tongue, telling himself that she could see that she'd likely have to burn her dress for the unnecessarily kind and definitely unappreciated effort to be companionable.

"If you want," Charlotte said, glaring at the window out of which she'd flung her chamber pot only minutes before.

Fiona pulled the bedding aside and found a relatively clean place on which to settle herself. Ian watched her, amazed that she'd chosen to sit so close; she could have easily reached out and touched his ward. At that short distance the smell had to be nearly overwhelming.

He was resisting the urge to take a step back when Fiona said, "I understand that you've been with His Grace only a few months."

"Sixty-three days, seventeen hours and . . ." Charlotte checked the watch pendant pinned to her grimy collar and then added, "Forty-eight and a half minutes."

Fiona pursed her lips and seemed to give the response considerable thought before she nodded and asked, "How long has it been since your parents were so tragically taken from us?"

"The fire was the thirteenth of October."

Fiona arched a brow and slowly nodded, then looked casually about the room. "I see that you paint."

"What you see," Charlotte said snidely, casting a hateful look his way, "is that Lord Dunsford bought me paints thinking that I can or might want to."

"I see needlework materials as well," Fiona bravely and cheerfully continued.

"I hate needlework. It makes my fingers sore."

She considered the full bookshelf on the opposite wall next and asked, "Do you not read, either?"

Charlotte's chin came up to a haughty angle. "I'm perfectly capable of reading. I just don't like to."

Again Fiona pursed her lips. Again she took a moment to think before she ever so breezily asked, "So what do you do with your days, Miss Charlotte?"

"I look out the window sometimes."

"At the gardens?"

"There isn't anything else to look at."

"Have you been down to see them more closely?"

"No," Charlotte snapped. "I haven't."

"Would you like to?"

"No."

For the first time since the two women had been introduced, Fiona looked over at him. She trailed the tip of her tongue over her her lower lip and took a long, slow deep breath. Ian didn't wait for her to speak. "Feel free to intervene in any way you see as having potential," he said. "God knows I haven't come up with any great ideas."

"Thank you," she said sweetly, before turning back to his petulant ward. "Whether or not His Grace and I eventually marry, it's clear that a firm hand is required here, Miss Charlotte. I can certainly appreciate that you're in need of understanding, given the sudden and horrible tragedies you've suffered. But I know from experience that unmitigated kindness and unrelenting tolerance simply aren't good for a person. There are some significant changes to be made in your world."

"I'm happy just the way I am," Charlotte declared.

"Whether that's true doesn't matter," Fiona replied evenly. "What does is that you're making everyone around you miserable." She rose from the bed with a gentle smile, saying, "His Grace and I are going to leave you now so that we may discuss the situation privately. We'll be back shortly."

Charlotte reached down, grabbed the wheels of her chair, and swung around to face him squarely while she snarled, "You're going to send me off somewhere, aren't you?"

Fiona answered before he could reassure his ward. "So you can be a petty tyrant in another place to other people?" she posed sweetly as she walked past him, heading toward the door. She stopped at the threshold and turned back. "No, Miss Charlotte. I'm sorry to disappoint you, but you aren't going anywhere. Now, if you'll excuse us for a few minutes."

And off she sailed, down the hall, leaving him to either suffer Charlotte's wrathful, resentful glares alone or trot after her like an adoring puppy. He went after her, pulling the door closed and telling himself that he wasn't so much adoring as he was desperate and clueless. He found her waiting for him not five feet from the room, shaking her head in silent rebuke.

"She's not happy," he said as he reached Fiona's side.

"Really?" she posed blithely. "I hadn't noticed."

All right, that hadn't been the most intelligent or sharply observant thing he could have said. Unfortunately, he really didn't have anything any more significant to offer. He opted for a confession. "I had no idea that you could be so . . . so . . ."

"Mean?" she suggested.

"Not at all!" he protested. "Deliberate. And coolly determined."

She chuckled. "Apparently pointing a pistol at your chest didn't make much of an impression."

"That was different. The heat of the moment and worry for your cat and all that. Which reminds me. How is Beeps doing today?"

"Eating and drinking happily," she assured him as a smile tickled the corners of her mouth, and her eyes sparkled with amusement. "He's grooming himself and is back to his usual place on my comforter. Shall we move down the hall so that Charlotte doesn't come out to interrupt our discussion?"

So much for the hope of a lengthy diversion. "We can move down to the window seat if you like, but only so we can sit and talk. Charlotte hasn't come out of that room since I carried her in there when she arrived," he said, moving down the hall. As Fiona fell in beside him, he added, "And yes, before you ask, she's been invited out countless times. She simply refuses to accept."

"The problem, Ian, lies in you giving her a choice in the matter. As I told her, kindness isn't always in a person's best interest."

"So I should drag her out?" he asked as they reached the window seat and Fiona gracefully settled herself on the cushion. "And take her where?"

"Well, to start," she replied, looking up at him, "to a dressmaker's. If what she's wearing now is typical of her wardrobe in general, the girl needs new clothes in the worst sort of way."

"I've repeatedly offered and she's refused. Adamantly."

"And you let her?"

He raked his fingers through his hair and with an honestly exasperated sigh, explained, "She's been through hell, Fiona. Orphaned and crippled and tossed into the home of a virtual stranger in a country she's never seen in her life. All within a span of a scant six months. Only an ogre would add to her misery."

She reached out and gently took his hand. Looking up at him, her eyes shimmered with a tenderness and compassion that squeezed the air from his lungs. He curled his fingers around hers, finding strength and calm in their touching.

"I know you've had only the best of intentions," she assured him softly, "but in letting her have her way on everything, you've inadvertently allowed her to create a life in which the only thing she has to do or think about is wallowing in anger and self-pity. It's not good for her and she needs to have her very able mind pushed in other directions."

"That's what I was thinking to do with getting her the paints, the needlework materials, and the books." God, did that sound as pathetic to her as it—

"You didn't push her, Ian. You provided and then let her choose to do nothing with them."

"So what do you suggest?" he asked, frustrated. "In addition, that is, to hauling her screaming and thrashing to a dressmaker's shop for clothes she doesn't want and is going to deliberately ruin."

His obvious bad attitude didn't faze her in the least. She smiled up at him, saying, "When Caroline and Drayton rescued me, I didn't talk. Why, I don't remember, but I managed to make my desires known in other ways and everyone willingly accommodated me. Until they discovered that I could speak and had simply chosen not to. After that, I wasn't allowed not to talk. I could point and look pleadingly all I wanted, but they refused to relent until I actually spoke. Even if it meant that I went without dinner a night or two or that Beeps spent the night in another room."

"They held your cat hostage? The beasts!"

She laughed softly and gave his hand a soft squeeze. "Beeps didn't suffer and I came into line with what, in hindsight, I can see were entirely reasonable expectations. Charlotte will do the same."

He leaned his shoulder against the window frame and countered morosely, "She doesn't have a cat."

"Which is a good thing because a cat isn't the right animal for her. They're entirely too sedentary during the day and too independent all of the time. She needs a dog. A young one who expects to be entertained for hours and hours on end and who thinks the sun rises and sets on her."

"How would she care for it?" he mused aloud. "It would need to be fed and watered and exercised outside."

"That's for her to figure out."

As though she would even make the effort. "I don't know, Fiona. Asking one of the staff to take the dog out several times a day would—"

"No, it would be *her* task to take the dog outside and to take care of all of its other needs, too."

"Asking one of the male staff to carry her up and down the stairs every time the dog needed to go out would . . ." He shook his head. "No, I can't ask them to take on another responsibility where Charlotte is concerned. If I did, they'd quit en masse in protest. And I wouldn't blame them in the least."

"Well, given what I saw in that room, your staff has the patience of saints and they've already served above and beyond reasonable expectations. They truly deserve to be spared from Charlotte's demands and tantrums."

"Agreed. How do you propose to accomplish that?"

She didn't hesitate, not even for a second. "You have massive amounts of space in this house, Ian. And, as I recall from our tour earlier, you have a second drawing room on the south side of the main floor."

"I think," he said, mentally walking through the lower floor, "that it's called a sunroom."

"Appropriately enough," she allowed brightly. "It's the most cheerful room you have. I can't see how Charlotte could possibly maintain her dismal attitude living in it."

Living? "Are you saying it should be converted into her bedroom?"

"Would you miss it as a public room?"

"No. Not at all," he admitted, stunned—and a bit embarrassed—that he hadn't thought of ensconcing her there the day she'd arrived.

"And if it were converted for her," Fiona went on, "she could easily manage to get her chair out of it and all through the rooms on the main floor. Why, she'd even be able to get herself to the dining room table for meals."

He didn't want to sound abysmal or defeated, but there were realities that couldn't be ignored. "Meals which are never to her liking."

"Then she can go hungry and hope the next one has something she does find to her liking. Eventually, sooner rather than later to my thinking, she'll become considerably less critical of what's put before her."

"All right," he allowed, trying to envision Charlotte rolling herself through the house *and* eating a meal in a civilized manner. Hope flickered, but he wasn't prepared to let it become a beacon in the storm of his daily existence. "But how would she manage a dog's outdoor requirements?"

Fiona closed her eyes and knitted her brows for a second. Ian watched her, wondering if perhaps she might be about to concede that the idea of getting

Charlotte a pet had been overly optimistic. Then she opened her eyes and smiled up at him. "If you could have one of your carpenters build a long, gently inclined ramp from the existing door down to the garden path, she could easily enter and leave the house as she wants and without having to impose on others to do it."

"You're very good at this," he observed, smiling, too.

"I have a great deal of experience at caring for injured and crippled animals. People aren't much different except that, unlike animals, they sometimes lack a natural instinct to adapt to the limitations. And when that's the situation, they have to be compelled, one way or another, to do it."

He saw the opportunity in her words and seized them. "Compelling Charlotte doesn't appear to be a task for which I have a natural instinct."

Fiona laughed softly, the sound adding to the newfound lightness of his heart. "Is that a roundabout way of asking me to oversee her social rehabilitation?"

"I'd be forever and undyingly grateful." And since there was no point in trying to appear nonchalant about her acceptance of the challenge, he immediately added, "How soon can we begin?"

"The transformation of her isn't going to go forward without a hitch or two, Ian," she countered calmly. "You know that, don't you?"

"It's that way with all major tasks."

"It will also involve some considerable expenses."

Jesus, when he thought about just the china and silver that had been destroyed in the last three months . . . "Money should never be one of your concerns. Please spend whatever you deem necessary. Actually, spend frivolously if you want to. I truly don't care what it costs."

"There'll be some changes to your life, as well."

"Such as?" he asked warily, suddenly remembering how she'd taken him apart by small pieces yesterday morning.

"To my thinking, Charlotte needs to have her mind engaged in something other than her losses and how much she hates being a burden to you."

"Why would she think that?" he asked, appalled. "I certainly don't think of her as a burden."

"No, you consider her a complete mystery and a problem for your staff."

Fiona, ever calm Fiona. She really was a wonder of patience and understanding. Very clear understanding. "You're absolutely right concerning my perception," he allowed. "And we do have to be fair in terms of how the staff sees her. She *does* create all kinds of additional work for them."

"She's fourteen, Ian. To her way of thinking at that age, every grumble, every reluctance and sigh of the staff is a message they're delivering from you."

"No," he countered in dumbfounded disbelief. "That's not at all true."

"I know it's not the case, but I'm not fourteen and dependent on your kindness. When was the last time that you sat down to share a meal with her?"

He cleared his throat to disguise a guilty groan.

Fiona arched a brow and smiled knowingly. "You should plan to share at least breakfast and the evening meal with her."

All right. He could do that. He had to eat somewhere; it might as well be at home. And if Charlotte wasn't going to be throwing the dishes and the food, he could be pleasant company. . . . God, he wished he had some solutions of his own on dealing with his ward, but he was well beyond his experience and the only thing to do was to cast himself on Fiona's wisdom and kindness. "What on earth will we talk about at meals?"

"Her dog," Fiona replied instantly. "The new draperies and rugs she's helped to select. The new furniture that she's helped to pick out and arrange. The dress designs the couturiere has suggested for her."

"You were serious about the expenses, weren't you? Not," he hurried to add, "that I have even the slightest qualm about it."

"She has to have some reason to come out of her room, Ian. Some reason to look forward to a new day and what it might have in store for her. When all you have to do in a day is stare out a window at a garden you can't get to with asking someone to be kind to you, what reason do you have to be cheerful and pleasant?"

"You are absolutely, utterly amazing."

Her cheeks flushed a soft pinky rose and her eyes sparkled. "And you might also," she said, "if you have a spare moment or two, offer to show her the garden and ask for her ideas."

"I could do that. Perhaps the three of us could do it together."

She nodded slightly and released his hand. "And if you happen to have any other interests, I'm sure she'd be willing to at least listen politely. I suspect that she was raised gently and to practice good manners. It would do her good to exercise them every now and again."

"My only other interests," he admitted, thinking it best not to let Fiona's hopes get too high, "are in medicine and in the building of the hospital. Hardly the sorts of things that a female—of any age—would find even remotely interesting."

She tipped her head to the side. "You're building a hospital?"

"Assuming that Mr. O'Connor, my manager for the project, is able to resolve the current permit problem with the Office of the Mayor of London, the actual hammer-and-saw work should begin tomorrow."

"Please tell me more," she asked prettily, sitting up straighter, her eyes bright. "What kind of hospital? Where?"

Well, someone had clearly taught Lady Fiona Turnbridge the finer points of showing polite interest. Charlotte could learn so much from her. "The building itself is one of the properties my father passed down to me," he explained. "It's the one where the man with the gangrenous leg was lying on the walkway."

"Yes, you told me about him."

"His name was Patrick O'Sullivan. I'm naming the hospital after him. The doors will be open to anyone who needs medical care regardless of who they are and their ability to pay."

"There will never be a moment when someone isn't there in desperate need. You'll be worked to death, Ian."

How very kind of her to consider his welfare. "I won't be alone in the venture," he assured her. "I've arranged with my fellow physicians for donations of time, materials and supplies. I've also worked out an agreement with the university so that medical students can gain practical experience under the guidance of those of us who volunteer there."

"I'd like to volunteer, too, Ian. I know a little—"

"I think, my dear Fiona," he interrupted kindly, "that you're going to have your hands full with Charlotte for the next eon or two. But I appreciate your enthusiastic support of the effort. You'd be amazed at how many people have told me that providing the poor with a free hospital is contrary to the way of Nature."

Sadness and disappointment clouded her eyes. Looking away, she shook her head and quietly observed, "People who have never wanted for anything can seldom imagine what it's like to be desperate and alone, of how curative it is just to know that someone cares."

"Beautiful, compassionate, determined *and* wise beyond your years."

Her smile seemed oddly, inexplicably strained, and he was wondering if her family ever gave her compliments, when she rose to her feet and turned to face him. "We don't have to wait overly long to begin with Charlotte," she said out of the blue. "If your staff could be imposed upon just a bit more on her behalf, we could have her and her belongings taken down to the sun room this afternoon."

"I'm sure they wouldn't mind," he allowed, still puzzling over her sudden change in manner. "Especially if there's even the slightest hope of less imposition as a result."

Smoothing her skirts, her gaze fixed on the door down the hall, she declared, "Then it's decided. If you'd be so kind as to go collect some strong arms and backs, I'll see to preparing Charlotte herself for the move."

"Gladly."

As she started away, a sense of unease bloomed in his chest. Something had gone wrong between them; what, he couldn't say, but he sensed a distance between them that hadn't been there at the start of their conversation. He didn't like it. Not at all.

"Thank you, Fiona," he called after her, hoping to somehow magically mend the rift. "From the bottom of my heart, forever and always, thank you."

"I'm not doing this for you," she said without looking back. "I'm doing it for Charlotte."

Ian was still searching for what had caused the change in her manner when she opened the door of his ward's bedroom and disappeared inside. Raking his fingers through his hair, he muttered, "Women," and then headed down the hall to do what he'd been asked.

Fiona stood just inside Charlotte's room, the door open behind her, the irascible young woman before her. Yes, she was doing this for Charlotte, for the girl who had lost everything and believed that she had no right—or chance—to be happy ever again. It had nothing to do with wanting to please Ian Cabott or make his life easier. It most certainly had nothing to do with how her heart skipped a beat and her blood warmed when he touched her. No, not at all.

But if Ian *did* happen to be impressed along the course of things . . . If it occurred to him that the woman he'd asked to be his duchess was more than a pretty face with a good bit of common sense . . . That he might discover that she had a good deal of intelligence, and no small amount of medical understanding, was a fragile hope, but one Fiona held in her heart anyway. And if he didn't . . .

If he couldn't be bothered to look past the surface and see who she really was, Fiona decided, giving Charlotte a smile, a skittering heartbeat and desire-heated blood wasn't reason enough to sign the settlement papers and commit the rest of her life to being nothing more than Ian Cabott's decorator, ward tender, and occasional, stoically dutiful lover.

Chapter Nine

Ian sat at the dining room table and considered the grease spot on the wall beside the fireplace. The blot that was just off the mantel and down a bit— where the cornish game hen had struck just moments into last night's dinner—seemed to have gotten bigger overnight. How that would be possible, though . . .

He looked to the right of it and considered the wide pattern of spatters. The yellow tint of them testified to a delicious curried rice pilaf having been sinfully wasted. And a perfectly good moire wallpaper utterly ruined. Which fairly well summed up the whole first attempt at bringing Charlotte back into the world of genteel dining and general civility.

Shaking his head, Ian thought back, wishing it had gone better and wondering just what he could have done differently. He'd been cheerful but pleasantly firm as he'd brought her from the sun room. Along the way to the dining room he'd clearly explained the expectations of her and then, just as clearly, laid out the consequences if she were to behave badly. Yes, she'd glowered at him as he'd taken his seat and rung for the food, but he hadn't detected even the slightest hint that she intended to go stark raving mad the minute the silver domes were lifted off their plates.

Apparently he'd been the only naive one, though. While he'd been inhaling deeply, appreciating the wonder of the meal and mentally framing his compliments to his cooks, the footmen had been discreetly scrambling out of the way. Their speed and awareness had saved their white shirt fronts while the rice had been falling off his all the way from the dining room to the sun room.

Wheeling Charlotte back to her room without supper hadn't been as difficult as he'd expected it to be, though. Not that it reflected well on him in the light of a new day, but at that moment he hadn't cared one whit that she was going to go to bed hungry. No, he'd been nothing but angry when he'd rolled her into the center of the room Fiona had had set up for her earlier in the day. He'd been determined when he'd left her sitting there, and, remembering Fiona's instructions, before closing the doors behind himself he'd paused to leave his glaring, ungrateful ward with a curt wish for a pleasant night and to express the hope that she might find breakfast more to her liking.

And now that breakfast was here . . . Ian sighed, reached for the silver coffee pot, and poured himself a cup of steaming black fortitude. Maybe she'd be a completely reformed person when she rolled herself into the dining room this morning. Gracious. Pleasant. Clean. Not that any of it was even remotely likely, but hope was all he had.

"Good morning, Your Grace."

He vaulted from his chair and turned toward . . . *Sunshine in a pale green and lavender house dress.* "Good morning, Fiona," he managed to get out past his thickening tongue. "You look lovely today."

"Thank you," she replied, kindly refraining from mentioning that the compliment rather implied that she hadn't looked lovely yesterday.

He dashed forward and pulled out a chair for her. As she settled herself in it and he moved her closer to the table, he resisted the urge to press a kiss to her ear and somehow found the mental wherewithal to offer her a cup of coffee.

It was while he was pouring out that she asked, "Has Charlotte already eaten and returned to her room?"

There was nothing to be but honest. Maybe, if he sounded desperate enough, she'd take pity on him and excuse him from any further involvement in the whole effort. Not that there was any more hope of that than of Charlotte having changed completely in the course of the night. "She hasn't been here yet. And I'll confess to almost hoping that she decides that she prefers to miss another meal."

"I gather that dinner last night wasn't an entirely smooth first effort?"

"Charlotte has a very smooth, very powerful pitch. The poor cornish game hen was utterly flattened. Honestly, I've seen things come out from under wagon wheels with more shape left to them than that bird had when it finally peeled off the wall and dropped to the carpet."

She arched a delicate brow and looked toward the window side of the room.

"Other side," he instructed, settling back in his chair and staring down at his boots. "By the nearest fireplace. Just a bit to the side and slightly below mantel level."

"Oh. That's not going to come out of the wall-paper."

"So Mrs. Pittman tells me," he allowed on a sigh. "I'm not sure, but I think Charlotte was aiming for my head. I just happened to lean forward to savor the scent of finely cooked food at the right moment, and she missed."

Fiona narrowed her eyes. "What was the yellow fare at dinner?"

"A delicious curried pilaf. Not that my dear ward bothered to sample it before she flung it after the chicken."

The ever unruffled angel of goodness nodded slightly and took a sip of her coffee before asking, "And what was your response to such horribly inappropriate behavior?"

"To my credit, I didn't throttle her," he provided. "Although I'll admit to being sorely tempted."

"Understandably."

"Instead, in a fit of maturity and reserve, I clenched my teeth, stood up, and proceeded to wheel her back to her room where I left her with a few terse words to the effect that I hoped today would go better."

"And what was her response?"

"I have no idea. I closed the door and walked away. And, as per your instructions, the staff left her to her own devices to prepare herself for bed."

Fiona smiled approvingly, warming his heart to a ridiculous degree and sending his spirits soaring to embarrassing heights. "Very well done, Your Grace."

He cleared his throat and reached for the coffee pot saying, "I do wish you'd call me Ian."

"I'll try to remember and make an effort."

Well, it was more accommodation than Charlotte was willing to offer him. And, truth be told, that Fiona would try was enough to satisfy him. His gaze trailed slowly over the finely carved features of her face, watching her sip daintily at her coffee and slowly realizing how delighted he was by Lady Fiona Turnbridge's mere presence at his table. And when she smiled at him, when she glanced his way and then blushed peachy pink . . .

How interesting, he mused, that he'd never before found innocence to be the least bit stirring. Actually, he silently amended, shifting uncomfortably in his chair, it was far more frustrating and perplexing than interesting. Having never felt this kind of attraction, he had no idea how to best go about the pursuit. Assuming that she did eventually forgive him for the Lady Baltrip incident and accept his proposal . . . Just how was he supposed to seduce such an innocent without shredding what made her so appealing and unique? Without scaring the bejeezus out of her and sending her running for home?

"Is something bothering you, Your . . . ?" She closed her eyes for a second and smiled. "*Ian.*"

He smiled in appreciation as his mind whirled through how to best respond to her question. Yes, he was bothered, but confessing that he was trying to figure out how to get her into his bed . . . No, honesty wasn't the best policy at the moment. "I was thinking of Charlotte," he lied silkily. "And wondering if I should go get her."

Tipping her head slightly to the side, she stared off toward the far end of the table. "It could be," she finally said, "that she's overslept. Perhaps we could go together and see if she needs to be awakened."

It crossed his mind to suggest that he offer to stay behind to order breakfast served, but as his conscience rebelled at the cowardice, he rose to his feet. Chivalrously stepping behind her chair, he inhaled the scent of her. Flowers, yes. But not the sickly sweet and dainty things that grew in hothouses. More like something that twined and flourished deep in the forest, something in which fairies made their beds. Scantily clad and delightfully wicked fairies.

He blinked to clear the image and completed his gentlemanly task as quickly as he could. Stuffing his hands into his pockets, he answered Fiona's puzzled look with a tight smile. "I will follow your lead."

She grinned, quipped, "If only I'd been able to talk my dancing masters into being so accommodating," and then glided past him, leaving him in a swirling eddy of a far too inviting scent. He stared down at the carpet, reminded himself that he was pledged to redeem himself, and then, ignoring his every natural instinct, trailed after her toward the sun room.

He stopped in the open doorway to first survey the situation and then to be thankful that he'd delayed in the dining room. If he'd been the one to open the doors and first step in, he'd have . . . Well, retching was still a distinct possibility. Charlotte sat in her chair in precisely the same spot he'd parked her last evening. She wore the same clothes she had last night. What was different this morning was that she'd repeatedly soiled both her clothes and the chair in the hours since he'd left her.

Fiona, to his amazement and chagrin, didn't appear to have the slightest aversion to putting herself squarely in front of his disgusting—and very wide awake—ward. Good God, how she could bear the smell . . .

"You are *mean*," Charlotte snarled at Fiona. "Mean! Vicious! Cruel!"

Ian had to swallow down his stomach and tell himself to pretend that he was in a military field hospital before he could get his feet to move. Not that either Fiona or Charlotte paid the least bit of attention to his tardy and obviously reluctant arrival.

Fiona nodded ever so slightly and leaned back against the mahogany bureau. "I can see how you might think so, Charlotte," she replied calmly, her fingers sweetly laced in front of her. "And if you were unable to use your entire body and if your mind were impaired, I'd be guilty as charged. However, you aren't entirely crippled and that makes all the difference in the world."

Ian stopped just a meter into the room, sensing that Fiona didn't need his intervention. Or his support, for that matter. For such a little slip of a thing, she had a presence about her. Steel. All soft and gentle and curvy on the outside. And on the inside, a spirit of finely tempered steel.

"You're perfectly capable of getting yourself out of that chair to see to your personal needs," she went on gently. "You could have rolled yourself to the commode chair at any time in the night. You could have taken yourself to the wardrobe and changed into your night clothes. You could have climbed into your bed and spent a night in peaceful, comfortable sleep. You chose not to do any of that. You chose to be miserable."

"I hate you!"

And there was a reason to love Charlotte? Pity her, yes. But love . . .

"I'd suggest," Fiona countered, utterly unruffled by his ward's venom, "that what you hate is the expectation that you abandon both your anger at the unfairness of life and your petty tyranny over His Grace and his staff."

"My parents are *dead*."

Again Fiona nodded sympathetically. "For which we're all truly sorry, Charlotte. If it were within our power to change what happened, we would in an instant. But we can't and there's nothing left for you to do but to accept your circumstances and carry on as your parents would expect of you."

"I don't want to!"

"That's apparent," Fiona replied smoothly. "And understandable. But it's also unacceptable, Charlotte. It wouldn't be at all kind of us to allow you to spend every moment of the rest of your life wallowing in misery over what you've lost."

"What do you know of loss? *Lady Perfect*."

"A great deal, Charlotte."

"What do you know about going through life crippled?"

Fiona seemed to contemplate the question for a moment before answering, "Enough to know that a happy life can be lived despite limitations and imperfections." She shrugged a shoulder and added, "If overcoming them is the path you choose to take."

"Well, I don't," Charlotte all but hissed. "I refuse."

Of all the stupid, obstinate for the sake of obstinacy declarations he'd ever heard, that one ranked as—

"It is entirely your choice," Fiona allowed serenely. "But please understand that we have a choice, too.

And ours is not to support you in the foolish wasting of your life. We're not going to rush in and prevent you from suffering the consequences of your decisions. If you choose not to eat at the table and in a civilized manner, you'll be allowed to go hungry. If you choose to sit in your chair all night instead of sleeping in the comfortable bed you've been provided, then you'll be allowed to be stiff and sore. If you choose to soil yourself rather than use your commode chair, then you'll be allowed to sit there and reek."

Oh, now that might be going a bit too—

"The matter of the horrible odor aside," Fiona went on, apparently unaware that his stomach was churning. "You should be aware of the fact that if you persist in soiling yourself and then sitting in it, your skin will ulcerate, your tissues will become infected, and you stand a good chance of dying. Painfully."

Charlotte appeared to at least be giving the idea some thought. Perhaps there was hope of reason finally prevailing. Although it might be difficult for her to admit that. Well, he noted, his optimism withering, she didn't appear to have any difficulty in wheeling that chair around to glare at him.

"You wouldn't let me die," she declared, her eyes sparking with angry defiance.

He was tempted to maintain that he would indeed, but quickly decided that flippancy wouldn't help resolve the problem. Instead, he opted for a general truth. "Doctors aren't God, Charlotte," he said in a tone that he hoped matched Fiona's for calm. "We can't save people from themselves. If you want to destroy yourself, you'll eventually succeed no matter how often I try to intervene or to convince you to do otherwise."

He took a deep breath and added, "I think it's only fair to point out to you that there comes a time when a sane person stops beating their head against a wall and accepts the necessity of letting matters run their inevitable course."

Her brows knit, her mouth puckered into a tiny, bloodless knot, Charlotte whirled the chair so that she faced neither of them. Ian glanced over at Fiona, hoping she'd give him a sign as to what he was supposed to say or do next. All he got was a brief smile of reassurance before her gaze shifted to Charlotte's back.

"Would you like to have some hot water brought in for a bath?" she kindly asked his ward. "We'll be glad to wait breakfast while you clean and dress yourself."

"No."

"It's your decision. And ours to allow it," she replied, unlacing her fingers and easing off the bureau's edge. Gliding smoothly across the room, she added, "If you should change your mind between now and luncheon, the bell cord is over here by the door. Please understand that the staff will be instructed to bring you only bath water."

"I want the floor cleaned!"

"I'm sure you do," Fiona cheerfully replied without

so much as a backward glance. She reached his side and stopped to smile up at him. "Shall we go to breakfast? I'm famished."

"So am I," he lied. He gestured toward the open door. "After you, my lady." He waited until Fiona was in the hall before he bowed slightly and said, "I hope you'll choose to bathe and then join us, Charlotte."

His ward said nothing and remained still as a post. Feeling defeated, he stepped into the hall and pulled the door quietly closed.

Fiona stood waiting for him, her normally bright eyes clouded with obvious concern. "I hope you don't think I was too brutal."

His every instinct wanted to wrap his arms around her slender shoulders and draw her close, to tip her face up and gently, slowly, thoroughly kiss away all her worries. "I think you handled the situation perfectly," he assured her, stuffing his hands into his pockets. "Far better than I have to this point. She needed to hear the things you said and—"

The crash was loud. And followed, in a mere flash of a second, by another. And another. Ian turned to study the door, his teeth clenched as he listened to the angry shrieking and sounds of destruction coming from the other side.

"Well," Fiona said softly as she, too, studied the door, "the good news is that she had to roll her chair over to the washbasin to get her hands on it. It's progress."

"Only a born and bred optimist," he groused,

"would see a violent temper tantrum as a positive sign."

"When there's nothing left for her to destroy," Fiona offered him in consolation, "and she realizes that no one's going to come in to either clean it up or provide her with new things to throw and break, she might actually have a revelation in the midst of the rubble."

Or not. He expelled a long, slow breath. "Assuming that there really are such things as miracles, how long do you think it might take?"

"I have no idea, Ian. It rather depends on how stubborn she is and how used she is to getting her way by behaving badly. Were her parents in the habit of granting her every whim?"

"Charlotte's parents were in the habit of largely ignoring her," he provided, offering his arm. She took it without hesitation, stepping to his side and placing her hand on his forearm. How such an innocent gesture could be so stunningly inviting, such a small and delicately structured appendage could produce such instant and compelling heat . . . His heart racing and his blood warming, he guided her down the hall.

"Dr. Masters was a distant, cold man who had his medical practice and his mistresses," he went on, more to distract himself than to enlighten Fiona. "Amanda hid in her social whirl and sought revenge in having her own affairs. Charlotte was an inconvenient object left to the servants to manage. And servants being there only to serve . . ."

"Then Charlotte's reformation could take a while."

Judging by her easy tone, the possibility of repeated frustrations didn't seem to distress Fiona in the least. She really was the most surprising woman, possessing so much more strength than anyone would reasonably expect by just looking at her. There was a surprising depth, a kind of quiet passion, to her, as well. He'd known a few women in his life whom he characterized as quietly passionate. If Fiona proved to be even half as exciting as they'd been in— Ian pushed the thought away, disgusted by his baser instincts.

"Is something wrong? Your muscles are suddenly tense."

He looked down into compassionate, searching green eyes. To lean down . . . She'd close her eyes as his lips brushed over hers. She'd murmur in consent and then melt against him, her murmurs becoming soft moans of pleasure as he explored—

Ian cleared his throat and lifted his chin. "I feel sorry for Charlotte," he said, offering up the first plausible explanation that stumbled past his awareness. "For the kind of childhood she's had to endure. For having to go through all the rest of her life crippled."

Mercifully, they reached the stairs and he withdrew his arm so that Fiona could manage her skirts.

"She'll only be as crippled, Ian," she replied, making her way down, "as she's willing to let an unhappy childhood overshadow all of the hope in her todays. As willing as she is to go through life letting her damaged legs determine what she wants to do."

"In other words, she'll only be as crippled as I allow her to be."

"And as she makes excuses for herself."

He followed her, marveling at how he could still feel the place on his arm where her hand had rested, could still feel the quickened beat of his heart. Cad that he was, he resented having the space suddenly between them. Ramming his hands back into his trouser pockets, he scowled at the carpeted steps as he made his way down into the foyer. What a cad he was. Fiona was expressing her concerns over the quality of another person's life while he was thinking about the way she'd feel in his arms, the luscious sounds she'd make as he made slow love to her.

Jesus. Physically mangled and personally humiliated didn't appear to make a damn bit of difference to him. Neither did his pledge to prove himself a decent, honorable man worthy of marriage to a good and sexually innocent woman. One touch, one look and he was teetering on the edge of completely ruining any chance of redemption he had left. God, the only real hope he had of resisting the temptation of his green-eyed beauty was to keep as much distance between them as possible. If he didn't . . . He didn't even want to think about how low her opinion of him would go.

"By the way, Beeps is able to jump up and down from the bed as he wants already," Fiona said cheerily from a circumspect distance as together they crossed the foyer and moved toward the dining room. "I removed his bandages last night. He had them half undone anyway."

"Doesn't anything ever discourage you?" he wondered aloud as they reached the table and he again helped her into a chair, as he again inhaled the heady scent of wicked fairy flowers.

"Not for very long. And you? Do you ever get discouraged, Ian?"

"Every now and then," he admitted, picking the bell up from the table and giving it a quick shake.

"Over what?"

"Any number of things," he supplied with a shrug as he took his own seat.

"Such as?"

Well, he'd been the one to open the conversational box; he couldn't very well refuse to answer her question. And, besides, thinking about other frustrations would distract him from the one of not being able to reach out and slowly open the little pearl buttons of her perfectly prim and proper bodice.

"Well, let's see," he began, gazing up at the ceiling. "There's the state of health among England's poor. My mother. Charlotte. The petty social expectations of being a duke. My mother. The starving children in India. In China. In Whitechapel. My mother. The incredible amount of paper one must file and the permissions one must beg for in order to do something not only charitable, but right and desperately necessary. And then there's my mother."

She chuckled. "I detect a reoccurring subject."

"Yes, my dear mother, the ever present cloud of gloom and disapproval waiting to drift over my life."

The footman arrived in the doorway with a bow. Ian acknowledged him with a dip of his chin and then said, "We're ready to be served breakfast. And please advise Mrs. Pittman and Cook that if Miss Charlotte pulls the bell cord, they're to take her only water for a bath. Nothing else. They're to fill the tub and leave. Under no circumstances are they to clean up the shambles she's made of her room or assist her in bathing or dressing."

"Yes, Your Grace."

Ian picked up the coffee pot. "More coffee, Fiona?"

"Please." She held out her cup and let him pour as she offered, "Surely there's something about you that your mother finds acceptable."

He couldn't think of what it might be so he simply shook his head, smiled and changed the subject. "What do you plan to do with the day if Charlotte decides not to come out of her room?"

"Plot the decorating changes to the sun room around her, chatting amiably and soliciting her opinion on colors and fabrics and such. She'll either be compelled to participate by my enthusiasm or by her horrified reaction to my suggestions."

Yes, a dyed in the wool, to the marrow optimist. "She could just decide to sit there and glower at you, you know."

"Yes, she could," Fiona allowed with an impish smile and a sparkle in her eyes. "But then she'd have to live in the middle of a tribute to British naval history."

"Naval history?" he asked warily.

"It's the most unfeminine thing I can think of. Yards and yards of Union Jack bunting, the bits and pieces of ships scattered here and there and tacked to the walls, all of it surrounding a portrait of Lord Nelson."

"Of course."

"Absolutely," she assured him, grinning. "*And* a huge painting depicting the Battle of Trafalgar, too."

God, he could just see it. And it was awful. Chuckling, he admonished, "Don't roll a real cannon in there, please. Not unless you plan to permanently spike it. She's done sufficient damage already."

"A cannon," Fiona whispered, delight dancing in her eyes. "That's positively inspired, Ian. Would you happen to know where I can get one?"

"No," he lied, enjoying their game. "But, if pressed, I could probably come up with a bilge rat or two."

She sat up a bit straighter and tilted her slightly to the side. "Properly bathed and—"

"I was joking! No one is going to bring rats into this house."

"We'd keep them in a cage."

"No rats!"

The corners of her eyes crinkled as her smile went bright and wide. Then she tipped her head back and laughed. The sound rippled through him, delighting his heart and buoying his spirit high. To have her laugh with that much joy as he swept her into his arms and carried her up the . . .

Oh, he was a man in trouble. Deep, deep trouble.

Chapter Ten

"Do you think we should thin out these flower beds?" Charlotte asked, using a light rake to brush an errant leaf from the newly greening shoots. "Perhaps we could transplant them to a new bed on the south side of the house."

Fiona smiled and walked over to where Charlotte had parked her chair, marveling at how much Ian's ward had changed in just the last few days. Admittedly the first week had been difficult for everyone, but eventually Charlotte had accepted that she really would be allowed to go to bed hungry and that she was going to have to roll herself out of the sun room if she wanted more than the companionship of her solitary thoughts. Once those two hurdles had been crossed . . .

"Don't you think so, Fiona?"

She stared down at what she thought might be irises. "Truth be told, I don't know a thing about when plants should be thinned, much less how to do it or where they should go next."

"Then why are you gardening?"

"Because I'm hoping you'll teach me what you know," she replied.

For a second Charlotte beamed up at her, and then her gaze abruptly darted toward the rear yard. Fiona didn't need to turn and look; she could hear the hoofbeats.

On the first full day of their plan for Charlotte's reformation, Ian had been here to greet her when she'd arrived. He'd spent most of the morning with her, growing ever more quiet and distant, and then, right after lunch, left to oversee the work on his hospital.

After that, she'd arrived every morning to find him leaving for a ride. And the rest of the day had become just as patterned. He rode for a couple of hours, returning home to bathe and change his clothes and then lock himself in his study with his medical books until lunch was served. He smiled tightly through the course of the meal, pretending to be interested in the things they'd done in his absence, and then, the very second that good manners permitted, he got up from the table and left the house. She went home before he returned in the evening.

This morning had gone slightly differently, though. His cousin Harry had sauntered into the dining room just as Ian was going through the ritual of wishing her and Charlotte a pleasant day. It had obviously chafed Ian's patience to go through the introductions, but his irritation had deepened to the point of outright glowering when Harry had settled himself at the table and, chatting happily away, reached for a slice of toast. Two minutes later, Harry, a piece of toast clutched in each hand, was heading out the door for a ride he didn't want to take.

"Isn't Ian simply the most incredible figure on horseback?" Charlotte asked. "My papa always said that Ian was born in the saddle."

Since it would seem odd not to, Fiona turned to watch Ian and his cousin return. The horses were lathered and had clearly earned their daily keep and feed. Fiona smiled, thinking that Harry looked as though he'd been dragged through a hedge or two. Ian, on the other hand, looked just as he had when he'd left, wearing the same dark and grim expression he had every morning, noon, and night, for the last week.

"Yes, he's very handsome," Fiona admitted, taking in the length of his legs, the width of his shoulders, the sureness of his hands on the reins. "And so very unfathomable."

"Maybe you need to spend some time alone together, Fiona," the girl suggested. "It's been days since you have."

Seven days to be precise. Not since they'd strolled to the end of the upstairs hall and discussed what to do about Charlotte. And to think that she'd walked away from that conversation feeling as though there was some real glimmer of hope that their relationship would blossom. She was such an optimist.

"Why don't you ask him for some ideas about the garden and take a little walk? I'll distract Lord Bettles for you."

Fiona didn't have a chance to either agree or disagree with the plan. Charlotte waved and called out to Harry, telling him that they'd baked lemon tarts while he'd been gone. Her heart in her throat, Fiona caught Ian's gaze and smiled in silent welcome and invitation.

Ian's pulse hammered through him at the sight of Fiona standing on the lawn, wisps of her golden hair escaping the confines of her bonnet, the breeze gently pressing the fabric of her silk skirt against the luscious curves of her hips and legs.

"Just shoot me," he muttered under his breath. "And put me out of my misery."

"Pardon?" Harry asked from beside him.

He was mercifully spared the need to reply by Charlotte's raised hand and call for Harry's attention. There was no such divine deliverance from his acute awareness of Fiona. Even as he narrowed the distance between them, he saw her gaze slide over him. God, the warm light in her eyes as she appraised the length of his legs, then visually caressed the width of his shoulders before coming to rest on his hands.

It took every bit of his self-control to swallow down the groan. He really should be getting better at ignoring her, he chastised himself. For God's sake, he'd spent countless hours in the last week exercising restraint. He knew that she didn't deliberately torment him, that she was completely unaware of how she affected him, but that didn't alter the truth— or his response—one bit; Fiona Turnbridge was a natural born seductress. All Fiona had to do was be herself and walk into a room or pass at the edge of awareness and . . . He could only hope that she had no idea of how many times she'd been only a heart-beat away from being swept into his arms and soundly, thoroughly kissed.

And to think that he'd considered himself to be safe from her appeal to his instincts, that the injuries and abuse he'd suffered for his foolishness at the Miller-Sandses' ball would prevent his mind from wandering along carnal paths long enough for him to change her opinion of him. If they handed out prizes for blind hope, he'd win one, hands down.

No, the plain truth was that he was never going to be battered and bruised enough to not know she was there. Hell, visions of holding Fiona and making love to her consumed him even when she wasn't anywhere around. And there was no distracting him-self, either. Riding didn't tire him enough. The work on the hospital could only put off the fantasies for a few minutes at a time.

And sleeping . . . He dreamed from the moment his head touched the pillow. Dreams that were filled with Fiona reaching out to caress his skin, her eyes dark green with desire, her lips swollen with the proof of his desperate passion.

Whether it was the restlessness and frustration of his sleep or the unending strain of trying to be a gentleman, the consequences were obvious; he couldn't concentrate well enough to practice medicine without endangering patients, he was drinking too much too often, he was a snarling bear to be around, and he was always on the brink of losing the battle against the little voice in the back of his head that whispered that he might as well surrender to temptation because sooner or later she was going to figure out what a single-minded cad he really was.

Staying as far away from Fiona as he could . . . It was his only hope. And he hated every minute of the sacrifice. It was only the certainty of what would happen if he didn't make the effort that kept him wandering the construction site and the halls of hospitals when all he could think about was how much he wanted to be home.

"Good morning, Ian."

He started and looked down, sucking a hard breadth when he found her standing not a hair's breath from his leg. She smiled up at him and used the back of her hand to push a silken wisp of hair from her cheek. "Did you and Harry have a pleasant ride?"

God, for the freedom to trace those cheekbones with his fingertips, his lips, to explore every sweet curve of her. He forced his thoughts away from temptation, cleared his throat and finally answered, "It was fine."

She nodded and moistened her lips with the tip of her tongue. Ian gripped the reins so tightly that the horse danced beneath him, nervous and tense.

"It'll be a little while before lunch is ready to be served," she said, using her hand to shade her eyes as she looked up at him. "Could I talk you into a stroll through the garden until we're summoned?"

Ian forced his awareness away from the fabric drawn taut over her breasts by her uplifted arm. "No," he answered tersely while swinging down from the saddle. "I have to settle my horse in the stable and then make myself presentable."

She smiled and tilted her head to the side in the way that accentuated the slender column of her throat and invited him to nibble at her nape.

"I'll go along with you to the stable," Fiona suggested happily.

Alone in the hay with Fiona . . . Ian clenched his teeth and sternly reminded himself that her reputation was far more important than his need. "Ladies stay out of stables. I'll meet you in the dining room after a bit," he said, drawing the reins down over the horse's head.

He saw the way her gaze touched his shoulders and back as he moved, saw the rise of her breasts as she caught her breath, saw the pulse quicken in the hollow of her throat. For a second he was tempted to say to hell with it all and reach for her, to take her hand and lead her upstairs to his room.

Again, the tattered scraps of decency stepped

between him and sweet temptation. He sucked in a
deep breath, lifted his chin and told himself that he'd
suffered worse deprivations in the course of his life.
Not that he could name one right at that moment.

"Really, Ian," she protested, the color rising in
her cheeks and her lower lip indignantly quivering
in a way that he found incredibly inviting. "I've been
to a stable before. Lots of times, in fact."

"Well, you're not going with me," he declared.
And then, before she could shred what little self-
restraint he still possessed, he walked away.

Fiona watched him leave her and tried to decide
whether she was more hurt or angry. Blinking back
tears, she lifted her chin and told herself that Ian's
rejection of her company didn't matter. When he'd
laid out his reasons for asking her to be his wife,
neither a grand passion nor a desire for emotional
intimacy had been on his list.

And despite the ease with which they'd devel-
oped the plan to help Charlotte a week ago, nothing
had fundamentally changed between them. His refusal to be alone with her really said it all; she didn't
appeal to him in any way, not intellectually, not
physically, and certainly not emotionally. She looked
down at her hands, wondering if he thought she
might be a carrier of some dreadful disease.

The ridiculousness of the very idea . . . Shaking
her head, Fiona turned back toward the house. Holding her hems above her ankles, she scampered up
the steps, her mind running through a myriad of

possible courses, all of them based on her refusal to be casually dismissed. If Dr. Ian Cabott thought he was going to go through life ignoring her, he had another think coming. She'd turn his house upside down and if he persisted in being a callous, distant fool . . . He might not regret having his settlement offer handed back to him unsigned, but it was a sure bet that he'd think of her every moment for the eternity it would take to erase her fingerprints from his world. One more week. She'd give him one more week, and if he didn't come to his senses . . .

Ian sent the carriage around to the back and paused on the walkway, considering his front door. It was lunchtime, he was hungry, and there was food inside. There was also chaos and constant temptation, both the consequence of his having encouraged one Lady Fiona Turnbridge to do whatever she wanted.

Five days since the "I'll go to the stable with you" incident . . . It had taken her all of five days to knock every single pin out from under life as he knew it. There were holes in his walls and barely a curtain left hanging at his windows. He never knew where he was going to find furniture in a room—if there was any furniture at all. There were workmen everywhere, piles of tools in every corner, and dust covering every single surface.

And amidst it all was Fiona, laughing and dashing from one room to the next, always bubbling in excitement and eager to show him the changes she was making, pressing him for his opinions and his preferences, and never once realizing how deeply and painfully she was torturing him in the process.

He was going to have to do something about her. Either move out of the house or . . . surrender. Just quit struggling to keep his fascination with her under control and within the bounds of propriety. Just give in to his desires and be done with the whole charade of being a decent man worthy of such a perfect woman. And then watch her run away, mortified and disgusted.

Squaring his shoulders, assuring himself that he could get through one more day, Ian walked up the steps. He smiled as the door magically opened at his approach. Ah, Rowan. The one last, undisrupted constant in his life.

"Good afternoon, Your Grace."

"Rowan," he said, gratefully. "How—" The sound of tiny, scrambling toenails. "Damn dog," Ian muttered as his butler closed the door behind him, and Jack, his ward's terrier, came careening around the corner of the foyer and toward him at a full run. A man shouldn't have to deal with an attacking dog the very second he entered his own home, Ian inwardly grumbled. His trousers were spared a shredding assault by the thankfully quick and perfectly timed arrival of Mrs. Pittman. She bent down and snatched the little monster into her arms.

Ian scowled and cocked a brow as Jack wiggled in delight and licked the housekeeper's chin. "An appreciated intervention, Mrs. Pittman," he said. He shrugged out of his coat and handed it over to Rowan as he asked, "Is Lady Fiona still here?"

"She's in the drawing room, Your Grace," Mrs. Pittman answered as Jack pinned his beady little gaze on Ian and growled. "Hard at work as always."

Ian nodded and stepped around the housekeeper, making sure to give Jack a wide berth. He and Fiona needed to come to an understanding about that ferocious little dog she'd acquired for Charlotte. It was hard to imagine that such a bad-tempered animal could come from someone so loving and sweet. Fiona was a nothing short of an angel; Jack was Genghis Khan with four spring-loaded legs and patchwork fur.

In his darker moments, Ian fantasized about Jack going for a long journey in box on a postal coach. Only the fact that both Charlotte and Fiona would be heartbroken at the loss kept him from paying for the dog's passage to the end of the Earth. At some point, very soon, he planned to suggest that maybe Jack would be happier terrorizing squirrels and other small animals at the country house than he was stalking the hallways of the townhouse, waiting for a chance to chew pant legs to rags. It was worth a try, anyway.

Ian's preoccupation with the dog came to an abrupt end as he passed the open doorway of the front parlor. He paused and let his gaze take in the changes being made. Certainly no British general had ever conducted a military campaign with the precision and determination with which Lady Fiona Turnbridge had undertaken the redecorating of his house.

He hardly recognized the place these days. She'd had the curtains taken down from the windows, and rooms that had been dark and gloomy were now flooded with the warmth and brilliance of sunlight. She'd rearranged every stick of the furniture in every room she'd assailed, creating little groupings of chairs and tables that she insisted would make for easier and more lively conversation. While he groused that no one except themselves and the household staff ever came into the rooms, he had to admit that the newly arranged furniture was definitely more pleasing to the eye.

His brows furrowed as he took in a pile of lumber neatly stacked against the far wall of the parlor, the handled wooden trays of wood-working tools set off to the side of the lumber. What was Fiona intending to have done with all that wood? Heaven only knew; Ian didn't have so much as the faintest inkling. He was certain, however, that she did indeed have a very specific plan and that in all likelihood it involved the employment of at least a dozen skilled carpenters for the next month.

Ian shook his head in wonder as he considered the room. Fiona had, for all intents and purposes, turned his home upside down in the week and a half since she'd agreed to help civilize Charlotte. But it was nothing, he reminded himself, nothing compared to what she had done to his life in the fortnight since she'd arrived on his doorstep with Beeps and a loaded pistol.

He didn't regret one little bit any of the changes Fiona had brought to his world. They were, without doubt or argument, the best of all the things that had ever happened to him. There wasn't a man in London—in all of England, for that matter—who wouldn't truly envy every facet of his life. He inhaled deeply with satisfaction, filling his senses with the light, sweet scent of Fiona's cologne.

He smiled, realizing that the scent of Fiona gently wafted through every corner of his swiftly changing world. Yes, his life was decidedly improving these days.

Charlotte had made considerable progress in the past twelve days. Far more than he'd believed to be even remotely possible in a lifetime. Yes, as Fiona had predicted, there had been some rough spots, but in looking back, he could see that they'd been brief and really not all that rough. And now . . .

They'd had nine straight days of her eating without so much as a whisper of complaint. Cook had reportedly fallen to her knees in gratitude after the first meal without broken china. Even more astoundingly, it was rumored that Aneesh, his Indian chef, had helped Cook to her feet and then, in his own delight with the situation, hugged her. And given the sudden breadth of variety of foods on the table since that moment, it appeared that the two of them had considered the event a cause for reaching both a territorial and culinary detente.

More importantly, Charlotte had been willing from the very first moment to take Jack out into the garden whenever he wanted to go. The light in Charlotte's eyes the instant Fiona had walked in the door with the little monster trotting so innocently on a leash at her side . . . For as long as he lived, that spark, that light, would define for him the transformative power of hope.

Ian reached the doorway to the drawing room and froze. Fiona stood on the top step of a ladder on the far side of the room, her dark green shawl sliding down one arm as she reached out at an impossible, precarious angle to unhook the draperies from the rod. Good God, the woman had absolutely no sense of self-preservation. If he didn't intervene, he'd be a widower before he was even a groom.

Afraid that a sudden warning would startle her and that she'd topple off the ladder, he quickly made his way across the room. Not that that was an easy task; she'd pushed all of the furnishings into a haphazard jumble in the center of it. She was wearing a pale yellow muslin dress with some sort of tiny print Ian absently noted as he went, the color beautifully complementing her porcelain skin and golden hair. He winced and silently cursed as he caught the rocker of a chair with his shin, but he didn't stop to inspect the injury.

The instant his hands slipped around her tiny waist, she gasped and spun about. He didn't bother to issue any instructions, but instead simply pulled her down off the ladder. Her hands instantly went to his shoulders and she grinned happily at him as he slowly lowered her to the floor.

Her body brushed against the length of him, remaining close enough, even after she stood on her feet for her light skirts to wrap about his booted ankles, for the warmth and scent of her skin to envelop his every sense. Her smile was mischievous and openly inviting, igniting his senses and heating his blood. He'd asked her to marry him, Desire whispered. And although she hadn't yet signed the settlement papers, she *was* redecorating his house. What harm could there be in kissing her? Just once.

His good judgment staggered to the fore, warning him for the countless time that once unleashed, his natural instincts might be damn near impossible to keep within the bounds of propriety, that a member of the household staff, or any one of the myriad numbers of hired workmen, could walk in on them. He couldn't in good conscience place Fiona in such an embarrassing and compromising situation. Especially since he was still trying to live down having been caught with her Aunt Jane.

Redemption be damned, Desire whispered.

Ian pulled his hands from around Fiona's waist, stepped away and took a long, slow, deep breath before saying, "Please stop endangering yourself,

Fiona. My heart can't take it. Just stand about and direct the staff or workers at the tasks you want done."

"Don't be ridiculous, Ian," she quickly countered, her eyes bright and her smile wide. "Carrie's had me climbing ladders, taking down and putting up curtains practically all of my life. I know what I'm doing and you have absolutely no reason to worry."

He shook his head. "Decorum suggests—"

"*Suggests* is the significant word," Fiona smilingly interrupted to point out. "It does *not* demand, thus allowing me room for my own interpretation of what is and what isn't appropriate behavior." Her smile broadened. "And at present I'm having such fun that I've decided to use a rather flexible meaning of the concept. Have you seen the front parlor, yet?"

It was virtually impossible to maintain righteous indignation in the face of her enthusiasm. He'd come back to the issue of her risk-taking later. "I paused to look on my way here. I assume there's a plan for all that lumber?"

"I'm having new crown molding milled. The old ones are so heavy that they make the ceiling feel as though it's pressing down on your shoulders."

"In other words, you're going to tear down the ceiling?"

"Well, not completely," she replied, smoothing her skirts and adjusting the drape of her shawl. "I'm sure some of the existing plaster will come down when the old moldings are removed, but the plasterer,

Mr. Stanley, has assured me that the repairs can be made without anyone ever knowing that they were patched. He really does the most marvelous work. Have you seen what he's doing in the dining room?"

Ian cocked a brow. "I assume that whatever it is, it's costing me a small fortune."

Fiona laughed softly. "He does have two sons who have expressed an interest in going up to Oxford."

"Well," Ian countered, nodding and enjoying their banter, "far be it from me to stand in the way of two young men trying to escape the world of plaster, trowels, and horse hair."

"Mr. and Mrs. Stanley have three daughters, too. Lydia, Dora, and Rachel."

Ian crossed his arms over his chest, broadened his stance, and attempted to look put upon. "Why do I have the impression that the Stanley boys aren't the only ones with aspirations?"

"Lydia wants to learn to ride," Fiona informed him with a pretty, happy grin. "Apparently she loves horses and is very good with them. She wants to train them for riding."

"Only for the really open-minded."

"Of course," Fiona allowed. "Dora wants her own dressmaker's shop. She makes all her family's clothes and what I've seen shows not only excellent skills and workmanship, but a real talent. She really could be as good as Carrie someday. And Rachel, the youngest, desperately wants to open a sweet shop."

"Mr. Stanley's brood's certainly an ambitious bunch. Couldn't you have hired a younger plasterer? Someone with no family?"

She looked up at him and pouted prettily while gazing at him through her lashes in a way that she no doubt considered playful. That he viewed her whole game as nothing short of a blatantly carnal invitation . . . Well, if nothing else it was nice to know that his abused body parts were fully functional again.

"You told me I could spend whatever I wanted in redoing the house, Ian. You said that I could spend frivolously if I wanted. Remember?"

Ian chuckled. "I seem to recall that at the time you said that you were going to go at the redecorating slowly. Take some time to see how the household functioned and all that. And that you'd discuss every single change with me before you made a discussion."

Fiona grinned and began to fold up the heavy brocade curtains she'd already removed from another window. "Well, that was then. In the meantime, I've made several important discoveries. The first of which is that Charlotte, despite her reluctance to openly display or admit it, has an artistic eye and an interest in decorating. In giving her something to do, I've discovered how much fun this is and why Carrie so enjoys it.

"And secondly," she went on, "how else am I going to see that Mr. Stanley's children have opportunities? Everyone should have a chance to reach for their dreams."

Ian laughed outright. "Sweetly generous, always optimistic Fiona . . . I truly don't care what you spend or who you help in the process. But would you please promise me that you and the esteemed Mr. Stanley will leave my study and office just the way they are? I know my cubbyholes aren't fashionable or even very well organized, but they are familiar and comfortable."

"Speaking of cubbyholes . . ."

"Oh, no." Ian glanced quickly around the room and made a production of swallowing hard. He was so enjoying the game with her. As long as he kept his hands to himself, there couldn't be any harm in continuing.

"Oh, yes," she blithely countered. "Mr. Pembroke, the dear old man in charge of the carpenters, showed me a drawing of the most wonderfully ingenious cabinet for storing dining room linens. They're going to be hidden in the walls of the dining room itself and with a concealed latch so that they're completely invisible. No one will know they're there and won't notice anything the least unusual about the wall panels hiding them. Mr. Pembroke thought of the idea and designed it himself. He says that no one else has such a thing."

Ian rolled his eyes. "We're so terribly fortunate."

"And the new space being created above the dining room is—"

"New space?" Ian repeated, cocking a brow. "I seem to recall that the old space was roof and then sky. Please don't tell me that you're having the roof removed so we can dine al fresco."

"No, of course not," she assured him, her hands on her hips and chin tilted at a pretty angle as she looked up to laughingly meet his gaze. "Mr. Stanley is putting in a false ceiling, lowering it so that the room isn't quite as cavernous and cold all the time. But in lowering it, a rather large space is created above it. Mr. Pembroke didn't think it at all proper that it should go to waste. He hates wasted space."

"Of course," Ian drawled, nodding. "And I'm sure that he sketched another drawing of a wonderfully unique idea whose construction isn't going to cost all that much in the grand scheme of things that no one else has."

"Mr. O'Connor recommended both Mr. Stanley and Mr. Pembroke," she informed him brightly. "He says they're the best craftsmen in London. I certainly believe him. As Drayton's always said, a certain degree of discerning vision and unusual creativity is the essence of what separates a quality artisan from the garden variety tradesman. I really do think you should feel incredibly honored that both Mr. Pembroke and Mr. Stanley are willing to work their magic to make your home so beautiful."

With a sigh, Ian grinned and held his hands up in mock surrender. "And so what has the illustrious Mr. Pembroke designed for what was formerly the upper portion of the formal dining room?"

She considered him for a long moment with

sparkling green eyes. "Perhaps it would be best if I showed you."

"Correct me if I'm wrong, Fiona," Ian said as she led him out of the drawing room, across the foyer and toward the wide stairway. "But doesn't a solid wall of the master's suite abut . . ." Suddenly a mental image filled his head and he knew precisely what she intended to do with that newly created room. His heart raced and his blood warmed.

She cast a bright smile over her shoulder as she continued to lead him up the stairs, but that was all the reply that he got.

He couldn't stand not having the answer. "Are you having that wall torn out, perchance?" he pressed.

"I'd say that the project is a bit further along than perchance. Although they did begin actual work on that phase of it only this morning," she supplied as they made their way down the the upstairs hallway. "Mr. Dylan tells me that they won't cut the new windows into the exterior walls until later in the week. Which, of course, means that for the time being your room is still recognizable."

And functional. "I gather then that you have plans to enlarge my sleeping quarters?"

She blushed prettily and avoided his gaze. "You're a very perceptive man, Ian Cabott," she answered quietly.

He couldn't resist the temptation. "Are you planning similar changes in your own suite?"

The color in her cheeks deepened. "I don't consider

any of the rooms mine," she began. She took a deep breath. "At least not at this point. But it has occurred to me that if we do decide to marry, we might be inclined to dispense with the entire notion of separate bedrooms."

The images suddenly filling his brain sent his blood pounding hot through his veins. Ian swallowed hard and deliberately forced his mind along a different track. "Won't that leave us with a large number of empty rooms on this floor? Or are you expecting a steady stream of houseguests?"

To his surprise her blush deepened even further. "Well, yes, there is the matter of accommodating overnight guests. But, actually, I was thinking about places to put children."

Children that had to be made before they needed to be put anywhere. Which meant, given that she was even thinking in that direction . . . Apparently Lady Fiona was reconsidering her initial aversion to the idea of bedding him. Proof that there was a reasonably understanding if not entirely benevolent God. Ian managed to stifle a groan of pure, frustrated desire, but just barely. "Oh," was the full extent of any pithy and witty commentary he could muster.

Thankfully, Fiona recovered her poise as they entered his room and before the silence between them could become any more awkward or painful.

"I'd like very much to know what you'd like to have in terms of colors and furniture styles," she said, passing the foot of his bed and keeping her gaze firmly fastened on the gaping hole in the wall ahead of them.

"I doubt very much whether my ideas on bedchamber decor would be either fashionable or aesthetic," he answered, following along in her wake, being just as careful not to look at his bed as she'd been. He told himself it was far better to avoid temptation altogether than briefly indulge it and then have to both fight frustrated desire for countless hours afterwards *and* spend the next month apologizing for being such a cad. And that was ignoring the very real chance that he'd lose control of the situation and undo all the trust he'd earned since the Miller-Sandses' ball.

Redemption be damned.

Ian clenched his teeth.

"I was thinking of using medium shades of blue and gold in here," she said, drawing his attention away from his inner turmoil. "Would that be all right with you, Ian?"

"I'm sure that whatever you choose will be absolutely, wonderfully perfect," he answered. "You have impeccable taste."

"Thank you," she murmured, turning to face him squarely and, as always, blushing a delicious shade of rosy peach. "But I really do want to hear your opinions. It seems to me that a husband and wife should share their lives completely, make decisions together. I want to share every aspect of my life with you and I hope that you feel the same way about sharing yours with me."

Well, yes, darling, it was a busy day today. I drained the pus out of an old man's leg, but I suspect that next week I'll either have to cut it off or call the undertaker for him. And there were three babies who didn't draw their first breaths today and two of the mothers who crossed into eternity with them in their arms. A kinder fate, though, than the ten-year-old boy whose head was crushed under the wheels of a train.

Ian pasted a smile on his face and pretended his thoughts were far lighter than they really were. "The desire to share our lives is a lovely sentiment, Fiona, and certainly worth trying to achieve. I just hope that you're not disappointed when reality falls short of the ideal from time to time."

She tilted her head and studied him. "Why would it fall short?"

Ian heard the cool distance edging her words, but he shrugged and offered her the only part of the truth he was willing to give her or anyone else. "I doubt you'd find the daily activities of a surgeon all that interesting. It tends be rather gory and, more often than not, depressing."

"If it's part of your world, Ian," she countered immediately and with obvious sincerity, "then I'd find it interesting."

He nodded and, knowing that nothing would be either gained or resolved by pursuing the course any further, chose to change the subject of their conversation. "Where is Charlotte this afternoon?" he asked, looking about—stupidly—as though she might be hiding behind a door. "I know she's not out in the garden because Genghis Jack met me at the front door. Only Mrs. Pittman's timely arrival saved another pair of my trouser legs from destruction."

Fiona bit the inside of her cheek and swallowed down the miserable lump in her throat. As long as she was being bubbly, he was happy. As long as she was decorating his home and managing the care of his ward, he was willing to tease and joke and talk to her. But the moment that she stepped beyond the roles of caretaker and adornment, the moment she asked to be let into the world he knew outside of this house, he closed down and all but physically pushed her away.

There was no denying that it hurt to know he considered her only a small part of his life. The part that had nothing to do with anything important. Telling herself that it had only been a few weeks since they'd met didn't assuage her wounded pride all that well. A few weeks was enough to have a sense of someone's true feelings.

Especially considering how much time they'd spent together in just the last week and a half. Yes, he still went riding in the morning and off to oversee the construction of the hospital after lunch, but in their sharing of the midday meal . . . And in all that time, he'd never come close to expressing any desire to know her better.

"Fiona?"

"Charlotte is with Madame Evaline," she supplied, lacing her trembling fingers behind her and trying to sound crisply efficient and not at all hurt.

"And who is Madame Evaline?"

"She's considered to be the premier coiffure stylist in London."

"Charlotte is having her hair styled?"

"Washed, cut and styled," Fiona clarified, dutiful in her role of caretaker. "This morning she said she hated her hair and asked if I'd shave her bald. I sent a servant for Madame Evaline with a note about the desperate need for her services. She dropped everything and rushed over."

He cocked a brow and smiled. "You don't think she'll let Charlotte talk her into anything rash or extreme, do you?"

"No, Ian," she assured him, moving toward the bedroom door. "Charlotte was actually delighted at the idea of being pampered and treated as though she were valued and special."

"Women do like that sort of thing," he observed as he followed her down the hall.

"Even the unpaid help and the strictly ornamental," she muttered under her breath.

"I'm sorry. I didn't hear you. What did you say?"

"Nothing," she assured him, reaching the bottom of the stairs, "of any importance." If he replied, she didn't hear him, not over the scrambling click of rapidly approaching canine toenails. For a scant second she thought about not warning him, but her conscience got the better of her. Pausing, she turned back just in time to see Jack slide around the corner of the stairs and launch himself at Ian's leg.

"Look—" was all she managed to get out before it was too late.

Ian stopped in his tracks, swore under his breath, and tried to shake Jack loose. Fiona arched a brow and wondered if he had any idea that Jack considered the shaking to be not only approval of the game, but active participation in it. As for all the Spawn of Satan comments . . . She couldn't help but wonder if Ian had ever had a dog of his own. He clearly had no idea how their minds worked, how they heard only their own names and considered everything else the equivalent of *Oh, let's play!*

"Your Grace?"

Ian stopped moving to meet his butler's gaze and ask over the growling, "Is the postal carrier here?"

"I beg your pardon, Your Grace?"

Good, Fiona thought, *at least I'm not the only one who doesn't know what he's talking about.*

Jack's feet slid on the marble floor as he unsuccessfully tried to brace himself to better whip his head and shred fabric.

"What is it, Rowan?" Ian asked over the sound of growling.

"A messenger from Dr. Mercer arrived just a

moment ago. There has been a crash in an underground portion of the city's railway and many severe injuries. He asked that you come as quickly as you can."

Fiona watched the color drain from Ian's face and his jaw turn to granite. She snapped her fingers and said quietly but crisply, "Heel."

The dog instantly ended his game and came to sit beside her, looking up at Ian hopefully. Whether or not the dog even crossed Ian's mind, Fiona couldn't tell, but she could clearly see the steely resolve in his eyes and the grim determination in the tightness of his lips as he turned to her.

"I'm sorry, Fiona," he said, his mind obviously miles away. "I doubt very much that I'm going to be able to attend the ball tonight at . . . at . . ."

"Lord and Lady Egan-Smythe's," she supplied.

He nodded and walked off, saying, "I'll take my horse, Rowan. It's faster. Have him saddled while I get my medical bag."

Jack started after him, but she snapped her fingers again and he circled about, came back and sat down beside her as the butler raced off to the rear of the house to have Ian's mount prepared.

Alone with the dog in the foyer, Fiona pursed her lips and arched a brow as she contemplated the situation. Drayton had begged out of the ball at breakfast this morning, saying that he had an important meeting concerning a law he was trying to get through Parliament. Simone had arrived at the house ten minutes after that to announce that Tristan had a ship coming into port and that he considered unloading it more important than going out for the evening. For her sisters, the lack of an attending husband actually made a difference in terms of their companionship for the evening. For her, though . . .

What difference did it make that Ian wasn't going to be there? She didn't dance, and since the day he'd proposed, Ian hadn't either. He came into the ballroom, got himself a glass of champagne, found her right away, and then after a few polite but utterly empty words that wouldn't offend anyone or provide the least bit of grit for the gossip mill, he offered to get her a cup of punch.

They sipped together, he looked pained, she felt pained, and they had some more inane conversation until their drinks were gone, and then Ian took the punch cup away on his way to meet his cousin at a gaming table.

That exceedingly polite, circumspect, and awkward exchange was the sum total of their attending a society event "together," and would be all that they were permitted until she formally accepted his proposal and he could officially escort her in through the door.

And to think that, in the seconds after being summoned to a horrific emergency, he'd stopped to apologize for not being there for their nightly "interlude." God, it had to mean a lot more to him than it did to her. Either that or he thought they meant a lot to her. Either way . . . Shaking her head, Fiona turned and walked back toward the kitchen to see how Charlotte was enjoying the attention and pampering. Maybe, she thought as she went, she'd see if Madame Evaline had the time to do something magical with her hair.

Or maybe not, she decided, thinking that she might be able to talk her sisters into staying home that night and enjoying the simple pleasure of one another's company without hundreds of other people getting in the way.

Chapter Eleven

Fiona sat on the carriage seat and smoothed her skirts, silently cursing the requirements of good manners. Her suggestion that no one would think it at all strange that the three of them had come down with an illness on the same night had been met with mixed reactions. Simone had laughed and called rights to morning sickness. Caroline had frowned and said that they couldn't cancel at such a late hour without wreaking havoc on Lady Egan-Smythe's dinner seating arrangements.

Pointing out that Drayton, Tristan and Ian having bowed out that day had already created the problem had been met with a cool pronouncement that while men were allowed to behave rudely, women were not. It had been followed immediately by The Look. And that had been that.

"So, tell us, Fiona," Simone said from the opposite seat as the coach began to roll down the drive. "Have you decided yet whether you're going to marry Dunsford?"

"It depends on what time of the day it is."

From beside her, Caroline asked, "What seems to be the sticking point?"

She looked back and forth between her sisters. "Ian."

Simone tipped her head back and laughed outright. Carrie simply looked at her, her brows slowly knitting. "What is about him that gives you second thoughts?" she finally asked.

Fiona sighed and tweaked the fringe of her shawl.

"Do you think he's being unfaithful?" her eldest sister pressed.

"I honestly don't think so," she admitted, "but I really don't know."

"All right," Simone said, her always meager patience clearly exhausted. "Enough of this dancing around. You're not accomplishing anything. Tell us what you like about him, what counts in his favor."

"He's handsome," she readily allowed. "Very handsome."

"That's a given," Simone countered. "So is the fact that he's a duke and incredibly wealthy."

"What's important, Simone, is that he uses his wealth for good and that he's not at all stingy. He's building a hospital, you know."

"No," Carrie answered, "I didn't."

"It's for the poor," Fiona explained. "He's having a tenement house he inherited from his father converted. Anyone who needs care will be able to get it there whether or not they have the money to pay for it."

Carrie smiled and observed, "So you're both very much alike."

"Not," she groused, "that he realizes that."

Simone arched a brow, but it was Caroline who asked, "And therein lies the problem?"

"Oh, there are so many problems, I don't know where to begin," Fiona admitted on a heavy sigh. "And quite honestly, I feel positively shrewish in even complaining. He's genuinely concerned about the welfare of his crippled ward and has freely and gladly given me a free hand to make improvements to his home so that her daily existence makes her happy. He's well mannered and gracious, tolerant of badly behaved animals and has a wonderful sense of humor. His sense of duty and service are noble and truly inspiring."

"And yet?" Carrie asked softly.

"He treats me as though I'm just *there*." As they both looked at her in silent puzzlement, she went on, the words and feelings suddenly flowing freely. "He constantly tells me how pretty I am. He compliments me on even the smallest of the successes with Charlotte and on all the changes she and I are making to his decor."

"Which was terribly dark and heavy," Carrie quickly explained to Simone.

"And as nice as the compliments are, that's all

they are," Fiona went on, her anger rising with every beat of her heart. "Words. Just words."

Simone leaned forward to lay a hand on her knee. "Are you saying that he hasn't so much as kissed you?"

"He can hardly bring himself to touch me."

Simone sank back into her seat, her mouth forming a tiny O. Carrie drew a long, slow, deep breath. They were shocked? No more than she was. "When I make even a small overture," she said, knowing and not caring that she sounded petulant, "he becomes tense and withdrawn and finds some way to end the contact as soon as he possibly can. In the one instance—just today, in fact—when he initiated a touch, he seemed inclined to take it a bit further, but then abruptly let me go and told me that decorum required ladies to order servants about and to resist climbing ladders themselves."

"Decorum, huh?" Carrie drawled.

Simone make a *tsk*ing sound and then said gently, "Well, in all fairness, Fiona, he's probably still in some pain from Aunt Jane's attack on his private person. Being stimulated might not be an altogether pleasant physical experience for him."

"And," Carrie added, "it could also be that he's being mindful of your innocence and restraining his natural impulses in an effort not to frighten you. In that light, what you see as disinterest might well be an indication of his respect for you."

Respect? "He doesn't respect me, Carrie," she

insisted hotly. "And that, I think, is the root of all my discontents. He's never asked me what my favorite color is."

"It's green," Simone said crisply. "It's obvious enough that asking would go into the inane conversation column. Give the man a little credit for being able to make an accurate observation on his own."

"It's more than the simple things like colors, Simone," she shot back. "He's never asked me what I like to read or what my interests might be beyond caring for injured animals. To him I'm nothing more than a superficial thing with a pretty face and a kind nature."

"In other words," Carrie offered, her tone even and calm, "he doesn't think that you're particularly intelligent or interesting."

"He considers me a typical society female, a genteel adornment whose only purpose and interest is in making his life easier. And, most importantly, he's made absolutely no effort to see if his assumptions might be wrong."

Simone shook her head and then brightened. "I could hit him upside the head with a blunt object if you think it would help him see how shallow he's being."

"Thank you, but no thank you," Fiona replied crisply and firmly. "If he can't see it for himself, then . . ."

For a long moment they rolled on through the streets of London in conversational silence. Caroline finally broke it by quietly asking, "How long are you going to give him to achieve enlightenment on his own?"

"I don't know," Fiona admitted, discouragement taking the place of her anger. "I keep hoping. Why, I don't know."

Carrie's smile was soft and almost knowing, "Perhaps it's because you see that he does have some qualities that are really quite remarkable and to his credit."

"It could be."

"That," Simone offered brightly from her side of the carriage, "and maybe a little bit of falling in love with him."

Fiona shook her head. "If something happened to him, if he were injured or killed, I'd feel horrible and I'd undoubtedly cry—but just as much about the cruelty of life as for the loss of Ian. Not exactly a clear sign of undying love and devotion."

Carrie chuckled and reached over to pat her on the hand. "A wise woman once told me that only weak and spineless girls died of lost love. And she was right, Fiona dear. I love Drayton dearly and with all my heart. But I wouldn't wither up and pass away of a broken heart and shattered spirit if he were taken from me. I'd cry and cry, yes, and then there would come a day when I straightened my shoulders and got on with living without him. Being able to live without a man isn't a measure of your love for him."

"Then what is?" she asked.

Simone replied breezily, "I'd say the real measure is how easy it is to tolerate his stupidities."

"Simone," Carrie chided. "The idea is to be helpful."

"Well, if she's thinking that a man in love with her is always going to be considerate and thoughtful and sensitive every day for the rest of her life, she really does need help. To my thinking, Fi," she went on, "the measure of our love for them is in how easily we can refrain from not only killing them in the moments when they're considerably less than likable, but also how easily we can forgive them for being decidedly, selfishly human."

Fiona had to admit that it was an intriguing way to look at the matter. Very Simone-esque.

"And I must say," her wild sister continued, "that you seem inclined to give Ian Cabott the benefit of the doubt more often than not. I'd suggest that the next time you see him, you grab him by the coat lapels, jerk his handsome face down to yours, kiss him senseless and see what happens next."

"Simone!" Caroline squeaked.

"Oh, for heaven's sakes, Carrie. I'm not suggesting that sweet little Fiona throw him to the ground and rip his clothes off of him." She grinned wickedly across the carriage at Fiona and quickly added, "Although I can tell you from experience that that's a great deal of fun.

"That reality aside," she said with a chuckle, "the 'what happens next' that I mean is to notice whether your toes are curled and he's suddenly the most perfect man God ever made. Even if the illusion lasts just a second, it's a sure sign that you love him."

Fiona nodded, wondering if Tristan had had any idea at the time of the handful he was marrying. God love the man; she was going to be extra nice to him from now on. As for taking Simone's advice on how to discover her feelings for Ian Cabott . . . Well, she might. But only if she were completely at her wits' end and her only other choice was to walk away and abandon all hope. Maybe he'd be different tomorrow, she offered herself. Maybe he'd realize how he'd been treating her and make everything right between them. Why she clung so resolutely to that hope, though . . .

Ian stood in the hospital garden, rolling his shoulders in an attempt to ease the tension from his aching muscles and trying not to analyze every decision he'd made in the chaotic rush of surgery. What was done was done and there was no going back to change his mind and do things differently. He'd trusted his instincts and known that the odds had been against all of his skills more often than not.

Despite that logic, that certainty, the failures weighed heavily on his soul. As they always did. He looked up at the stars, hoping that his mind would empty as his gaze wandered across the sparkling heavens.

A smile lifted the corners of his mouth. He was

going to have to buy Fiona some diamond necklaces. Not that she needed them to be beautiful. No, if ever there was a woman who could outshine a king's ransom in jewels . . . God, he could see her lying in the sheets, wearing only a satisfied smile and a delicate strand of diamonds and emeralds. The pendant would drop low, to lay just at the top of the valley between her creamy breasts. A beacon to . . .

Ian sighed and shook his head to dispel the vision. He was so tired of fighting himself and how much longer propriety could hope to win . . . Every day his desire for Fiona deepened while his ability to marshal gentlemanly restraint frayed a little bit more. There wasn't much left of it at this point.

He'd told himself it was merely a matter of their recent close proximity—that Fiona's redecorating of his house and their shared meals with Charlotte brought them into too much contact. Staying away as much as he could hadn't helped, though. The instant he went home all the rational explanations fell apart and his determination to keep a safe distance ebbed away. Her smiles and obvious pleasure at the task of transforming his world warmed his heart and relentlessly shredded his resolve.

Yes, he was losing the battle. So badly that he'd been thinking lately about how it wasn't at all uncommon for husbands and wives to present big, healthy, bouncing babies to the world a month or two "prematurely."

As though Fiona deserved those whispers on top

of all the others swirling through London's Society. That he'd asked her to marry him was common social knowledge already. That she was still seriously considering his proposal after the Lady Baltrip debacle . . . Everyone thought she was crazy for giving him the benefit of the doubt.

From out of the darkness, William Mercer came to stand beside him and roll his own shoulders. A fine surgeon, Mercer was. And a good and caring man who had no doubt been put on this earth for only two reasons: to be a doctor and the world's best father and grandfather.

After several long moments, Ian's colleague said quietly, "We did the best we could."

"Yes, we did. Sometimes that's the only consolation."

Mercer nodded in silent agreement and looked up into the stars. "My wife tells me that you've asked Lady Fiona Turnbridge to marry you."

Apparently everyone in London knew. "I have. She hasn't accepted, though."

"You've made an excellent choice. I hope you think she's worth the wait for a decision."

It took a moment for the man's words to penetrate the fog in his mind. "Oh?" he asked carefully. "What have you heard about her?"

Mercer chuckled. "I've actually met her. Several times, in fact. I'd seen her at my lectures a half dozen times before she first approached me. She always sits in the very back and well away from the other students. At first having a female, and such an attractive one at that, in attendance created quite a stir, but she handily rebuffed the untoward advances and conveyed the seriousness of her interest.

"She never speaks, of course," Mercer went on, seemingly oblivious to the fact that Ian's jaw was slowly sagging. "Never draws attention to herself in any way. But even before we spoke, I knew in watching her that she was the best of my students. Always a full tick ahead of everyone else. Always has the answer while the others are still turning the question over in their minds."

Ian closed his mouth, moistened his lower lip and then dragged enough air into his lungs to ask, "You are talking about your internal anatomy lectures, aren't you?"

"Well, yes. It is my specialty."

"And Fiona has attended."

Mercer nodded enthusiastically. "Not just attended. She listened carefully, took copious notes, made the most incredibly detailed drawings, and then, later in the course, approached me after dismissal to ask some of the best questions I've ever been posed. She's keenly intelligent and I have to confess that I had true regrets and second thoughts every time I denied her request to attend the operating theater. If she weren't a female, she'd make one of the best physicians in England. She's amazing. Just amazing."

He'd always known that she was amazing, but he hadn't had the slightest inkling as to just how amazing. Not the slightest. He thought back, remembering bits and pieces of conversations he hadn't fully understood or appreciated at the time, the mysterious shadows that had darkened her eyes when he'd ever so blithely dismissed her efforts to tell him about herself and her abilities.

Mercer laid a hand on his shoulder and gently asked, "You didn't know any of this, did you, Dunsford?"

"No, I didn't," he had to admit. "And that I didn't reflects poorly on me."

"She hasn't mentioned her interest in medicine to you?"

"I haven't been listening." He swallowed down the thickening lump in his throat and reached for his pocket watch. "Mercer," he said, noting the time and quickly putting the timepiece away, "would you mind overly much if I lit out of here on you?"

"Not at all," the other man assured him. "They say they've brought everyone in who had a chance. I think we're done for the time being. Tomorrow, though . . ." He shrugged.

"If you have to go back in on someone sooner, send a runner," Ian instructed. "For the next hour, I'll be at my home. After that I'll be at Lord Egan-Smythe's. Don't let a ball deter you from sending a runner there if need arises."

His colleague shook his head and offered him a tired smile. "I'm impressed that you have the strength to even consider dancing."

"I'm not going to dance, Mercer. I'm going to grovel for forgiveness."

"Good luck to you, then. If it helps any, I can't think of any other woman—excepting Mrs. Mercer, of course—who would be worth the sacrifice of dignity."

"Thank you," Ian replied as he headed for the stable at the rear of the hospital. Calling back over his shoulder, he added, "And send for me if you need to."

Mercer waved him on, then turned and went back inside.

It took just a few minutes for Ian to be on his way. The fatigue that had gripped his mind as he'd come out of the surgery was gone, replaced by a driving sense of clear purpose. He had been an idiot. A presumptive, self-absorbed idiot who, when he wasn't wallowing in the misery of his every waking moment, had spent the last two weeks being surly and resentful to a decent, caring human being.

Well, there were degrees of humanity and degrees of caring. And until Mercer had ever-so-unknowingly smacked him right between the eyes a moment ago, he'd had no idea that he'd been so damned shallow. God Almighty, it was a miracle that Fiona hadn't killed him.

Fiona sighed and leaned her elbows on the balcony balustrade. She'd spent so much time on ballroom balconies in the last two weeks . . . People were going to start thinking of her as a human gargoyle.

Better that, she supposed morosely, than being considered the pathetic little mouse who dutifully went to the ball while the Duke of Dunsford cavorted about London with God only knew who and doing what God and everyone else knew good and well. If she saw one more pitying glance tonight she was going to . . . to . . . Well, she didn't know what she was going to do other than be even more unhappy than she already was.

A shadow fell across the marble tiles of the balcony. She arched a brow as she watched it advance slowly. Hopefully, it belonged to one of the hordes of randy, badly mannered bachelors who haunted balls looking for easy prey. She was very much in the mood to blacken an eye or two. Maybe even mercilessly mash some toes. All she needed was the slightest provocation.

The shadow stopped just as a breeze wrapped the scent of a familiar cologne around her senses. She straightened, her heart thundering and her knees weak. Gazing out over the garden below, she wrapped her fingers around the granite railing and waited for him to step to her side.

"It's a lovely night, isn't it?" he said, remaining behind her.

His voice sounded very different than usual. There was a softness to the deep timbre that she'd never heard before. "The stars are very close," she answered. "It looks as though you could reach right out and pull one down. I hope that the crash wasn't as bad as everyone thought at the beginning."

She heard him sigh. "It was probably worse," he supplied, easing to stand beside her at the railing. His gaze still fixed on the stars, he added, "We did what we could, as best as we could, but sometimes life and death are in hands more powerful and determined than our own."

Deep in her soul, an ache bloomed. "I'm sorry, Ian. It has to be very difficult to try so hard and fail."

He nodded slowly and then softly cleared his throat. "Dr. Mercer sends his regards."

"How nice of him," she said as her heart skittered.

"He told me that he always regretted and had second thoughts about denying you permission to attend his operating theater lectures."

Yes, the Beeps was definitely out of the bag. And since there was no point in claiming that the esteemed Dr. William Mercer was mistaken, she accepted the situation with all the grace and nonchalance that she could muster. "I suspect that he's the only one of the teaching physicians who has regrets. When I asked Dr. Turner if I could attend a circulatory dissection, he not only told me no, but also barred me from his lecture hall."

"Narrow-minded and close-minded men are everywhere."

"That's very true."

"And sometimes people are just blindly stupid,"

he went on, sounding sad. "Largely out of making groundless assumptions and because they're so pre-occupied with their own thoughts and feelings and hopes that it never crosses their mind that others might have them, too."

"That's true, as well," she agreed, the ache in her soul deepening with his every word.

He turned to face her and lifted his chin to swallow. "Fiona," he said gently, "I've been a complete ass. Not once in the last fortnight . . ." He paused as she turned to face him.

After a quick deep breath, he went on, saying earnestly, "To my everlasting shame, not once since we met has it occurred to me that you were more than a beautiful, kind, and domestically capable woman. I've spent the days since my proposal consumed by the effort to behave in an exemplary fashion and keep my hands to myself, to impress you with my generosity and compassion, and to shield you from the dark and grisly aspects of my life's work.

"I've been so consumed with presenting myself well that I didn't even think to ask after your interests and intellectual passions. In the clarity of hindsight, I realize that you've tried several times to share them with me and, again to my shame, I haven't been at all willing to listen."

"Ian, I—"

He held up his hand, effectively cutting her off. "I completely understand your hesitation to accept my proposal. So far, all I've done is display extraordinarily bad judgment and inexcusably self-centered, chauvinistic attitudes. Then, on top of that, I've taken considerable advantage of your kind heart to resolve the problems with Charlotte. Considering the rather lengthy list of my appalling shortcomings . . ." He smiled tightly. "Well, I wouldn't marry me, either."

"But you can see your mistakes and that counts in your favor," she offered sincerely. "As does your ability to offer a sincere apology."

"Yes," he allowed with a slight shrug, "but it remains to be seen whether I'm capable of changing my behavior and attitudes. It could well be that marriage to me would be nothing more than a long string of deep frustrations and backhanded insults, punctuated every now and again with an apology that doesn't change a thing in the aftermath. That's hardly the kind of domestic situation I'd find the least bit appealing on a day-to-day basis."

Confident in the kindness of his heart and the content of his character, she considered the one and only other concern she had. Modesty suggested that she just trust to luck and hope it all worked out for the best. Honesty compelled her to say, "May I ask you a question, Ian?"

"Of course. Ask whatever you'd like."

"Do you find me at all physically appealing?"

His jaw went slack as his brows shot up. It took him a moment to recover enough to offer a strangled sounding, "God, yes."

"I mean in a way more than being reasonably pretty," she pressed, hoping she wasn't being too indelicate about it all. "It's just that I don't seem to inspire you in the same way that . . ."

"Your Aunt Jane did?" he finished for her after a long second.

"Well, yes."

Slowly trailing his fingertip along her jaw and down her throat, he whispered, "Apparently I've been trying too hard to redeem myself."

The simple caress melted the last of her doubts. A delicious heat warming her blood, Fiona laid her hands on the lapel of his jacket and looked up into his gaze to say, "I would deeply appreciate it, Ian, if you'd consider yourself fully redeemed and stop trying to be a saint."

"I'd be delighted." He leaned forward and pressed a slow kiss to her lips. His arms slowly slipped around her, drawing her to him, then tightened, holding her close as his possession deepened and her senses were swept upward in a swift, exhilarating spiral. She melted into the hard planes of his chest, happily surrendering to the desire he so easily and quickly fanned to life within her.

"Oh, do pardon me."

Ian drew back, cast a quick glance toward the now vacant doorway, and then smiled down at her, his chest rising and falling in the same quick cadence as her own. Fiona gently brushed a lock of ebony hair from his forehead. God, was there any more magnificent man in the world? And to think that he was willing to be hers.

"Well," he drawled, grinning. "That puts a kink in things. I came out here intending to offer a withdrawal of my proposal. But having been caught together, in a passionate embrace, I find myself in the position of having to propose again."

"It's really not necessary, Ian," she assured him. "Not at all."

"Yes, it is." He drew back, bringing his arms from around her to take her hands in his. "Lady Fiona Turnbridge," he said, earnestly gazing into her eyes, "may I have the honor of protecting your reputation and delightfully delicious personage for the rest of my life?"

Her heart melted. Her soul soared. "You may."

Grinning, he reached into the inside breast pocket of his coat, saying, "I've been carrying this around with me every day, prepared to capitalize on the first weak moment you might have." He offered her a small dark green velvet box as he added, "I hope you like it."

Ian watched her eyes widen as she took the box from him with trembling fingers and slowly opened it. A quiet gasp slipped past her lips as she stared at the diamond-and-emerald engagement ring nestled in black satin. Her eyes, bright with awed delight, slowly lifted to meet his, touching his very soul and taking his breath away.

"It's absolutely exquisite, Ian," she whispered. "Thank you."

"I don't think an engagement is really official until the prospective groom puts the ring on his lady's finger," he said.

She grinned and handed him back the ring box, waiting until he'd removed the band from its nesting place before extending her left hand. Gently cradling it with his own left, he slipped the gem-encrusted band onto to her tiny finger. It fit perfectly—just as he'd known that it would the second he'd seen it in the jeweler's case.

"It's almost too magnificent to wear," she said quietly, openly admiring the way it looked on her hand.

"But I hope you will."

She beamed up at him. "I'll never take it off."

Ian considered his options. Engaging her in conversation, lively and witty or otherwise, wasn't one of them. Telling himself that as long as he exercised some common sense and self-control . . . "I hear that it's also customary and perfectly acceptable at this point for the prospective bride and groom to kiss."

"Well, we can't defy custom," Fiona answered, her eyes sparkling, her smile inviting. She reached out to slip her arms around his waist as she added, "We certainly don't want people talking, do we?"

"I don't care if they do," he replied softly, wrapping her in his arms and lowering his mouth to hers.

Common sense was staggering and gasping when Ian finally heard its desperate pleading and released his claim to Fiona's sweet lips. She sighed in contentment, her eyes huge as she looked up at him, their color deepened by the fires of desire their kiss had kindled.

Ian softly cleared his throat and cocked a brow. "I think that our interlude had best stop now. I've pledged to protect your reputation, not do my best to destroy it."

She nodded and stepped from his arms as he loosened his hold on her. "I suppose that you're going to see me delivered back into the ballroom," she said, adjusting first her dress bodice and then the drape of her shawl.

"You suppose correctly, my Lady Fiona." He offered her his arm as he added, "But I must say that I'm really looking forward to the time when we can decline invitations to gala public events. I think we can find much more enjoyable private pastimes."

The pink shading her cheeks darkened ever so slightly as she smiled, put her hand on his forearm, and let him escort her off the balcony and back to the ball.

Chapter Twelve

Fiona sighed, kicked off her elegant shoes, and dropped down on the edge of the parlor settee, heedless of wrinkling her ball gown.

"You're very pleased with yourself, aren't you, Fiona?" teased Simone as she, too, kicked off her shoes. She placed her fan on the mantel before dropping unceremoniously into a chair beside the hearth.

"And why wouldn't I be?" Fiona replied, stretching out the full length of the sofa and sighing in contentment. "It was a spectacular evening. Ian apologized beyond my wildest dreams and asked me to marry him all over again. This time with genuine feeling and sincerity."

She held out her hand and wiggled her finger so that the firelight danced off the brilliant gemstones. "I have a beautiful ring from the most wonderful man on Earth and I was escorted through the evening by the most handsome man in all of London. There wasn't a woman there who wasn't wildly jealous of me."

"From angry and uncertain to flushed with giddy happiness in the span of a single evening," Caroline observed as she came into the parlor. "I gather that he finally kissed you?"

Fiona lifted her head just far enough to see her eldest sister's face and then collapsed back into the settee with a broad smile. "Soundly and repeatedly."

"And did it curl your toes?" Simone asked, laughing silently.

"I don't know. My toes never crossed my mind," she admitted.

"We won't inquire as to what parts of your body you were aware of," Caroline teased, settling into the other chair by the hearth.

Simone grinned. "I will."

"You can ask all you want," Fiona countered, "but I'm not telling you. I will, however, admit that you were right about there being a moment in which I realized how utterly magnificent and beyond perfection he is."

"Really?" Caroline said, leaning back and settling her shoulders. "How long did it last?"

Fiona grinned up at the ceiling. "He's still magnificent and perfect."

"Well, that puts him head and shoulders above every other man who was there this evening," Simone quipped. "Talk about dull, duller and dullest. Since Tristan wasn't there and I didn't need to beat the tarts off of him all evening, I had plenty of time and opportunity to watch what was going on around me."

"Oh, really?" Caroline taunted, a smile tugging at the corner of her mouth. "Do tell us everything you saw, Simone dear. Everything."

"Yes, and don't spare the slightest detail," Fiona added, happily joining the game. "And start at the beginning."

"That would be the point where Haywood was announced. Which was right after you went out to hide on the balcony. I'm telling you, every woman under the age of seventy . . . Well, I've never seen so much fan-fluttering and near swoons."

"Haywood?" Fiona asked, mystified as to why Drayton's ever-single friend would suddenly elicit such female awe. It wasn't as though he ever had before.

"He's dyed his hair," Caroline answered dryly. "And let it grow longer."

"You're kidding me."

"Oh, no we're not," Simone hurriedly assured her. "Jet black and almost to his shoulders. Personally, I think he looks like a skunk without the stripe, but then, I'm not exactly open-minded about the whole thing."

"I happen to agree with you," Carrie said. "But the two of us seem to be the only ones who think he's making a complete fool of himself. I overheard Lady St. Regis say that she thought he looked like a dashing, romantic pirate who could, *and I quote,* swash her buckle and jolly her roger any time he wanted to."

"Oh, my God!" Fiona cried, lifting her head from

the sofa to stare in amazement at their eldest sister. "The Queen of the Rumor Mongers really said that?"

"She did indeed."

Simone snorted as she waved her hand dismissively. "Oh, that wasn't the best. When he handed back Lady Philben her dance card, she kissed it and then grabbed his waistband and shoved it in. And judging by the look on Haywood's face, quite a ways down."

Struggling to contain her laughter just long enough to speak, Fiona asked, "What did he do?"

"He walked away like a pirate. A pale, eighty-year-old, decidedly arthritic, bowlegged pirate."

"His timbers," Caroline added sweetly, "having been shivered. Or shaved."

Poor Haywood. It really wasn't very nice to laugh at his misfortune, but since he'd invited it . . . Fiona wiped the tears from the corner of her eyes and drew a steadying breath. "And aside from Haywood setting all sense of matronly decorum and decency on its ear," Fiona said, "what else did you see this evening?"

"Lord and Lady Quinn came in shortly after that."

"Dear God," Caroline sputtered, "I thought I was going to die."

"What happened?" Fiona demanded, grinning.

Caroline, laughing silently, motioned for Simone to start the tale. "Well," their dark-haired sister drawled, "they were announced and strode in, her under a huge crane plume headdress and him looking—and walking—like a severely trussed penguin. They step up to be received by Lord and Lady Egan-Smythe."

Caroline chortled and quickly pressed her hands over her mouth.

"Lady Quinn does her curtsy to both of them. Lord Quinn shakes Lord Egan-Smythe's hand and then steps over to pay his respects to Lady Egan-Smythe. She presents her hand, he leans over it and . . ." She grinned and shook her head.

"Thar he blew!" Caroline exclaimed. "Oh, Lord, Fiona. His corset laces popped right up the line. One right after the other. Everyone in the ballroom turned. It was that loud. And then, right before our eyes, his jacket gave way at the seams and he plumped and plumped."

"Like a biscuit in a hot oven," Simone said, picking up the story. "So, undoubtedly seeing far more than she ever wanted to of Lord Quinn, Lady Egan-Smythe is mincing sideways to put some distance between them, looking horrified in a dignified sort of way. Lady Quinn is just standing there looking horrified."

"Dignified was beyond her."

"Lord Quinn, still bent over double, decides he's going to make an escape just as the waistband on his trousers starts to go. He whirls around looking for a way out, accidentally puts his head in Lady Quinn's rump and, before he can stop his momentum, gives her a big heave ho."

"She grabbed her crane-plumed hat," Carrie said,

gazing off into the memory, "and then holding on to it for dear life, her eyes as big as saucers . . . she went over like a tree."

Fiona looked back and forth between them. "She wasn't hurt, was she?"

"Naw," Simone said with another dismissive wave of her hand. "Lady Egan-Smythe's timing was perfect. Ever the considerate hostess, she was in just the right place at the right time to cushion Lady Quinn's impact. If she hadn't squealed and thrashed all the way down, she could have claimed that she deliberately sacrificed herself. Unfortunately, she just wasn't thinking ahead at that particular moment."

"All this while I was on the balcony?"

Caroline nodded. "You were out there a very long time."

"Was all this before or after Ian arrived?"

"He came in," Simone answered, "just as Lord Egan-Smythe was pulling his wife out from under Lady Quinn. And with his arrival, everyone forgot all about the Quinns."

"Oh, please," Fiona instantly protested, lifting her head to toss a skeptical look at her sister. "I hardly believe that."

Simone arched a raven brow. "Fiona," she began in the tone she always used when launching into a subject on which she considered herself far better informed than most. "Ian Cabott walked into the room and practically every woman took two steps forward and raised her hand."

Of all the ridiculous—

"The exceptions being me and Carrie, of course. And Aunt Jane. She took off in the other direction like a shot."

Well, that was definitely nice to know.

"The fact that they didn't do anything more than drool and ogle him—none too discreetly, I might add—from across the room is only because he made a beeline for me. Didn't look left, didn't look right."

"You?"

"To ask me where you were. He was utterly single-minded and . . . primed."

Primed was a very good way to describe him. Fiona felt herself blushing and smiled.

"You do know, don't you, that he's likely to explode before the wedding?" Simone went on.

Well, yes. And if they happened to have the chance to kiss somewhere private and at a time when they weren't likely to be interrupted, she might explode herself. In fact, she was looking forward to it. But since there were some matters one simply didn't share with one's sisters, no matter how close the relationship, she kept the admission to herself and simply grinned in anticipation.

Ian sighed as the coach rolled toward home. His bones creaked as the vehicle rocked on its springs, reminding him that he'd spent hours leaning over a surgical table earlier in the evening. How long ago it seemed now, how far away. Even the pain of losing to Death wasn't as raw as it had been. It really was amazing what the favor of a good woman could do for the soul.

Well, he amended, the favor of a good woman, the cleansing of a well-done grovel, and the end of his penance for Lady Jane Baltrip. He couldn't say that he and Fiona were in love with each other, but for the moment he could be quite content with a mutual and breathless lust. The odds were good that they could build a happy marriage out of that.

Yes, if he took the train wreck out of consideration, he could say that it had been a wonderful evening. It would have been perfect if he and Fiona could have slipped off to spend it alone, seeing just how fevered they could make each other. Lord knew she could set his blood on fire with just a playful bat of her eyelashes. For a woman who had never been kissed before, she was remarkably skilled at it. Once she had some experience . . . Ian expelled a long breath to ease the tension of anticipation.

Just a while longer, he reminded himself. "For the thousandth time tonight," he muttered as the carriage eased to a stop along the walkway in front of his house. The engagement ball was a mere three days away and the wedding itself just under a month. Having lasted this long, he could be patient just a little bit longer.

Of course, he allowed as he climbed down the carriage steps and started up the walk, it was going to be damn difficult to be patient if he had to spend every night of the next month escorting her to parties and balls and galas. Resisting her was one thing in the daytime. She wore demure house dresses that covered her from neck to ankle to wrist. And while the bodices certainly didn't hang on her like sacks, they more hinted at the delights under them than accented them.

But when the sun went down . . . Tonight she'd been wearing a pale green-colored silk ball gown, its overskirt ruched up at the sides to show a slightly darker underskirt of some filmy sort of fabric. There hadn't been any sleeves to the thing. And the neckline . . . If her intent was to torture him with glimpses of creamy swells that he couldn't touch, with shadows of an inviting cleavage that promised delights he couldn't sample yet, then she'd more than succeeded. Well, to a point, he allowed, smiling as he remembered the feel of her pressed against his chest.

The very sight of her so temptingly dressed always put him on pins and needles and made the conversation over a champagne and punch excruciatingly difficult to endure. But tonight, having held her, having tasted just the smallest measure of her passion . . . Watching her smile in conversations with other men had very nearly undone him. He'd spent most of the evening with his teeth clenched and alternating between reminding himself that there wasn't anything untoward in a man exchanging polite greetings with her and fighting the urge to draw her outside and along the garden paths.

There was, however, considerable consolation to be had in knowing that he was envied by every man in attendance that evening. Fiona had finally agreed to become his wife. He'd claimed for himself the most beautiful and kindest woman in the Empire. And that Fiona had delighted in showing her sisters her ring, grinning and wiggling her finger. . . . Deciding that he had every reason to be the happiest man of all time, he pushed open the front door of his house and strode inside.

Genghis Jack was nowhere in sight. Rowan was the one coming around the corner to meet him. That the man was still up at this late hour didn't bode well.

"There is a problem with Charlotte?" he asked, removing his greatcoat and handing it over.

"Miss Charlotte is fine. Her Grace, the Dowager Duchess, is here to see you."

Ian's good mood evaporated in an instant. In the next his stomach turned to lead.

"She arrived some hours ago and has refused to leave until she's spoken to you. We've placed her in your study, Your Grace, since it is the only room not under construction."

"The proper decision, Rowan," Ian assured the man while considering the closed door of his study. "Thank you. Now please don't worry about her any further and retire for the evening. If I need anything, I'll see to it myself."

"Yes, Your Grace," he replied with a nod of his head but clear misgiving shining in his eyes.

Ian waited until the butler was gone before striding across the foyer and turning the knob on the door. He'd barely stepped over the threshold when a voice came from the darkened corner of the room.

"Good evening, Ian. I'd like to talk to you about your choice of a bride."

She didn't look one bit different than she had the last time he'd seen her. What had it been? Two years? Almost. It had been at his father's funeral. Thin, gray, a bit stooped over at the shoulders. A buzzard in human form. "Good evening, Mother," he replied as he headed for the decanters on the credenza. "You may talk all you like, but it's my choice as to whether or not I listen and reply."

"I've had my agents investigate her past."

Of course. He poured himself a glass of whiskey. "I'm sure it was a very short, very dull report. I hope it cost you a fortune."

"The current Duke of Ryland was not born into the peerage and served in her Majesty's Artillery Corps. He became the duke only because there were no surviving males in the direct lineage."

So?

"And the woman he married. She is illegitimate, Ian. And the duke's cousin. She was a dressmaker before she presumed to pass herself off as a lady."

He took a healthy swig of his drink, remembering the times he'd met Drayton and Caroline. They'd been nothing but gracious and polite. He liked them and considered them to be two of the most honest and decent people he knew.

"There is another sister, also illegitimate, who is rumored to have killed several people prior to marrying a man in trade."

He couldn't decide which she thought was worse, the murders or the marrying a man in trade. As curious as he was, though, he knew better than to ask. He sipped his drink and studied the clock on the mantel. Almost three? Well, the night had been clipping right along until just a few minutes ago.

"He claims the title of marquis, but he has spent a good deal of his life in America."

How those two things went together to damn the man, he didn't have a clue. But having spoken with Lord Lockwood a time or two in the gaming rooms, he couldn't see that—

"In trade."

Of course. Tristan might have been forgiven for having left English soil if he'd spent his time across the pond shooting helpless animals of one sort or another and attending parties at the homes of America's wealthiest men. But that he'd actually used his time and hands and mind to make money . . . Very bad form.

"And this creature you think is suitable to be a duchess," his mother said crisply, "is cut from the same bolt of cloth as her sisters. Her half-sisters, actually."

"A dressmaker and a brigand from the same bolt," he mused aloud. "I can't wait to hear what Fiona's been fashioned into."

"She is a whore."

He simply stared at his mother, his mind too stunned and outraged to even think of a retort, silent or otherwise.

"Her mother was a common strumpet, walking the streets and offering herself to anyone for a tuppence."

"And Fiona is to be painted with the same brush you so self-righteously wield against her mother?" he asked as his anger got the better of his restraint. "A dead woman who can't defend herself against the accusations? A woman whose early circumstances and choices you know absolutely nothing about?"

"My agent reports that this Fiona girl worked in the brothel with her mother."

"Your agent is padding his bill."

"My agent is a diligent man, Ian. He reports that she not only continues the practice into which she was led by her mother, but is blatant in the public display of her moral failings."

"Oh, do tell, Mother," he snarled. "What might she do that's so incredibly heinous?"

"She frequents, unchaperoned and for obviously unseemly purposes, places reserved for men."

Places reserved for men. . . . Only an agent paid by the pound for sleaze would twist a laudable circumstance so viciously. "Good God," he muttered. "It's an unbelievable low."

"Well, I am relieved to know that you finally understand just how horribly unsuitable she is to be your duchess. You will withdraw your proposal immediately, of course. First thing in the morning."

"Did your agent mention just what kind of *male haunts* Fiona frequents?"

"Of course not. There is no need to shock or offend to inform."

"Lady Fiona has a mind for medical study. She attends teaching lectures by prominent physicians. By my colleagues, Mother. She doesn't go there to solicit medical students."

"Just to find one foolish and blind enough to marry her."

"That's not where we met, Mother."

"Wipe the stardust from your eyes, Ian. You are a duke. You do not have the luxury of being a romantic."

"I'm a man and I'll do as I damn well please."

She arched a white brow and said with icy firmness, "She is no lady, Ian. I will not accept her as a daughter-in-law."

So be it and thank you for the deliverance. He lifted his whiskey glass in salute, saying, "We'll miss you at family gatherings, Mother. We'll send you announcements of our children's births, of course. And, just for the sake of decency, the occasional note to keep you abreast of their milestones and accomplishments." He smiled tautly. "Shall I have your coach brought around front now?"

"I sent my driver on for the night with instructions to return late in the morning. Your housekeeper has prepared me a room."

Well, Rowan could have damned well warned him about that. Standing there holding a whiskey glass, and gaping like the village idiot, wasn't anywhere near a position of strength. And with his mother, any little weakness could lead to scars that lasted for a lifetime. He threw the whiskey down his throat in a show of manly mastery that he hoped would disguise how fast and desperately the wheels of his mind were whirling.

Of one thing he was absolutely, positively certain: he needed to be at Lord Ryland's early enough tomorrow morning to head off Fiona. If she sailed in through the door of this house while his mother was still here . . . God, he didn't even want to think about how deeply she'd be hurt.

Oh, Jesus. And Charlotte. The damage his mother could do to a young soul . . . And one so fragile . . .

Chapter Thirteen

Fiona propped her elbow on the dining room table, put her head in her hand, and smiled into her cup of coffee.

"Satisfied with life?" Drayton asked as he came to the table with his breakfast plate.

She sighed and looked up at her brother-in-law. "Supremely."

"That's quite the ring you have on your finger."

"Isn't it, though?" she agreed, twisting the band so that the light danced through the brilliant facets. "I spent all night just looking at it. Beeps is most impressed, by the way. He said he'd always thought the best of Dr. Cabott."

From the sideboard, Caroline chuckled and asked, "Did you sleep at all?"

"I don't think so," she admitted. "I'm exhausted this morning." Sitting up to sample her coffee, she added, "Happy, but exhausted."

Carrie joined them at the table with her plate.

"Maybe you should think about going back to bed for a bit."

Oh, what a tempting thought. "I can't," Fiona lamented. "Charlotte and I are digging up a garden bed today. And the plasterers are planning to set the medallion on the new dining room ceiling. I have to be there for that. Mr. Gebhart is bringing his wallpaper sample books over this afternoon so that Charlotte and I can go through them and make selections for the drawing room, dining room and three of the bedrooms. I don't have time to go back to bed."

Caroline arched a brow without comment and laid her napkin across her lap. Drayton shook his head and picked up the morning paper. Left with her coffee, her ring, and her newfound happiness, Fiona sighed silently and hoped she could find the energy somewhere to get her through her list of tasks that day. That hope, though, paled beside the one for time alone with Ian. What a difference a night made. One conversation, actually. One honest, direct conversation. On a starlit balcony with the soft notes of a waltz drifting around them.

Ian did care about her. About *her*, not just what she could do to make his life easier and his day-to-day world run more smoothly. Had a man ever so easily seen and accepted the error of his ways? And then apologized so deeply and sincerely? Had a woman ever been held so passionately? Kissed so thoroughly? In such a gently ravenous, heartfelt way?

"Good morning, Fiona!"

She started at the familiar voice and, not quite believing it possible, looked toward the dining room doorway. "Charlotte!" she exclaimed, gaining her feet. "Ian!"

Ian, his eyes sparkling as they skimmed down the length of her, grinned and eased the wheeled chair into the dining room.

"Surprised?" Charlotte asked, beaming up at her.

"Delightfully so."

"I told you it would be more fun to announce ourselves," Charlotte triumphantly declared, looking up over her shoulder at her guardian. "You owe me a horseback ride."

"Tomorrow morning."

A horseback ride? Well, why not? Ian would figure out how to do it safely. He was magnificently resourceful. And kind. And handsome and witty and—

"Ahem."

Fiona started at Drayton's subtle intrusion and hurried to practice good manners. "Charlotte," she said cheerily, stepping over to stand beside the girl, "I'd like for you meet my sister and brother-in-law, the Duke and Duchess of Ryland. For formal purposes. At home, they're simply Drayton and Caroline."

"It's a pleasure," Charlotte replied, looking between the two and bowing her head ever so slightly in acknowledgment. "Lady Fiona talks about you all the time."

Drayton bowed. Carrie sailed into the moment with a wide smile. "As she does you, Charlotte. We're so glad to have you pay us a visit. Have you had breakfast yet?"

"No, we haven't," the girl replied brightly while Ian situated her at the table. "We're running for our lives. We only took the time to get dressed."

"Oh?" Carrie pressed, a smile tickling the corners of her mouth.

"It's only a slight exaggeration," Ian supplied, accepting Carrie's gesture toward the warming trays on the sideboard. "My mother's encamped in one of my guest rooms. She was waiting for me when I returned home last night. Discretion being the better part of valor and all that, we've gone into hiding until she gives up and goes home."

Fiona went to get Charlotte a plate of food, asking, "But what about all the workmen that are going to be there today?"

"For ten pounds for every insult they endure from my mother, Rowan and Mrs. Pittman have volunteered to oversee the workers while we find other places to be."

"Oh, Ian," she protested. "Your mother can't be that bad."

He slid a look her way and cocked a brow. Drayton snorted. Caroline discreetly cleared her throat and then asked, "Did she happen to mention whether or not she plans to attend the engagement ball?"

"I very much doubt it," he replied, helping himself to scrambled eggs. "And sincerely hope not."

"She doesn't approve of me, does she?"

He put down the serving spoon and turned to face her. Placing his fingertips under her chin, he tipped her face up until her gaze met his. "Fiona, darling," he said softly, earnestly, "I swear on the family Bible that it's nothing personal. My mother doesn't approve of anyone except herself."

"But—"

"No," he interrupted firmly. "I can see the direction your thoughts are going. My mother can't be changed, Fiona. Don't even think about wasting your incredible kindness on her. We'll all be happier for her absence."

She was about to insist that she be at least allowed to make a case for herself when the footman arrived at the dining room doorway and announced, "The morning post has arrived, Your Grace."

Ian smiled reassuringly, winked, and released her as Caroline accepted the mail with murmured thanks. Fiona followed her husband-to-be down the sideboard, filling the plate for Charlotte while wondering how she might go about building a bridge between him and his mother. It was simply unacceptable to have children grow up without ever meeting, much less knowing, their grandmother. Surely even the dowager duchess would have a soft spot for darling, beautiful, innocent children.

"Lady Rhoades has written," Carrie announced, pulling an envelope out of the pile of correspondence. She broke the seal, opened the flap and pulled out the inside sheet. "She's remembering Fiona at her ball last Season and hoping that we'll plan to attend again this year."

Fiona suppressed a shudder and called herself uncharitable.

"And I'll bet," Drayton said dryly, "that in the very next sentence she gushes on about how she's always felt that Fiona would make the perfect wife for her doughy son."

"Actually, they're in the same sentence," Carrie admitted, shaking her head. "The poor thing actually sounds desperate."

"She is desperate," Drayton countered. "For God's sakes, Dudley has to be pushing forty. And he's still living at home. Probably in the nursery."

"I feel sorry for him," Fiona said with a sigh as she placed the plate in front of Charlotte.

"Oh, please, Fiona!" Ian snorted as his ward smiled her thanks and placed a napkin in her lap. "Dudley looks like he's been floating in the Thames for a week. If he didn't actually move from time to time, we'd have to check him for pulse."

"When he does move it's with incredible speed and focus, though," Drayton offered, his smile widening. "I've seen him knock as many as a half dozen men into potted palms when dinner's announced."

Ian closed his eyes and shook his head. "I've been one of them."

"I think that it's horribly sad that food is the only thing Dudley finds even remotely exciting," Fiona said, taking her seat. "It must be terrible to have nothing else to do with your life except eat. Nothing else to look forward to beyond the three meals a day."

"Three?" Ian posed. "For Dudley, the day is one long, never-ending meal."

Drayton nodded and then added, "He does have a purpose, Fiona. He spends day after day with tailors having his seams let out and new suits made to accommodate his increasing size. It's enough to wear a weak man to a nubbin."

Carrie sighed and shot both Drayton and Ian a warning look that managed to slowly erase the grins from their faces. "Speaking of tailors," she said, taking a paper-wrapped bundle form the pile and pulling the string. "In today's post we have received a catalog of Madame Dupree's latest drawings. Would anyone care to see them?"

Ian and Drayton both shook their heads emphatically. Fiona was silently waving the offer off when Charlotte asked, "Who is Madame Dupree?"

"A dress designer," Carrie explained, handing her the packet of colorized sketches. She waited a few moments, giving her time to leaf through the pages as she ate. Fiona lifted her cup and smiled around the rim, knowing exactly what her sister was planning.

"So," Carrie began ever so smoothly. "What do you think of her ideas, Charlotte?"

"Well," the girl began, carefully restacking the pictures and then neatening the edges as she obviously searched for something diplomatic to say. "Fashions are very different in England," she finally offered. "No one in India ever dresses like this."

"Madame Dupree has a unique vision," Carrie assured her, chuckling. "Even for England."

"I do like the color of this one," Charlotte allowed, flipping back through the pages until she came to a ridiculously bustled, hugely sleeved creation in vivid royal blue. "We had peacocks at home, and while they weren't very nice, I always thought that they were very, very pretty."

Caroline leaned over to look at the gown and then sat back in her chair to consider Charlotte from a bit of a distance. "Your coloring is suited for the tones," she said, nodding with certainty. "You could wear them easily." She smiled and added, "Of course, then Ian would have to glower at all the males whose heads you turn, so it would be something of a mixed blessing."

Charlotte beamed. And then, in a single instant, her face fell. "That's kind of you to say, Your Grace," she replied, summoning a weak and tremulous smile. "But no one's going to give me a second look. At least not in a way that would be a compliment."

Fiona watched Ian's eyes cloud with sadness. Even as he opened his mouth to offer his ward a kind word, Caroline spared him the need to intervene.

"Oh, dear Charlotte," she countered happily, reaching out to lay her hand on the girl's forearm. "You are selling yourself so very short. And so needlessly." She looked across the table at Ian and smiled.

"Do you have specific plans made for the day, Ian?"

He blinked, the dazed and uncertain look in his eyes suggesting that he'd only just realized that there was a well-calculated current swirling around him. "Nothing beyond our initial escape," he answered cautiously. "I thought that we'd see what Fiona would like to do."

"Beautifully handed off," Drayton muttered as he scooped up his paper. "A natural born husband."

"Fiona?" Carrie asked, smiling sweetly.

"I'm open to any suggestions you might offer," she replied on cue.

"Well, I'm sure Ian wouldn't find it at all interesting, but I think it would be great fun for Charlotte and I to spend the day designing her an all new wardrobe."

"Oh, no," Charlotte gasped, her eyes wide. A flicker of hope brightened the darkness of her eyes. And beneath the hope eddied the unmistakable light of regret, of the suspicion that hoping really wasn't possible. "That isn't—"

"Carrie's the designer that Madame Dupree would love to be," Fiona leaned close to say softly. "Trust me, Charlotte. You *do* want to do this."

She swallowed and drew a deep breath. "It wouldn't be an imposition?"

"Not in the least," Caroline declared, beaming in victorious satisfaction. "Finish your breakfast, dear. You're going to need your strength. We have a grand and glorious adventure ahead of us today."

Charlotte looked down at her plate, grinned and laid her fork aside, declaring, "I couldn't eat another bite."

"Then gather up Madame Dupree's drawings and we'll be off," Caroline instructed as she tucked her napkin under the edge of her plate. She rose, picked up the stack of mail, and handed it over to Drayton. "Here, darling, you finish going through the mail."

He sat there blankly looking at it as Caroline drew Charlotte's chair back from the table and then wheeled her out of the dining room.

Amazed by how the bounds of propriety loosened once there was a ring on a woman's finger, Fiona considered the unexpected possibilities of the day. The most delightful of them was the chance to spend time alone with Ian. It was also the most reckless. "I hear," she offered, "that Dr. Fuller is delivering a lecture on the causes and treatment of gout this afternoon."

Ian snorted and replied dryly, "Well, he should know all about gout."

"I take it it that you're not all that interested in attending."

"He just wants everyone to look at his toes and feel sorry for him."

"You two," Drayton drawled, setting the mail aside and going back to his morning newspaper, "have the most interesting conversations."

They didn't seem the least bit strange to her and, given the way Ian's brows were knitted, he didn't consider them odd, either. "Crossing a dubious medical lecture off the list," she mulled aloud. They needed something in public so that tongues didn't wag, but not so public that they'd be required to share their time with others. "How would you feel about going for a picnic at the zoo?"

"I like that," he said, his eyes sparkling, a slow grin lifting the corners of his mouth. He reined it in to slide his gaze over to Drayton and ask, "Do you have any objections to the idea, Your Grace?"

"It's *Drayton*," he corrected without looking up from the paper. "And no objections. Just a word of advice. Stay well back from the monkey exhibit. They throw things."

Ian chuckled. "Duly noted."

Before Drayton could change his mind or offer to go along as a chaperone, Fiona rose from her chair and headed for the kitchen saying, "I'll go talk to Cook and see about getting a hamper packed. I'll be back shortly."

Ian watched her go, mesmerized by the sway of her skirts, and thankful that the goddesses of fashion dictated designs that so perfectly displayed narrow waists and the sweeping curves of delightful hips. He could do without the buttoned-to-the-neck design of day dresses, but the close fit of the bodices tended to compensate enough to keep his imagination from starving to death.

"Ahem."

Jesus. Caught ogling the man's sister-in-law. He

swallowed and softly cleared his throat. "Despite appearances, I'm trying very hard to be a gentleman. I've been keeping my hands to myself."

"I've fought the good fight, too," Drayton said, nodding slowly. "And lost it just like you're going to." He met Ian's gaze from across the table and cocked a brow. "I can't expect you to be any more of a saint than I managed to be. We're all human. But understand that when you cross the line, you're committed to meeting *my* expectations."

"Which, in the larger scheme of things, aren't at all at odds with my own." Ian smiled. "Your warning has been duly noted, Your Grace."

"Are you interested in politics?"

Ian weighed honesty against the requirements of family harmony and struck a balance. "I'm interested in certain areas of social reform. If being involved in politics could achieve the ends, I might be interested."

Drayton laid aside his newspaper, propped his forearms on the edge of the table and slowly smiled. Ian drew a slow breath, and knowing just how a bird felt when trapped by the cat, sacrificed himself for the sake of making a more positive impression on his future brother-in-law.

I'm sure you'll find some like-minded men in the reform circle. Open-minded men who, while they have their own pet concerns, understand that not everyone feels the same sort of passion as they do, and appreciate the necessity of trading support for support. Take Thacker, for instance."

His Grace went on, but Ian only vaguely heard the rumble of his voice. And to think that he'd asked the woman standing in the doorway to marry him simply because he'd resolved to pick a wife on the same night that she'd needed a surgeon for her cat. Fate had more than smiled on him, She'd handed him the most beautiful, most angelic woman in all Creation.

"I'm ready to go any time you are, Ian," she said as he somehow managed to remember good manners and get to his feet. "Cook had the hamper taken out to your carriage while I changed my clothes."

She wasn't wearing green. For the first time since he'd met her, she wasn't wearing a green dress of one sort or another. Why she'd chosen to wear a smokey rose–colored walking outfit with a matching short cape, he couldn't guess, but he did know that somehow her eyes were larger and greener, her skin more alabaster, and the curls piled atop her head, and peeking out from under her hat, even more golden.

"Pick up your jaw and put one foot in front of the other," he heard Drayton quietly instruct from behind him.

He snapped his mouth closed, slightly shifted his shoulders to adjust the sudden tightness of his shirt collar, and then drew a deep breath. Not that any of that did much to slow his racing heartbeat or calm the tremors in his knees.

For God's sake, he railed at himself. He was a man of considerable worldly experience. He'd seen beauty before. More times than he could count. He'd seen innocence, too. Maybe not nearly as often as beauty, but still . . . Why, the sight of Lady Fiona Turnbridge wearing a perfectly respectable walking outfit and smiling happily, invitingly at him turned him into a . . . well, a goddamned bumbling, blushing schoolboy . . .

"Move."

It wasn't as much the quiet order that put him into motion as it was the embarrassment of it having to be issued. That and the desperation to get away from someone who knew all too well just exactly how flummoxed he was. Stepping forward, he presented his arm, said something stupidly inane about how good she looked in pink, and then suggested that they be on their way.

She arched a brow as she took his arm and there was no mistaking the effort she made to keep her smile under control. Looking back over her shoulder as they left the dining room, she assured her brother-in-law that they'd be back to collect Charlotte before tea time.

Charlotte. God, he'd forgotten all about his ward. He'd passed her off to Lady Ryland and promptly forgotten that she existed. He was a miserable excuse for a human being. Shallow and utterly thoughtless. Well, thoughtless as in not being considerate. He had thoughts all the time. Most of them having to do with leaving Fiona with only a vague recollection of carnal innocence.

"I hope Drayton didn't badger you too badly," Fiona said as he handed her up into his carriage. "He can be incredibly single-minded at times."

Ian climbed in and took the rear facing, opposite seat with a shrug and a smile. "Actually," he admitted as the driver moved them out into traffic, "it was interesting. And at least he was honest about the chances of enacting significant reforms in the short term."

"What about the long term?" she asked as she reached up and removed her hat pin.

"Slow and incremental change seems to be the way things are done if Parliament's involved." She was taking off her hat? Why? "I got the distinct impression that politics is often like a shell game," he went on, watching her place it on the seat beside her. "Put a pea under a walnut half, shuffle it around until everyone loses track of it, and then call for a vote while they're all watching the card sharp slipping aces up his sleeve."

She tugged at the fingers of her glove. "That doesn't sound terribly above board."

"It apparently gets things done, though. In small steps that don't alarm anyone enough to mount an opposition that could derail you. In the end, it's the results that matter."

"I suppose you're right," she allowed as she put her gloves on the seat beside her hat. "Are there any health reforms under walnut shells at the moment?"

"Not that Drayton knew of," Ian replied absently as she undid the frog at the collar of her cape. "But that's not to say that I can't propose one down the road."

"After you've supported other men's reform interests?"

"You're a very perceptive woman, Fiona Turnbridge."

She laughed softly. "Guessing at the hows of Parliamentary action isn't all that difficult. Any group of men who play shell games and hide aces are likely to play tit for tat, too."

Ian cocked a brow. They were discussing the nature of British politics while she . . . While she was practically undressing in front of him. Christ on a crutch; this was ridiculous in the extreme. "Can you really read minds, Fiona?"

She sat back in the seat, her smile instantly gone. "What?"

"Harry thinks you can see things that other people can't," he explained. "That you can read minds and see the future."

"Well," she drawled, clearly hedging.

"You can?" he pressed, exhilarated by the possibility and more than slightly appalled by it, too. The things he's been thinking for the last few weeks . . .

"I don't read minds, Ian," she replied, her smile

returning. "I'm simply observant. For example, I saw the look on your face when we were in the dining room and I suggested a picnic. I had the distinct impression that you were entertaining thoughts of sharing more than a companionable meal on a blanket in full public view on the lawn at the London Zoo."

All right. He'd been thinking of a secluded spot and wondering just how daring he could talk her into being. But since she had apparently guessed that and it didn't seem to offend her tender sensibilities . . . "Oh? Just what sorts of sharing did I have in mind?"

She sighed. "Considering the fact that you're still on your side of the carriage and behaving like a perfect gentleman despite the fact that I've removed my hat and gloves and opened my cape, I was obviously mistaken." She shrugged. "So much for my impressive mind-reading abilities."

Damn. If he'd been any more thick-headed, she'd have had to send him an engraved invitation. *Lady Fiona Turnbridge requests that you stop being a tight-laced unnecessarily suffering idiot. She is wearing your ring, you know.*

Ian chuckled and slipped across the carriage to sit beside her. Sliding his arm around her and drawing her close to his side, he whispered, "You know me better than I know myself."

"Then I was right? You were entertaining more intimate thoughts?"

"Where you're concerned, Fiona, I'm always entertaining intimate thoughts."

"Really?" she drawled, looking up at him. "Would you be willing to prove that?"

"Here? Now? In the carriage, Fiona?" he teased, cocking a brow in feigned shock. "That would be exceedingly improper."

"Well, of course," she allowed as he felt her pulse quicken. "But is it really possible in such a small space? I have no personal experience in these matters, you know."

"You're presuming that I do?"

"Actually, it's less presuming than fervently hoping."

"We'd be courting scandal."

Fiona laughed and twined her fingers through the hair at his nape. "By doing what," she asked on slightly ragged breath, "precisely?"

"I can think of several possibilities," he answered, tracing her lower lip with a fingertip. "One leading quite naturally to another."

"Do you think I might enjoy them?"

"I'm certainly willing to find out," he replied, lowering his hand and very slowly and deliberately skimming his palm over the curve of her breast. "Do you like that?"

"Yes," she whispered, her eyelids fluttering closed. "But I think it would be even more pleasant if my dress weren't in the way."

God, she was his every dream come true. "Let's see if you're right," he murmured, his voice husky as he lowered his lips to hers and began to undo her buttons.

Fiona quickly decided that if the measure of the heat consuming her was any indication, she thoroughly enjoyed Ian's notions of courting scandal in a carriage. And that was just the first of several quick and exhilarating discoveries, not the least of which was the fact that she was capable of complete abandon. And that rows of bodice buttons and yards of petticoats and skirts weren't much of an obstacle to a man determined to make his way past them. She also found, to her great delight and considerable pleasure, that coat and shirt buttons were undone with equal ease, and that it took almost no effort at all to get them slipped off broad shoulders and down well-muscled arms. And God, the feel of heated skin against heated skin . . .

Ian touched her everywhere, no part of her beyond his tasting and teasing. His lips followed the tracings of his hands, making her breathless, pulling gasps of pleasure from her soul and making her squirm in the delightful heat of ever-building desire.

And that she could do the same to him, that she could drag ragged moans past his lips and trigger an ever-deeper intensity to his explorations . . . To realize that giving pleasure could bring so much pleasure . . . She selfishly touched him with her hands

and her lips and was rewarded with the most exquisite spirals of heady sensation and tiny, taunting
glimpses of a mysteriously compelling summit.
God, for the chance to spend every minute of the rest
of her life feeling so wondrously, wickedly alive.

Ian's conscience and good judgment tried to hold
him in check, but the feel and taste of Fiona . . . Her
lusciously deep-throated moaning sighs, the touch
of her hands on his bare skin, the heat of her body
and the unstinted expressions of her pleasure . . .
She gave at his merest touch, her responses so in-
stinctive, so honest that his every good intention was
incinerated. He was on the brink of losing control.
He knew it. And he didn't care. All that mattered
was making love with Fiona. Now. And then again.
And again and again.

And then the carriage slowed, turned, and bounced
over a rut. The sudden motion momentarily cleared
his senses and allowed the shrill cries of his conscience to be heard above the rasp of their breathing.
He blinked and swallowed as reality tore through the
haze of desire.

Fiona lay on the seat, her eyes closed and her
long blond hair cascading over the cushions. Her
shoulders and breasts were bared for his feasting,
her skirts bunched up around her waist, her shoes,
stockings and garters somewhere on the floor with
his coat and shirt. He knelt between her knees, his
hands caressing the bare skin of her silken thighs

and he knew that she wanted him to satisfy her hunger, that she would wrap her legs around his hips and welcome him into her. Ian also knew that she deserved more from him this first time than being ravaged on the seat of a carriage.

Closing his eyes, Ian gathered together the tattered remnants of his good judgment. He reminded himself that there would come a time when he could complete their union without a thought as to where they were and how fast he took her, a time when he could mate them in a breathless stolen second of wicked pleasure and smooth her skirts in the next. But that time wasn't this time.

"Ian . . ."

He opened his eyes to find her gazing at him, her eyes large and shimmering with unfulfilled desire. Her lips, swollen from his kisses, were invitingly parted. Her breasts, firm and taut and hard peaked, rose and fell, tempting him to return for another taste. Ian groaned and shook his head.

"We've turned off the main road," he said, his voice raspy with frustration and tortured resolve. "We're almost to the zoo."

"I really don't care about a picnic at the zoo."

"Me, either," he admitted, his gaze slowly trailing over her, his conscience again struggling against his hunger and need.

"Do you think your mother might have gone on her way yet?"

"And taken all the workmen and my servants with her?"

"You could ask the driver to just roll around London for a while."

He smiled as the solution flashed through his brain. "Or . . ." He rose from the floor, putting a knee on the seat and reached up to slide open the small panel in the front wall of the carriage. "Leon," he called into it, "we've changed our minds. Please take us to the Mayfair house."

"Mayfair?" she asked as he rammed the panel closed.

"The house that'll be yours once you sign the settlement papers."

"I really do need to do that, don't I?"

He grinned. "If you wouldn't mind too terribly much," he said, leaning forward to suckle her breast for a long, languorous moment. She moaned and arched up against him, twining her arms around his neck and trying to draw him even closer.

Ian slowly released his claim and eased back to take her hands in his and murmur, "I think we should at least put some of our clothes back on before we get there."

"If we must," she replied, smiling up at him. She freed one hand and trailed her fingertips down his chest. "I never imagined."

Ian caught her hand when she neared the waistband of his trousers and brought her fingertips to his lips. He gently nipped at them as he looked deep into her eyes. "By the time I'm done with you, my darling Fiona, you'll have little left to your imagination and more than a passing acquaintance with a delightful range of carnal pleasure."

She made a purring sound deep in her throat and her eyes sparked with a fire that sent searing waves of desire through his loins. Ian groaned again and managed to smile through his noble frustration. "I'm trying to be a considerate, sensitive lover, Fiona. But if you persist in looking at me like that, the driver is going to pull open the door and discover what an absolute cad I am."

"Not to mention that your fiancée is a thoroughly, irredeemably wanton woman," she laughingly added.

"Yes, and that, too," he admitted, chuckling and pushing himself back until he settled on the opposite seat. "Dressing would give us a better chance of maintaining our reputations."

She stretched and with a long sigh of resignation swung her legs over the side of the seat. "I suppose you're right," she conceded, sitting up and tucking her breasts back into her corset. "But I must admit that I'm not all that thrilled by the idea of having to start all over again."

Ian grinned and winked. "Capes are the most marvelous things, darling. They hide so much." At her arched brow he added, "I'm not in the mood to waste time, either."

Her smile was sweetly, deliciously wicked. "Then I probably shouldn't bother with putting my stockings and garters back on, should I?"

"You can if you want. They're not going to be in my way."

She laughed and reached down to pluck one of the white silk stockings from the floor of the carriage. With deliberate slowness she gathered it in her hands and then, watching him all the while, began the process of rolling it up the length of her leg.

"You're torturing me, Fiona," he said thickly, blindly pulling on his shirt.

"And you're enjoying every moment of it," she countered, wildly excited by the power she had over him. "Would you like to help me with my garter?"

Ian fastened his buttons. "Fiona," he warned, unable to keep his gaze from the slow, sinuous progress of the lace garter.

"I suppose you're planning to exact revenge for this, aren't you, Ian?"

"Oh, yes." He picked his coat up off the carriage floor. Laying it on the seat beside him, he warned, "And if you don't stop, it's likely to be all of a half meter inside the front door."

She trailed her fingertips down her throat to the top of her cleavage. "Promise?"

Jesus. If only she had any real idea of what she was asking for. "I was thinking of taking just enough time to find a bed for us."

"You think too much."

"Apparently," he admitted, sliding to the edge of the seat. "I'll stop, if you'd like."

"I'd like."

He undid the waistband button on his trousers and began to stuff in his shirt tail. "You actually think that you want to make love on the foyer floor?"

"On the front step if you're so inclined."

Still trying to get his shirt properly arranged, he chuckled and looked over at her. Watching as she twisted her hair into a knot atop her head and pinned her hat back into place, he shook his head in wonder and murmured, "You are the absolute light of my life."

Her grin was pure wicked delight. "How long before we arrive at the house?"

"Not long enough to make love to you properly, if that's what you're hoping."

"What about improperly?" she asked as she slid off the seat and onto her knees in front of him.

"Fiona," he warned, his heart tripping in excitement, his hands shaking. "Darling, what are you thinking?"

"I'm not," she blithely replied, reaching out and undoing the rest of the buttons of his trousers. "And you promised me that you'd stop."

"I did, didn't I?" he ground out as her fingertips brushed aside fabric. He swallowed a groan as she ever so deliberately traced the hardened length of him with a fingertip.

"Does that hurt?"

"Not at all." He closed his eyes and tipped his head back, awash in brilliantly keen pleasure as her hand closed around him. How she knew . . . Hell, he didn't care. It felt too good to care about anything else.

"Am I doing it right?"

"I don't think there's a wrong way," he growled as his last remaining brain cells frantically told him to stop her before it was too late, before she drove him so close to the brink that all of London looking in the carriage door wouldn't make a difference. But God Almighty, it felt so good and he was soaring so fast that—

"Oh, drat," she whispered, her hand abruptly stilling. "We must be about there. The carriage is slowing."

His mind reeled, desperation, desire and rationale twisting into one certainty in a single beat of his hammering heart. Reaching down, he wrapped his hand around hers and whispered, "Then we'll have to hurry this, my wicked darling. If you don't mind."

Chapter Fourteen

Fiona snuggled against the warmth of Ian's body and watched the dust motes dance in the sunlight spilling through the bedroom window. Almost two, she judged. Time to be thinking about returning to the world. Or at least going down to the foyer and rummaging through the picnic hamper.

"Are you cold?" he asked, drawing her closer and pulling the dust cover over her shoulders and hip. "I could try to find some real bed coverings, a blanket. They have to be here somewhere."

Fiona pressed a kiss to his bare shoulder and drew her leg over his. "I'm quite comfortable," she assured him. She wiggled closer and added, "Now, anyway."

"I hope it didn't hurt too badly."

Lord. Her deflowering . . . *Again.* It mattered so much to him that she didn't hate him for it. It was almost as though he thought that it was the worst thing that had ever happened to her. Or ever would happen to her. His sense of guilt and responsibility was endearingly sweet in a way. Thoroughly maddening in another. She'd already assured him—twice—that she didn't loathe him and that she'd live without traumatic memories and emotional scars. Since words hadn't soothed his conscience the least little bit, there was only one other course to take.

She trailed her fingers over the sculpted planes of his bare chest. "The pain was fleeting, Ian. And ever so much smaller in measure than the satisfaction. Briefer in duration, too." Pushing herself up onto her elbow, she leaned forward to feather a kiss over his lips. "But this time, you can dispense with the gentlemanly restraint. It tends to be frustrating."

"This time?" he murmured, his hands skimming down her back. "I didn't sate your hunger?"

"The deeper and more complete the sating, Ian, the greater the desire."

"Really?" he drawled, his eyes twinkling.

She arched a brow. "It doesn't work that way for men?"

Chuckling, the sound of his happiness rippling through and warming her blood, he drew her atop him and settled her across his hips. "Contrary to what all the decorum experts say, and a good many doctors claim as fact, the sexes are more alike in terms of desire than they are different."

"I know," she admitted, leaning down to nip at his chin.

He laughed again and nipped back. "And may I ask just how you know that? Have you been slipping into the racier medical lectures?"

"I have two happily married sisters. And, in case you haven't noticed, neither one of them is inclined to be prudish or to mince words. All I've had to do was sit there, do my needlework, listen and make mental notes."

"Bless Caroline and Simone."

"Speaking of family . . ."

"Let's not," he countered, skimming his hands up her back. Twining his fingers in her hair, he drew her lips down to his. "Let's pretend we're all alone in the world."

She could do that. Easily. Happily. For a while, anyway.

L ife was good, Ian mused as he tossed the crust of his sandwich toward the open hamper on the carriage floor.

"You missed," observed the delectable blond morsel lying on the seat between his outstretched legs, her back nestled against his chest.

He gave her a quick hug. "Only because I'm weak with exhaustion."

She laughed and launched her own crust toward the basket. It hit the edge, flipped into the air, and then neatly dropped inside.

"You haven't had enough wine," he declared,

grinning and nudging her half-full glass toward her lips. "I've downed my share and done my part to maintain the picnic charade. You can't be a piker."

"A lady never guzzles her way to the bottom of a glass."

"Then sip purposefully," he admonished, chuckling. "We don't have all that much farther to go." He glanced down into the basket. "And we have to do something about those tiny little cakes before we get there, too. They'll think it odd that we didn't eat them."

"They're called petit fours. Do you want me to get one for you?"

"That would require you to sit up, wouldn't it?" he asked, lazily contemplating his options.

"I can manage sitting up, Ian."

He tightened his arms around her and bent down to press a kiss into her hair and murmur, "Yes, but I can't manage letting you go. I can live without cake."

She shifted in his arms, half turning so that she could offer him her lips. He smiled, pleased to his marrow, and bent his head lower. His lips feathered over hers and whether he was the one who sighed or—

The movement was sudden, even more violent for being completely unexpected. *Can't fall on her*, his mind barked as together they pitched forward and off the seat. In the split second of her startled cry, he pushed her down and away from him, twisting his body and grasping for something—anything—solid, for an anchor that would keep him from toppling down onto her.

His fingertips brushed the velvet of a seat cushion and he strained for a handful. For a heartbeat he had one, and then the carriage pitched hard to the side, flinging him away amidst the pelting hail of debris. He came to an abrupt halt, the door handle rammed into the center of his back and driving the air from his lungs.

"Fiona!" he gasped, struggling to get his feet under him and to make himself breathe.

"I'm all right, Ian," she said, grabbing a seat cushion and trying to leverage herself up off the carriage floor. "Are you—"

"I'm fine," he assured her, his senses overfilling with sights and sounds as he reached out and pulled her to the seat. Horses neighing in panic, the screams and shouts of men and women. And over it all rolled the rumbling and crashing and dust-laden belching of a giant going down. He turned and pushed open the door and froze as his heart slammed into his throat and his stomach filled with dread.

"Jesus. Aw, Jesus," he muttered, trying to decide where he was likely to be needed most, where the greatest chance was of finding survivors. "Leon!"

"Here, Your Grace!" his coachman called from a short distance up the street. "I'm right here with the horses!"

"What's happened, Ian?"

"Stay in the carriage, Fiona," he ordered, his gaze still sweeping the carnage. "Just sit there. I'll be back as soon as I can." He had one foot on the step when Fiona caught his coat tail and tried to hold him back.

"What's happened?" she demanded.

Pausing, turning back to meet her frightened gaze, he crisply explained, "A building's collapsed into the street. There are serious injuries. Stay here where you're safe."

Fiona watched him vault down the steps, heard him call out, "Leon, stay with Her Ladyship! Don't leave her for an instant!" and then the door was closed, leaving her with only the quick and fragmented images of dust swirls, mounds of brick and scrambling people.

There are serious injuries. Yes, there would be. Cuts from the glass, crushing and contusions from the bricks. Choking from the dust. People would need help. No one who could offer aid should be sitting in a carriage.

She reached down, grabbed the picnic hamper and dumped the few remaining items out on the carriage floor. The big white linen table cloth was easy enough to find, and while it took a second to find the little knife Cook had packed for slicing the apples, once she had it in hand she made quick work of turning the fine Irish cloth into bandages.

Her ears ringing with the frantic cries of the injured, the precious seconds ticking away in her mind, Fiona stood, opened her shirt front at the waist, reached inside, and pulled the drawstring on her petticoat. Even as it pooled around her ankles, she dropped back down onto the seat, kicked it free of her hems and snatched up the knife again.

"No, Lady Fiona," Leon said, moving to block her way as she started out of the carriage with the basket. "I heard what His Grace told you to do."

Yes, well, Ian had been focused on the immediate needs of the the moment and not thinking past his own obligations to the injured. She gave his coachman the best smile she could muster. "I'm not going to sit in that dark little cocoon and do nothing more than listen to the screaming, Leon. Step aside, please." When he didn't move, she firmly added, "Now."

"Your Ladyship, I beg you. Get back in the carriage as His Grace expects."

Hoping that Ian was close enough to call off his dedicated and dutifully obedient employee, Fiona looked past the driver, searching among the rescuers for him. He was nowhere in sight. But what she could see . . . Her little basket of bandages would be empty within minutes. Still, better a few bandages than none at all.

Her mind raced along the course of what needed to be done and how best to do it. The first task was to get past Ian's driver. "Are our horses injured?" she asked.

"Cal's got a bad gash in his right front leg. Flying glass. Meg's got a couple knicks and knocks from bouncing bricks, but nothing too bad. She can still pull. Not that we're going anywhere for a while. Please get back in the carriage."

"Here," she said, taking linen strips from the basket and thrusting them into his hands. "Take care of Cal."

"Only if you'll get back in the carriage."

"All right," she agreed, vaulting up the step and inside. She turned back, grabbed the door handle, said crisply, "Now see to His Grace's horse," and yanked the door closed.

"Sit in the carriage," she muttered as she silently counted to ten, her hand still wrapped around the door handle. "Why not just tell me to eat little cakes?"

She opened the door and stepped down, casting a quick glance toward the front of the carriage. Seeing Ian's coachman fully occupied in tending his injured animal, Fiona adjusted her grip on the wicker handle, lifted her hems, and strode off into the destruction and mayhem, determined to do whatever she could to help.

People were really the most amazingly wonderful creatures, she mused as she tied a compress over an old man's badly cut arm. The instant her fingers finished tying the knot, she stepped back and let two younger men carry him off toward one of the many wagons being quickly filled with other patients.

No one had had to issue orders. No one had had to make a plea for assistance. They had just come from everywhere, bringing wagons and blankets and anything that could be used to help strangers in desperate need. Lengths of wood from the collapsed building had been salvaged and piled for quick splinting of broken bones. Doors had been pulled from the wreckage to become stretchers.

Men climbed up and pawed through the rubble, clearing it away to bring out the injured they found. Women sacrificed their skirts and their petticoats for bandages and darted among the injured, rendering immediate aid to those with minor wounds and comforting those who cradled others beyond earthly help.

"Got a bad one over here, lady!"

Yes, people were truly at their best in the worst of circumstances, she decided as she hiked her skirts and jumped over a fallen beam to answer the summons. A testament to—

Bad? Dear God. The blood arced in a feeble spurt from the boy's groin, spattering slowly across her skirt. Her mind clicking crisply through the certainties, her heart scrambling in frantic hope, she dropped to her knees beside the makeshift litter and plunged her hand into the mass of ravaged flesh. His eyes opened as she found the severed end of the vital artery and squeezed it closed. Blue eyes. A beautiful blue. So young. Maybe fifteen.

"What's your name?" she asked, finding him a reassuring smile.

"Louis," he whispered. "Have you seen my brother?"

No other critical injuries that she could see. "I'll look for him after I help you." With her free hand she smoothed a lock of dust-caked brown hair off his forehead, brushed bits of crumbled brick from the corner of his mouth.

"Please find my brother."

"I will, Louis. I promise. What's his name?"

He smiled and closed his eyes. For a second her heart sank and then the faint beat of his valiant heart pulsed against the palm of her hand.

"Move out of the way, lady, so we can get him to the surgery."

She looked up into the dusty and grimy face of one of the rough and beefy men who had been carrying away the injured. "I can't let go," she explained. "If I do, he'll bleed to death before you get him into the wagon. You'll have to transport him with me attached."

"Lady, let go."

"No."

"Damn, woman," he snarled with a shake of his head. He bent down to grasp the corners of the door, saying, "Get the other end, Russ. I got his feet. Lady, you're on your own for hangin' on."

She scrambled to her feet, one hand firmly clamped around the artery, the other fisted in her skirt, and then half stumbled and half ran beside the litter as Russ and his fellow angel all but sprinted for the back of a cart.

Ian flinched at the long, high-pitched splintering of timber and then instinctively leaned forward, covering his patient's body with his own just as more timbers sang and another wall of brick roared down the mountain of those that had already collapsed. The dust rolled over him and he held his breath, his lungs already burning for having learned the lesson a half dozen breaths too late.

And then, as it always did, the worst of the airborne debris settled to the ground and the air became breathable. Ian pushed himself upright and went back to work on the man whose shoulder had been run through by a huge sharp wooden stave.

"Your Grace?"

He blinked and looked up in the same moment, stunned and instantly filled with dread. "What the hell are you doing here, Leon? I told you—"

"She slipped away while I was tending Cal."

"What?" he demanded even as his soul was crying, *No, no, no.*

"I don't know where she is, Your Grace. I've looked everywhere."

"Look everywhere again!" he barked, half turning to scan what he could of the chaos swirling around him.

"Maybe she went on home, Your Grace. She wasn't liking the screaming."

Home? Not on a bet. The gurgling sound penetrated his fear and he looked back at his patient, at the bubble of blood forming between the man's pale lips. "She's somewhere around here, Leon," he snapped, furiously going back to work. "Find her!"

Fiona counted the beats of Louis' heart, measuring the slowing cadence and willing his spirit to fight as they rolled up to the door of the hospital, one wagon in a long, long line of them bearing hope and desperation, the wailing and the silent. Two blood-spattered men dashed from a knot of others just as grisly and grabbed the end of the door on which Louis lay. In a heartbeat they were pulling him from the bed of the wagon. Fiona squeaked and scrambled, yanking at her skirts and stretching to keep her hold as they hurried to get the boy inside.

An arm clamped around her waist, lifted her up, and then roughly dropped her on her feet outside the wagon. She ran, holding on and glancing back over her shoulder to meet the gaze of the burly man who had told her she'd be on her own. "Thank you," she mouthed. He dipped his chin and touched the brim of his wool hat, and then turned away to climb back into his wagon.

"Lady Fiona?"

She started, whipping her attention from the wagon to the chaos into which she'd blindly run. "Dr. Mercer," she gasped in relief. "The artery's been cut. He's still with us, but just barely."

He glanced down, nodded crisply, and stepped to her side saying, "Slide to your left and let me get my hand in there."

"His name is Louis," she supplied as she did as instructed and the doctor smoothed his hand downward along hers. "He has a brother somewhere."

"I have it," he replied. "You can ease away."

Fiona willed her hand to slowly relax, willed a deep breath into her lungs, and stepped back.

"Jonas!" the doctor called as he motioned for the men bearing the litter to move along. "Clear us a path!"

Fiona stood and watched them go, vaguely aware that her knees were shaking and the world was swaying gently to and fro. *He'll be all right,* her heart whispered. *Dr. Mercer is very good.*

And then the men bearing Louis' litter slowed and her heart knew. They stopped and she watched Dr. Mercer ease his hand away and bow his head. She closed her eyes for a second and then opened them, lifting her chin and squaring her shoulders. Gazing up at the plaster ceiling, she sternly reminded herself that crying wouldn't bring Louis back, wouldn't accomplish anything other than to add more tears to the flood that was already too deep. There was more work to be done, more people to be tended and brought here. Crying wouldn't help them, either.

The gentle hand on her shoulder almost undid her. "You did everything right, Lady Fiona, and everything within the power of man. Or woman." She nodded because she knew she was supposed to and Dr. Mercer added, softly and kindly, "Let me get someone to take you home."

"I need to go back to the accident," she said, stepping out from under his caring hand. She dragged a breath into her too-tight and aching lungs. "Ian will be worried if he can't find me there."

"Then let me find someone to escort you."

"That's very kind of you, Dr. Mercer," she countered, stepping backwards toward the door. "But I think that everyone here has more important things to do. I'll be fine on my own."

She could see that he had doubts, but he nodded anyway and gave her a gentle smile. "You did everything you could. No one could have done more or done better."

"Thank you."

Someday, she told herself as she went in search of a wagon heading back to the collapsed building, someday his assurances and approval would make her feel better about failing. Someday she'd be able to look back and accept that the span of a life was written and that no man or woman could change it. But that day wasn't today. No, today she was angry at the injustice of a young, barely begun life being over. At the unfairness that such beautiful blue eyes were closed forever. If only she'd been faster . . . Stronger . . . If she'd willed him to hang on harder . . .

Your Grace!" Leon exclaimed, stumbling over a pile of bricks in his haste to reach his side. "There she is!" he added, reeling and pointing wildly. "Over in that wagon!"

It took Ian a heart-thundering second to find the one Leon meant. At the sight of her, the air flooded out of his lungs in a shuddering sigh of relief. He locked his knees and threw his shoulders back to keep himself upright, willed his mind to look past the blood to critically appraise her from hair pins to hems.

She was a mess, he allowed, quickly making his way through the rubble toward her, watching her check the damage on a man being loaded into another wagon. There weren't any hair pins left. Her dress was torn and stained and caked. She looked a bit dazed, like so many soldiers did when the heat of the battle was over and the reality of having survived was hard to grasp. But she was moving well, no halting steps or shortened gestures that would suggest she'd been injured in the course of her ill-considered dash into the maw of a bloody, god-awful disaster.

Which was good, he allowed, as she looked in his direction and found his gaze. Because he'd have felt terrible about chewing her up one side and down the other if she'd been hurt. He ignored her faltering smile, pretended he didn't see her lean toward him and raise her arms.

"I told you to stay in the carriage!"

She blinked once and then let her arms fall back to her sides as she shook her head and replied, "I couldn't."

So soft, so certain of herself and the rightness of her defiance. So damned oblivious to the danger she'd put herself in and how mercilessly she'd battered his heart and wrenched his soul. He clenched his hands into fists at his side, struggling hard against the the urge to grab her by the shoulders, shake her, and then haul her against him and never let her go.

"It is my duty and my responsibility to keep you safe," he ground out. "What if you'd blithely walked up to one of the walls just before it collapsed?"

"Blithely?" She arched a brow. "*Blithely?*"

"How the hell would I have faced your family if you'd been killed?"

She took a step back. "Do you think I'm that stupid?"

"I think you're reckless and foolish—"

"*Foolish?*"

"And presumptive!" he finished, purposefully closing the distance she kept trying to put between them. "You've attended a few goddamned medical lectures, taken some notes and drawn some pretty pictures. That doesn't make you a doctor. The only thing it qualifies you to do is follow instructions."

Her chin came up. Fire danced in her eyes. "I'm perfectly capa—"

"To sit where you've been told to sit and stay where you've been told to stay," he snapped, his heart hammering and tears clawing their way up his throat. "Out of the way and out of harm's way." He raked his fingers through his hair. "Jesus Christ. Do you have any idea at all of how—"

"Doctor!" someone called from the rubble. Ian whipped around just as a man was dragged out from under a heavy beam. "Over here, Doc! Hurry!"

In that instant, Fiona felt a certainty wrap around her heart. It was neither hot nor cold. Neither good nor bad. It just *was*. While his back was turned and his tirade was stemmed, Fiona turned on her heel, lifted her chin and her hems, and walked away.

"Where are you going, Fiona?" Ian shouted after her. "The carriage is that way!"

She knew exactly where the carriage was. She also knew that that way lay compliance and docility, forever lived inside a comfortable, pretty little box with no doors or windows. She kept moving, not looking back, stepping over bricks and skirting the pools of blood and shattered glass.

"Fiona! Don't you dare leave here! I have work to do!"

And she wouldn't keep him from it. It was important work; lives depended on him. It was perfectly understandable that he wouldn't come after her. He couldn't. And just as she knew that he had no choice, she also knew that even if he did have a choice, she wouldn't be his first one. And what hurt most of all was the certainty that no matter how much she learned, no matter how good she was or what kind of help she could ably provide, he would never see her as anything but a woman who kept his bed warm and made his less important life easier.

She swallowed back hot tears, putting one foot in front of the other and telling herself that crying over the loss of Ian wouldn't change the inevitable course any more than crying would bring Louis back to life.

Fiona noted Simone's footman's wide-eyed shock and stepped across the threshold saying, "I'm fine. Where might I find my sister?"

He stammered and then gestured toward the drawing room. With a muttered thanks for his assistance, Fiona made her way there. She was all of two steps into the room when Simone dropped the book in her hands and ran toward her.

"Oh, my God! Where are you—"

"It's not my blood."

Simone grabbed her by the shoulders and looked her up and down. "You're sure it's not yours?"

"Yes."

"Did you kill Ian?"

For some perverse reason, the thought amused her. She chuckled and arched a brow. "Not yet."

"What happened? Whose blood is it?"

"Mostly Louis'," she answered, the memories flooding back.

"Who's Louis?"

She tried to breathe, tried to swallow, tried to lift her chin and banish the tears.

"*What* happened, Fiona?"

Words wouldn't come. But the tears did. And as they poured in a hot torrent down her cheeks, Simone wrapped her in her arms and murmured, "Such a brave, tender heart."

Chapter Fifteen

Yes, he might have handled the situation with a bit more patience, Ian admitted, shooting his cuffs as he walked up to the Rylands' townhouse door. But the basic facts were the basic facts: Fiona had endangered herself. And while her intentions had been kind and noble and good, he had absolutely no intention whatsoever of spending the rest of his life trying to do his best in a crisis while worrying that one of the mangled victims presented to him would be his beautiful wife.

The door opened and he was bowed inside, his coat and gloves taken without a word. Escorted to the parlor and left to wait, he lifted his chin and silently framed, yet again, what he needed to say. A genuinely caring inquiry into her well-being. An apology for having been curt with her that afternoon. A clear and succinct explanation of how her actions had led to his very natural reaction. At that point he'd pause to let her express her regret for having been so short-sighted and unthinking. Then he'd lay down carefully detailed parameters for her conduct should anything like today ever happen again. Once that was all done, he'd accept her invitation to stay for dinner and afterwards they'd go for a lovely private stroll in the garden where they could put all of today's ugliness and tensions behind them.

But only, he reminded himself at the swishing sound of approaching skirts, after she understood that she was never ever again going to put him through the wringer as she had that afternoon.

"Good evening, Lady Ryland," he said, offering her polite bow as she came to a stop just inside the room. He glanced past her, expecting to see his errant fiancée in tow.

"Fiona isn't here."

This was not part of his carefully crafted plan. He cleared his throat. "Is she all right?"

Caroline shrugged. "She's unharmed physically. Emotionally . . . She's very angry and very, very hurt."

Hurt? Of all the . . . He stuffed down his own anger and dredged up what he hoped would be considered a diplomatic response. "I'm afraid that I didn't handle the situation this afternoon as well as I could have. I should have used a bit more tact than I did."

"That's certainly the impression I've been given," Caroline said softly, nodding. She reached into her dress pocket and then stepped forward, her hand extended, saying, "I sincerely hope that you find some tact and perhaps a bit of grace to deal with the consequences of it."

Ian stared disbelievingly at the glittering object in the palm of Fiona's sister's hand. "She's breaking our engagement?"

"I do believe that's what returning the ring traditionally means," she replied evenly, still holding out the ring for him to take back.

Because he'd yelled at her? Because he'd been angry because she'd scared him? Well, he wasn't going to take the ring back. "Where is she?"

"She doesn't want you to know and we'll abide by her wishes."

"But—"

"Good evening, Your Grace," she said coolly, stepping forward and dropping the ring into the breast pocket of his jacket. "Thank you for calling to inquire after my sister's well-being. I will relay your concern the next time we speak."

Ian stood there for a long moment after she swept out of the room, his anger flaring white hot. And then, as suddenly as it had engulfed him, it was extinguished. His heart slowly sinking into the pit of his heaving stomach, he turned and left before his quivering knees could give out on him.

A man had a right to be angry, he told himself as he poured himself another glass of whiskey. When a woman did something foolhardly and reckless, he had every right—no, obligation!—to point out her mistake and insist that she not do anything so thoughtless again. For her to be indignant about such a perfectly logical and considerate reaction was beyond ridiculous. And then to break an engagement over a little tiff like that . . .

God, he was really lucky to have discovered this inexcusable flaw in Fiona's character now rather than after they were married till death did them part. Yes, lucky. Beyond anything he deserved.

He tossed the whiskey down his throat and reached for the decanter again. And maybe, by the time he got to the bottom of the cut crystal bottle, he'd be rid of the inexplicable feeling that he was lying to himself. And with it would be gone the infuriating, maddening, niggling notion that it was all his fault. God, what she'd done to his mind . . . It should be criminal. Maybe, once he sobered up, he'd think about sponsoring a law in Parliament that would forbid women from making men feel guilty about being reasonable, rational, logical and commanding creatures. Yes, that was a bloody good idea. He'd call it Fiona's Law in honor of how badly and thoroughly and forever she'd mangled his heart.

Someone was stealing his whiskey. Ian opened one eye and glared—as best he could, given how little of the whiskey there was left to steal—at his cousin.

"Good Lord," Harry drawled, filling a glass, "what a long face. Did your favorite horse die?"

There was no point in lying. She'd probably taken out an advertisement in the evening paper to announce the crushing of his every hope. "Fiona broke off our engagement."

"Oh, well. There are plenty more fishes in the sea."

Fiona wasn't a fish. And there weren't any other like her. "Harry, you're an idiot."

"No, Ian. I'm a realist." He sat down on the arm of the other wingback chair. "You're not a prince with world alliances and the fate of a kingdom to consider. Your pockets have plenty of coins in them. For you, one woman will do just as well as any other when it comes to taking a wife. There's nothing terribly special about Lady Fiona Turnbridge."

Harry wouldn't think that if he really knew her, had he ever seen the little wicked edge to her innocent smile. "Go away, Harry."

"Let's go clubbing," his cousin said brightly. "It'll take your mind off this little setback. We'll find some pretty skirts and—"

"I don't—"

"By the time the sun rises you'll be saying, 'Fiona who?'"

He'd go to his grave whispering Fiona's name. "Harry, I'm not nearly as shallow as you are."

"Yes, you are," his cousin shot back with a shrug. "You just like to pretend that you're not. It's all that education, service to the Crown, and higher purpose falderal. Scratch past it and you're a man with the same sorts of needs and wants as any other."

"I'm a duke." Why the world swayed when he announced that . . .

"All that means is that you get your wants and needs met without working nearly as hard for it as the rest of us."

The world was really getting wobbly.

"How about a suggestion?" he heard Harry say from somewhere that sounded far enough away to be . . . Africa?

"You send Lady Fiona some pretty things along with a note or two professing your regrets for whatever it was that you did wrong and ask her to reconsider marrying you."

"Fiona doesn't care about pretty things." *She gave me back my ring.*

"She's female. She cares."

His head fell against the padding at the back of the chair. The impact was still rippling around in the front part of his brain when he observed, "It's no wonder you're single, Harry."

"And even if she doesn't particularly care, those around her are bound to be impressed and might be inclined to observe that there are worse fates than being a wealthy duchess. If she has even the slightest regrets about so rashly throwing you over, their influence might be enough to tip her back to exercising good judgment."

That made sense. In a way that required a bit of peculiar twisting. And the Rylands were a peculiar lot.

"All right, Ian," Harry said, droning ever on.

"Consider it groveling for forgiveness in an aristocratic, dignified way."

What was *it*? What were they talking about? Oh, yes, groveling. "I need to grovel in person."

"Then do it and get it over, one way or the other."

"She won't see me." *She hates me. I don't know why.*

"Well, then sending her an unending stream of expensive gifts and well-crafted notes is your only other choice, isn't it? Other than shrugging and going out to find someone to replace her."

"I don't want to replace her."

Harry balled up his fist and struck himself in the forehead while moaning, "God, I'm getting a headache."

Ian winced. "You *are* a headache."

"You've never been a very happy drunk, you know."

"So?"

"So things aren't really as bad as you think they are," Harry asserted from an ocean and a continent away. "Your outlook and decisions aren't as much a matter of fact as they're the reflection of the level of whiskey left in the bottle."

"That might make sense in the morning. Maybe." How interesting. When he cocked a brow, the whole side of his face moved. He tried it again. And the top of his head moved, too.

"In the meantime, let's go out. There's nothing more pathetic than a man sitting around, drinking himself blind, and sobbing about having been thrown over."

"I'm not sobbing."

"But you look pathetic. For God's sakes, at least have some pride, Ian. Do you want everyone to think that you let yourself get wrapped around her little finger?"

"No." He was going to write Fiona's Law to prove it.

"All right, then," Harry said, taking away his whiskey glass and standing up. He set both their glasses on the side table and then held out his hand. In a way a bit like Caroline had held out hers when she'd been giving the ring back. He shouldn't have let her put it in his pocket. A ring that wasn't returned meant . . . meant . . .

"Give me your hand, Ian, and I'll help you get to your feet."

"If I can't stand on my own," he protested, rocking slightly forward as he swayed back and forth, "I have no business going out."

He had no recollection of getting to his feet, but Harry beamed and called "Ta-dah!" so he must have done it when he'd been thinking about the possibility of going over to the Rylands' and seeing if maybe Fiona had come home yet.

"Now come along," Harry said, handing him his jacket. "There's no reason for you to put yourself on a shelf while you wait for fickle Fiona to come to her senses."

"If she hears of me going out—"

"Maybe she'll be bitten by the green-eyed monster."

"And take me back. So others can't have me." There was something he wasn't seeing, a facet he wasn't considering. He should be able to. It was obvious. He could sense it right there, but just out of reach. "That is a possibility, isn't it?"

"Well, I'd certainly think so."

"Something's not . . ."

"You know, if we hurry just a bit," Harry said, picking up their glasses, "there's enough time in the day to stop by a jeweler's. And a florist shop or two. You can make the arrangements for a tidal wave of sparkly and pretty-smelling things, then sit back, enjoy yourself, and let matters run their course without giving the campaign another thought."

"And if it doesn't work?"

"Then you'll be especially glad that you didn't sit at home pining away. Women love to suckle wounded warriors to their breasts, you know."

"Fiona," he whispered, remembering, wishing with all his heart.

"Here," Harry said firmly, thrusting his glass in his hand. "Finish this up and drown your false sense of nobility so that we can get on with having a good time."

Drowning. Yes, they said that was a lovely, very peaceful way to go.

Chapter Sixteen

Fiona climbed into the waiting Ryland carriage, thinking that Simone's bout of morning sickness had been just a bit too conveniently timed. One minute she'd been fine and suggesting new ways to get even with Ian, and in the next the note from Caroline had arrived and Simone was gagging and running out of the room.

As notes went, it couldn't have been any shorter. *Come home. NOW.* As the threat of dire consequences went, it was all there—clearly and bluntly implied—in black and white and the firmness of Carrie's script. There would be no more hiding, no more crying and feeling sorry for herself. No more imagining that Ian would crawl to her feet and beg forgiveness, promise her that he'd become a better man, and beg her to take him back.

Fiona plucked at the trim on her dress, remembering how at one time, seemingly so long ago, she'd intended to weave her feminine wiles and then leave Ian mourning for what he'd lost. Why she'd wanted to do that, though . . . It probably served her right that, in the end, she was the one alone and regretting what couldn't be.

With a half smile, she smoothed the trim and wondered if there was such a thing as masculine wiles. Surely there had to be. What else could account for the willingness of women to forgive them so often and for so much? Not to mention to so happily assume responsibility for the smooth functioning of their worlds. She'd tamed his ward, redecorated his home, cleaned out his flower beds, and . . .

Fiona arched a brow. And rolled around with him in his bed. All quite contentedly, quite hopefully. All while believing that Ian would be able to see and deeply appreciate that she was more than domestically competent.

The family carriage rolled to a stop, and she opened the door and let herself out. Before her, just up the short walkway, was the same house she'd left three days ago. How perfect her life had been that morning. How blindly optimistic she'd been.

Shaking her head, she made her way to the door and inside. At least, she consoled herself as she made her way across the foyer, she'd realized her folly before the engagement ball, before she'd signed the settlement papers. Carrie and Drayton had to be relieved by the timing of it all.

"I'm here," she announced, entering the dining room. "As summoned."

"Thank God," Drayton said from behind his paper. "The parlor is going to burst."

Fiona stepped up to the buffet and picked up a plate. "What's wrong with the parlor?"

Carrie rose from the table, took the plate from her hand and returned it to the buffet. "Follow me," she said crisply as she walked out of the dining room.

Fiona followed, noting that her sister was wearing a walking outfit instead of her usual morning house dress. Obviously she intended to go out and pay a social call or two. Fiona frowned, hoping that she wasn't going to be expected to go along. She wanted to crawl into her own bed, wanted to snuggle up with Beeps and tell him the whole sad tale. He'd be disappointed to hear that they weren't going to go live with Dr. Cabott, but his heart belonged to her and he'd love her no matter what. Ian could have learned a lot from Beeps.

Caroline paused at the double parlor doors, pushed them both open at the same time, and then stepped aside, gesturing with a flourish. "It's all from Ian."

Fiona stared, thinking that it looked as though Christmas had come early and decidedly run amok. There were vases and vases of flowers, boxes of all sizes, all of them wrapped in green paper and tied with fluffy bows, little green velvet boxes with no bows at all. There wasn't a single flat surface in the room that was stacked high and crowded to the point of toppling. All of it from Ian.

What was he thinking? That she'd be so dazzled

and delighted by pretty things that she'd forget how he'd treated her? That she'd decide that, in exchange for things, she was willing to be a thing herself?

"Send it all back," she said wearily, turning away.

Carrie caught her arm and stayed her. "I'm not doing anything, Fiona," she said calmly and firmly. "You're the one who ended the relationship. It's your responsibility to clean up the debris that decision has created."

"I didn't ask him to send me all this stuff."

"But he did and you will not only graciously deal with every piece of it, but convey to him, personally, that you want the tide of apology stopped."

Apology? This wasn't an apology; it was a full-scale bribery campaign. "I don't want to see him."

Carrie arched a brow and gave her The Look. "Then write him a letter and arrange for every single one of the gifts to be returned. Before lunch today. I'm off to call on Lady Barnes and coo over her new baby. I expect to find this room back to its normal appearance when I return."

Carrie waited. No doubt for formal and meek acquiescence. Fiona folded her arms across her midriff. "Why are you angry with me?"

"I'm not angry, Fiona," her sister replied. "I'm disappointed."

Disappointed? "At what?"

Carrie studied the floor for a moment, then lifted her gaze to give her a small but patient smile. "No relationship ever runs smoothly all the time. There are ups and there are downs."

"And," Fiona countered, "just as there are beginnings, there are ends, too."

"True. And the measure of one's maturity and character lies in how one handles life's inevitable less-than-happy moments. You've been hiding at Simone's for the last three days, simmering in your anger, letting Ian wallow alone in his misery, and expecting everyone else in your world to manage the unpleasant consequences and obligations you don't want to deal with. It's time to grow up, Fiona."

Ian wasn't miserable. And she hadn't expected anyone to deal with all this flotsam because she hadn't known it was here. The only thing she'd asked of anyone was that Carrie return the ring to Ian if he happened to call, and that her animals be fed and watered.

"Ogre sister that I am," Carrie went on, "I expect you to be done with the process by noon today so that I can advise my guests in advance of tomorrow night's ball that the engagement has been called off."

"You haven't done that yet?" Fiona asked, stunned.

"I've been waiting to see if you would change your mind. The only thing worse than calling off an engagement at the last moment is announcing, at an even later moment, that it's back on again."

Fiona gestured toward the mountain of gifts. "You thought all of this would make a difference?"

"I thought that perhaps you might come to your senses and realize that you love Ian."

"Ha!"

Carrie turned and walked away, saying, "I'm off to see Lady Barnes."

"Love Ian," Fiona muttered, glaring at the decorated boxes and vases of flowers. She stepped into the overflowing parlor, looking for any sign of a note. The first one she found was tucked amongst the fern fronds in a large vase of red roses sitting on the sideboard. "Let's see," she muttered, yanking it out, "if he's once—just once!—mentioned the word *love*."

She opened it to find an elegant and obviously feminine script announcing—with the distinct sound of a trumpet fanfare in the distance—that the flowers were from His Grace, Dr. Ian Cabott, the Duke of Dunsford.

"She was obviously impressed," Fiona groused, wadding up the note and tossing it down. Looking around, she saw another note. This one accompanied a smallish box with a big white bow.

I'd like seeeee you in thi . . . I. Fiona arched a brow and read it again. His pen had shaken, he'd left out words, and he'd trailed off at the end, not even bothering to finish the thought. And *I*? What, writing out his full name had been too much for him to do? Well, probably, she allowed, her teeth clenched. He'd clearly been three sheets to the wind when he'd picked up the pen.

She tossed the note down and considered the box, tempted to open it just to see what a drunkard considered an appropriate wooing gift. Given how small the box was . . . Gloves and scarf. Or maybe a shawl. She had lots of those already. She sighed and wandered on through the maze of male stupidity.

The clock was chiming the half hour when Fiona dropped down onto the settee and tossed the collection of notes on the side table. Seven were fanfare announcements from florists. Four were from perfumers who expressed His Grace's hope that she found their wares to her liking. The jewelers hadn't written notes; they'd just included their finely, tastefully engraved cards. There was only the one drunken note from Ian himself. The one where he'd mentioned the word "like." Hardly the heartfelt declaration of adoration she'd been hoping to find.

And the truth was, she had to admit, blinking back yet another wave of tears, she had wanted very much to find a word or two on which to hang her fragile hope. Her fading hope. And to think that only a few weeks ago she'd been hoping that Ian would withdraw his marriage proposal and leave her alone to enjoy her comfortably patterned life. How odd that it didn't feel quite so comfortable anymore, that it felt a bit hollow and . . . well, expectant. As though she were simply going through familiar motions while biding her time until something important happened.

Until Ian accepted the notion that marriage was a

partnership of equals. Or until she decided that she cared enough about him to risk herself, to overlook his faults and marry him in the hope that, over time, his perceptions could be remolded. If only she thought there might be reasonable odds of succeeding at that.

He really was a remarkable man. Intelligent and handsome. Kind and compassionate and generous. He was a socially progressive thinker—at least when it came to the practice of medicine and public health. And while she didn't have any other lovers to measure him against, she honestly couldn't imagine that there could ever be anyone more intriguing, anyone who could make her feel freer or happier, or satisfy her more thoroughly.

If only he understood that she—

"Pardon the intrusion, Lady Fiona."

She looked up to meet the gaze of the footman standing in the parlor doorway. "It's all right," she said, wearily rising and gathering up the notes. "Do you have a match?"

He cocked a brow and then intoned, "Her Grace, the Dowager Duchess Dunsford."

He'd sent his mother to plead his case? God, why? It suggested a sense of complete desperation. Or maybe a last, final effort so that he could say he'd gone the full measure. Of course, why he'd consider it important to do that . . .

An older woman—maybe sixty or so, if Fiona had been pressed to guess—glided into the room.

Only the slightest bit stooped at the shoulders by age, she was regal and perfectly dressed, perfectly coiffed. She came to a stop at the midpoint of the parlor and waited.

"Hello, Your Grace," Fiona offered.

Ian's mother sniffed and lifted her chin so that she could look down her nose. "You are supposed to curtsy at being presented to me."

The daughter of a duke, the sister-in-law of a duke. The wife of a duke, the mother of a duke. They seemed fairly evenly anointed to her. And the idea of kowtowing on command . . . Fiona leaned back against the sideboard and crossed her arms over her midriff. "Is there a particular reason you've called this morning, Your Grace?"

She drew herself up by slow, even degrees, then pointedly slid her gaze over the contents of the room. "You appear to have a great many ardent suitors."

"It's all from Ian."

"Ah, ever overly generous," she said through a tight, obviously forced smile. "I have a great many things to do today and so I will be direct. Ian's only true purpose in life is to be a disappointment, embarrassment, and irritant to me. I have long expected his choice of duchess to follow in the same vein as the other choices he has made and for the same reasons. I must say, however, that choosing you was a spectacular low, even for him."

Well, if Ian had sent her to plead for him, she'd apparently thrown the script out the carriage window along the way. "The truly direct version of that, Your Grace, would be to say that you don't approve of me."

Her lips were thin and bloodless as she opened her reticule. "Two thousand pounds," she said, removing a stack of banded, pristine bank notes and tossing it down on the seat of the nearest chair.

"For?" Fiona asked warily.

"Ending your overreaching relationship with my son."

She doesn't know. Ian didn't send her. Sadness weighting her heart, Fiona shook her head. "I'm not interested in your money."

Her Grace took another stack from her reticule and tossed it atop the other one. "Three thousand."

"I'm not for sale, Your Grace."

"How much do you want?" the other woman asked frostily.

It really was no wonder that Ian's view of relationships was so limited. In his world, everything could be had for the right price, and nothing had value beyond what had been paid for it or what it could be sold for. "Just out of curiosity . . . How many would-be duchesses have you purchased over the years?"

"I have lost count."

Too ready, too quick to answer. Not even the slightest pause to remember. She was lying. "How many have refused your offer?" Fiona asked, oddly strengthened by the certainty that she was at least one kind of first in Ian's experience.

"None."

"The correct answer, Your Grace," Fiona said kindly but firmly, "is *one*." And, given the way the woman blinked, she was apparently a first for his mother, too.

"You can either choose to take the money or suffer the consequences."

Her tone was the same, still icy and imperious. But the cadence of her speech was drastically different: faster, the words less separated and measured. Ian's mother was off her stride. "And what might those consequences be?" Fiona asked, truly curious about what was the worst that could happen in Ian's world.

"I will see that your name is dropped from the invitation list of every Society event."

"For free?" Fiona asked before she could think better of it.

"I beg your pardon?"

"I loathe parties," Fiona explained. "I'd be willing to pay you—handsomely—if you could arrange it so that I didn't have to go to any more."

"No worthy designer will ever make your gowns."

She considered this a dire threat? "My sister designs my gowns. She always has and always will."

"You will never wear the Dunsford family jewelry."

Fiona had to suck in her cheeks to keep from grinning. "I'll probably cry myself to sleep tonight over that one," she replied, failing miserably in the effort to keep her amusement out of her voice.

"Sarcasm is most unbecoming."

"No more so than bribery and bullying," Fiona blithely shot back.

"You are impudent."

Better than being impotent, she silently retorted. The insight was swift, and despite being wholly unexpected, crystalline and certain. Fiona chewed the inside of her lip and considered the elderly woman, weighing what each of them stood to gain by honesty. In the end she decided that there wasn't anything to be gained in keeping silent. It wasn't as though they were ever going to be part of the same family. And maybe, just maybe, Ian's mother would look at the world just differently enough to understand that she could be a happier person.

"I know that you have places to go, Your Grace, so I'll be direct, as well," she began. "I broke off my engagement to your son three days ago. All of this has arrived here since then. His attempt to apologize and convince me to change my mind."

"Which, when the value becomes large enough to suit you, you will."

"No, Your Grace, I won't," she countered softly. "All of this will be returned to him this afternoon."

"There is no other man in the kingdom who can give you more."

"It's not *things* that matter, Your Grace. Money and status and pretty baubles mean nothing without respect. I don't want to go through the rest of my days being considered a socially necessary but not particularly valuable ornament in a man's life. It strikes me as a very sad and empty and lonely way to live."

"As is being a spinster," she haughtily countered.

Fiona shrugged. "At least spinsters don't have to spend their lives with someone who dismisses their hopes and dreams, thoughts and opinions as being unimportant simply because they're those of a female. They can be more than merely a wife, more than a person as easily and quickly replaced as any member of the household staff."

The duchess slowly arched a white brow. "Young women today have such overly inflated expectations of marriage."

"I think that it's more a matter of understanding that they have worth on their own and that being happy is just as important as being married."

Ian's mother made a tiny *hrumph*ing sound. "And what would happen to the world if women were to choose their happiness over marriage?"

Fiona smiled. "Men will either have to pay housekeepers a *lot* more, or they'll have to adjust their thinking as to what makes an acceptable husband and then decide whether they want to make a sincere effort to become one, or live alone."

One corner of her mouth twitched ever so slightly. "What an intriguing notion." Then, as though she felt guilty for having enjoyed the thought of males losing some of their kingly prerogatives, she added, "Not, of course, that there is the remotest chance of it ever coming to pass."

"Well, to be perfectly honest, Your Grace," Fiona replied with a tiny shrug, "I'm not the least interested in changing the way the world works for everyone. Most people are quite content to go along, to accept matters as they are and have always been. I'm simply not one of them. I want more for myself. Yes, it's selfish. But . . ."

She managed a smile that she hoped didn't look as sad as she suddenly felt. "It's become apparent that your son is very traditional in his thinking. His life would run ever so much more smoothly if he marries a woman of like mind."

The duchess openly considered her while nodding and quietly replying, "Yes, it would."

Well, it would have been nice if the woman had disagreed and suggested that her son's life would be happier if he married her. Nice, yes, and not at all surprising that she hadn't. "Is there anything else we need to discuss, Your Grace?" Fiona asked, stepping over to the chair and picking up the banded stacks of currency.

"I believe we are concluded, Lady Fiona."

She handed the money back to Ian's mother and then dipped her chin in acknowledgment. "Good day then, Your Grace. I'm glad that we had the opportunity to meet."

"Good day, Lady Fiona," she said, bowing her

head slightly before turning and sweeping out of the room every bit as regally as she'd entered it.

Fiona watched her go, her heart growing heavier with every beat. The woman wasn't the ogre everyone had painted her to be. Yes, she was distant and frosty and formal. But given the world in which she lived, the world in which she'd been a young woman, a wife and mother . . . Ice was often a good thing; Nature's way of protecting tender growth from the ravages of harsh, uncaring winter winds. It was sad, though, that spring had never come for Ian's mother. Perhaps, if the two of them could have traveled down the road of life together for a while . . .

Fiona dragged a breath deep into her lungs and squared her shoulders. There was no point in wishing, in hoping for a road she couldn't take. The ruts of social expectation in it had been worn deep, and she knew that, in time and despite her every effort, she'd fall into them and never be able to climb out. In time, married to Ian, she'd become just as lonely and empty and angrily impotent as his mother. And Ian would be so busy with his life that he'd never notice that in her tiny, limited world it was always winter.

Swiping away the tears, Fiona left the parlor to find some packing boxes.

His head was in pieces. He could feel the air whistling between them. God, it was loud. Loud enough to make him wince. And that made all the pieces throb and ache all that much more. Actually, they weren't so much aching as they were wailing. Well, some were wailing. Others were growling about needing a drink, but it was hard to hear them over the frantic blubbering.

"Ahem."

Damn. He wasn't alone. Someone was there. Someone who probably thought he was capable of opening his eyes and carrying on a conversation. What a mean expectation. Then again, it might be Harry. And Harry might have another bottle of whiskey. Ian cracked open an eye. If his lashes weren't in the way . . . No, even with his lashes in the way, it was his bedroom ceiling. And now that the blubbering and growling in his brain wasn't so bad, he could smell plaster dust. Definitely his bedroom.

"Ahem."

All right, he'd managed to get an eye open. He could probably gather up his wits enough to turn his head and glare for a gulp of the whiskey. *His* whiskey. God knew Harry never bought any. His hair scraping over the linen of the pillow created a godawful racket that vibrated all the way . . . He pushed his tongue up between his teeth and his upper lip. Somebody had knitted little sweaters for his teeth.

"Ian."

His eyes flew open. Sunlight flooded in and stabbed what few functional brain cells he had left. He threw an arm across the top of his face and groaned. He heard his mother sigh. Her heavy, greatly pained and irritated sigh. "Where's Harry?" he asked, desperately hoping that a rescue was imminent.

"I ordered him out hours ago. I have no idea where he went. More importantly, I do not care."

He swallowed a whimper. "Why are you here?"

"I am here to ensure that you are well and truly miserable."

"I am," he admitted. "You may leave now."

"I will not leave until I have expressed my opinion on several matters."

God. Someday he was going to arrive at the gates of hell and find that his mother was the head guard. "Go ahead. Get it done."

"I insist that you be reasonably sober before I start, Ian." Her skirts rustled like a plague of locusts as she stood up. "Your valet is preparing your bath and your shaving mug. A tray of bread and cheese and black coffee will be arriving shortly. When you are presentable and capable of reaching the parlor without breaking your neck along the way, I will be waiting there for you."

The plague rustled toward the door, mercifully sounding softer and softer as it went. Maybe, if he took forever, she'd get tired of waiting and go away. But probably not. She'd probably come back to his room and beat him with something. He cocked a brow and winced.

"Conners?" he whispered. Nothing. Ian lifted his hands and held the sides of his head. "Conners?" he called softly.

"Here, Your Grace."

Thank God. If he'd had to make his voice any louder, what was left of his brain would have exploded. "Slit my throat for me."

"Your bath is ready, Your Grace. Do you need assistance in getting to the tub?"

"No."

Well, actually, he probably did, he admitted to himself as he slid off the bed and his legs threatened to buckle under him. He grabbed the headboard post to steady himself and waited for the world to stop spinning so damned wildly. Perhaps . . . No. The idea of asking Conners to walk him to the tub, to help him undress . . . No. He'd get to the bathing room and into the tub on his own or die trying. The latter being a distinct and highly likely possibility, he allowed as he let go of the bed post and staggered forward.

It might have been the effects of the hot bath water. Or time. Or food. But he was inclined to think that the thick black coffee had done the best job of dragging him back to the edge of the real world. Yes, he could see the outlines of it from here. And while it wasn't at all pretty, he suspected that where he'd been of late was even worse.

"Conners?"

"Yes, Your Grace?"

"How long has the binge been?"

"Three days."

Three? Jesus. He didn't remember a thing. Well, not after Harry had shown up and suggested that they go clubbing and skirt . . . His stomach twisted in dread. A liter of coffee sloshed upward. "Have I brought any women here?"

"*You* have not, Your Grace."

He hadn't. Good news in a way, but not quite what he'd been hoping to hear. "Somebody else brought the women?"

"Lord Bettles has been . . . entertaining . . . during your incapacitation."

All right, Harry had been the procurer. Not surprising news. "Just how incapacitated have I been?"

"Severely, Your Grace. In fact, Mrs. Pittman summoned Dr. Mercer last night out of fear that you might be close to death."

Ian nodded, one part of his brain stunned and amazed that he could do it without the whole world moving, and the other half of his brain calmly assuring him that *severely incapacitated* implied that he'd been utterly incapable of even the least bit of carnal frolicking.

"It was at Dr. Mercer's suggestion, Your Grace," Conner went on, "that the remaining spirits were placed where you couldn't reach them."

"Forcing me to travel the road back to consciousness."

"Yes, Your Grace."

It would have been nice if someone had thought to drag him to the edge of the road to let him sober up instead of leaving him lying in the middle of it to be run over by every horse cart in the Empire. God, he ached in places he didn't know he had. The last time he'd hurt this badly had been the day after Lady Baltrip's assault. It was going to be a while before he rode a horse again. Hopefully Char—

"Uh-oh," he drawled as a particularly unpleasant possibility bloomed in his awareness. "Miss Charlotte. Has she been aware of . . ."

"The debauchery?"

He tried not to groan out loud. "It was that bad?"

"It was confined to this level of the house, Your Grace. Rowan posted a footman at both the main and servants' stairs to keep Lord Bettles and his companions from dubiously enlightening Miss Charlotte."

"That's a relief."

"Miss Charlotte is, however, very much aware of your wedding to Lady Fiona having been called off, Your Grace. She has been discussing with your solicitor the possibility of taking up residence elsewhere."

Fiona. His chest tightened and his throat thickened. "Damnation," he said, forcing himself to think of something else. He'd intended to tell Charlotte himself. To explain. Now it was going to be one helluva fence to mend. "Anything else I need to know about before I face the dragon in the parlor?"

"Lady Fiona has returned all of your gifts," Conners said, running the razor up and down the strop.

Gifts? "What gifts?"

"I have not inventoried them, Your Grace."

"A general description will do."

"Flowers, candies, jewelry, perfumes. The usual things, Your Grace."

Flowers. He had a vague recollection of clutching some roses to his chest and talking about steel fairies and wicked beds deep in the woods. There were a few other bits and pieces of odd scenes tumbling around with that one in his brain. "What about clothes?"

"I am not aware of any larger boxes, Your Grace."

Which didn't mean a damned thing if the foggy memory was anywhere near accurate. The way he remembered it, the little white wisp of a peignoir would have fit inside the average tea tin. God, she would look utterly delectable in it. Well, for as long as she'd have the thing on before he tore it off of her. Maybe . . .

"Can you tell if she opened the boxes?"

Conners brought the shaving mug and the razor to the side of the tub, replying, "They appear to have been returned unexamined, Your Grace."

Trying to decide whether that was good or bad, Ian extended his hand for the mug and the brush.

Conners obediently handed them over. On the one hand, Ian mused as he soaped three days' worth of beard, if she'd opened the boxes, appraised everything and then sent it back, it would suggest that none of it was to her liking and that he simply needed to find out what was. He still had a chance to mend the bridge between them. On the other hand, if she hadn't cared enough to be even a little curious about what he'd sent her . . . He handed back the mug and brush, wondering if she'd shoot him if he dared to try to apologize in person.

"I can shave myself," he protested as Conners leaned down with the razor. His valet handed it over, looking decidedly amused. Ian considered the way the sharp edge was shaking and handed it back, adding, "Tomorrow."

The corners of the man's mouth were definitely twitching as he replied, "A wise and prudent decision, Your Grace."

"It's the only decent one I've made lately," Ian admitted as he leaned back in the tub and presented his neck.

Someone had turned his parlor into a forlorn lover's desperation gift and sweet shop. Ian scanned the long line of floral arrangements on the sideboard and the stacks and stacks of gaily wrapped boxes on the floor in front of it. Had he sent all of this to Fiona? Good God. She had to think he'd gone insane.

"You still look terrible."

"Thank you, Mother," he said, dropping down onto the chair opposite the settee. "As usual, you've shored up my battered and flagging spirits."

She put her teacup back into the saucer. Holding both pieces in perfect fashion, she asked, "Why have you spent the last three days drinking yourself into a stupor?"

"It seemed the thing to do."

She contemplated that for the count of two entire seconds. "I would appreciate a serious and truthful answer, Ian."

"It was the easiest and least painful thing to do."

"As compared to what?"

He sighed and pinched the bridge of his nose. "Let's get to the heart of the matter, Mother, so you can be properly pleased." He dropped his hand and met her gaze. "Fiona has returned my ring. We will not be marrying. Feel free to select whoever you'd like to be the next duchess and advise me of when and where to be for the wedding."

"I have already made my selection, Ian."

"Well, you certainly didn't waste any time," he observed testily as he watched her set her cup and saucer aside. "Do I know her?"

"I have chosen Lady Fiona."

Oh, for the love of Christ. He snapped his jaw closed and told himself that despite the temptation, getting himself a drink was *not* a good idea.

"I called on her this morning," his mother said,

primly lacing her fingers in her lap, "determined to do whatever had to be done to end your dalliance with her. She was in the process of returning all of this to you. We had a brief and highly interesting conversation. At the end of which, I concluded that she has a considerable number of redeeming qualities. Not the least among them being a healthy sense of pride and a good measure of common sense."

"Well, Mother," he drawled, "it's a little late for your approval to make a difference. I'm afraid that I have again managed to disappoint you. I find it amazing how things *always* work out that way."

"I found myself contemplating her words long after I left Lord Ryland's," she went on, either unaware that he'd said anything or choosing to ignore him. "Lady Fiona is also uncommonly wise for her years. I wish that I had had a friend of her mind and self-confidence when I was a young woman. I can not help but think that my life would have taken a very different path, that I would be a person very different from the one I have become."

Stunned, he ran her words back through his mind. Yes, it certainly sounded as though she'd just said that she'd made mistakes in her life. Surely not, though. Not the Dowager Duchess Dunsford. Either his brain had been truly pickled, or his mother had fallen and rattled hers. "You have regrets?" he asked cautiously.

"A great, great many, Ian."

Dear Lord Almighty. If he hadn't been sitting

down, he would have fallen down. "Such as?"

"I should not have married your father without setting some very clear guidelines as to how I wanted—and expected—to be treated."

Why he'd thought she'd talk about dresses and shoes. . . . "I don't recall him as a cruel man," Ian replied, too shocked to be capable of anything except outright honesty. "Was he an ogre in private?"

"He was an indifferent man, Ian. Both publicly and privately. I was merely a convenient ornament in his life. Had I died or left him, he would have replaced me as easily and quickly as he would have a member of the household staff."

Ian shook his head in wonder. "That sounds like something Fiona would say."

"Undoubtedly because she did say it," his mother quipped. "To me. This morning. We were discussing her most fundamental requirements for entering into marriage."

"And how I don't meet them?" he asked, his wonder withering.

"Actually, Ian," she replied cheerfully, "the specifics of your personal shortcomings were never mentioned. We were discussing, in a general way, the nature of marriage and what should be considered reasonable expectations of the female half. In listening to her, I realized that I could not fault her for wanting to be happy. I could not wish upon her the kind of shallow marriage that I and so many women of my age have endured."

"She thinks our marriage would be shallow?" he asked numbly.

"What did you do, Ian, that led Lady Fiona to break off your engagement?"

The memory was there in an instant, full and crisp and horribly, horribly vivid. "I said things I shouldn't have said."

"All men do, Ian. Women know and accept that men are often incapable of working their brain and their mouth at the same time with any degree of competence. That is why we usually listen with only half an ear. Our willingness to be partially deaf allows men to live longer lives."

"I had no idea."

"Well, now you do," she said crisply, picking up her teacup again. "What did you say that Fiona found not only impossible to ignore, but also unforgivable?"

He'd called her reckless and foolish. He'd reprimanded her for having disobeyed his orders. He'd told her that she was presumptive in thinking that . . . Realization came in a long, slow instant that crushed the air from his lungs and tore through his heart.

"I displayed a phenomenal and inexcusable disregard for her intelligence, skills and abilities," he said softly. "I treated her as though she were nothing more than a pretty ornament."

"And how have you gone about offering her your

apology for having been so insulting, disrespectful, and wrong headed?"

"I sent her . . ." He gestured toward the overloaded sideboard.

"Ornaments?"

"Oh," he whispered as the dawn of realization continued to illuminate the incredible depth and breadth of his stupidity. "Oh, damn."

"Alcohol," his mother offered blithely, "when combined with Harry's instincts and encouragement, makes for very poor decisions."

"Unfortunately," he drawled, closing his eyes, "it's only after sobering up that that's obvious."

"Would you care for a bit of maternal advice?"

As though there was anything he could do to salvage the wreckage. Chuckling darkly, he shrugged. "Is it going to make any difference whether I do or not?"

"No," she answered, chuckling herself.

She was laughing? Ian opened his eyes, trying to remember if he'd ever in his life heard her laugh.

"I can not turn over an entirely new leaf all at once," she told him. "Aside from that, I happen to be very good at giving advice. You need to take yourself to Lord Ryland's townhouse, apologize profusely and sincerely to Lady Fiona, and then beg her, preferably while on your knees, to give you a second chance."

"It would be a third chance," he clarified while a

vision of Fiona shooting him played through his mind.

"Third?"

"My second chance followed the Lady Baltrip debacle."

"Ah, yes. I had forgotten."

"I doubt that Fiona has."

She apparently mulled that over for a moment and then said, "If it helps any to know, Ian, I think Lady Fiona is probably the only woman who would be able to sincerely forgive you for your repeated stupidity, and allow you a chance to start over."

Yes, Fiona probably was the only woman on earth with a heart that big, that loving and compassionate. But the question was *why* she'd be at all interested in forgiving him. *Again.*

"Of course, I am assuming that you have a true preference for her as your duchess. If any woman will do, please disregard my advice."

"No," he assured her. "No other woman will do, Mother."

"Why is that?"

He *hated* questions like that. To condense an ethereal something the size and complexity of the universe into a few common words . . . "Fiona's everything to me," he offered lamely. "She makes me laugh. She makes me think. She makes me proud. She makes me happy a thousand times a day in a hundred thousand ways. I can't imagine living without her." He paused, and for the sake of honesty, added, "Well, actually, I can imagine life without Fiona. It's awful enough to drive a man to drink himself to death."

She nodded and looked off across the room. "Do you think you might love her?"

He sighed in frustration. "Of course I love Fiona. Didn't I just say that?"

His mother arched a brow and brought her gaze slowly back to him. "No, Ian, you did not."

"Well, in as many words," he offered in defense.

"There are times, Ian, when fewer words are more expressive than many."

She put her teacup on the side table again and placed her hand on the arm of the settee. Ian, recognizing the sign, vaulted to his feet—not nearly as smoothly as he would have if he hadn't spent the last three days swimming in alcohol—and wobbled forward to offer her his assistance in rising.

"I will wish you luck and be on my way," she said as she steadied him. She was walking toward the parlor door when she added, "Do let me know how it all works out."

It was going to take a miracle, but he had to try. He couldn't walk away without having stood in front of Fiona and telling her that he—

"Oh, Ian?"

He looked over toward the threshold. "Yes, Mother?"

"I realize that you may be tempted to dash forth in the moment and pledge your undying love and devotion to Lady Fiona, but it would behoove your cause to wait a bit. At least until the distillery has largely passed from your person. Your breath is horribly offensive."

Some things never changed. "Thank you, Mother."

"You are most welcome."

Chapter Seventeen

While he was championing his cause, he needed to do what he could to clean up the shambles he'd made of the rest of his life in the last three days. Ian glanced in his study, noted the piles of papers on his desk, and continued on his way to the rear of the house. He'd barely reached the open sunroom door and lifted his hand to knock when Genghis Jack raised his head off the bed and sprang into action.

With the snarling dog firmly attached to his trouser leg, he waited until Charlotte turned her chair to face him. "May I come in?" he asked.

"It's your house," she said, giving him a hard look before turning her back on him.

It was exactly the reception he'd expected to get. But if ever there was such a thing as the perfect opening to a necessary conversation . . . "I hear," he said, dragging Jack back into the room, "that you've been talking to my solicitor about establishing your own residence."

"I have. I think it would be for the best."

Yes, but she was fourteen and she was female. The solicitor was listening to her only to be polite. "Would you be considering a house of your own if Fiona and I were still going to marry?"

"No. But since you're not, and you seem to have decided to live a libertine existence, I think—"

"Harry was the libertine," he corrected. "I was the drunk." She shrugged. Jack's toenails scraped on the floor as he growled and ruthlessly shook Ian's trouser leg. "I'm going to apologize to Fiona and ask her to reconsider my proposal."

She wheeled around. "When?"

"As soon as I'm far enough into sober that my breath won't knock her over."

Charlotte moved the chair back, saying, "It could be next week."

"It's that bad?"

She looked away, made a tiny O with her lips, and then glanced at him with a painful expression to reply, "There's a peppermint patch in the herb garden. I suggest that you graze awhile before you go anywhere."

He nodded. Jack growled and succeeded in tearing Ian's trouser leg.

"How was your dress designing session with Lady Ryland?" Ian asked, glaring down at the Hound From Hell. "I'll bet this thing was owned by a tailor," he grumbled. "And he trained him to shred trouser legs so he'd have more business."

Charlotte snapped her fingers. "Heel, Jack!" The dog instantly released what was left of his trouser leg and trotted to the side of her chair. He sat down and grinned up at Ian.

"Highly enjoyable and productive," his ward said, answering his question. "Considerably better than your afternoon with Fiona turned out."

Since she seemed to be fairly well informed . . . "Have you talked to her since that day?"

"No. Fiona's been staying at her other sister's house. Lady Ryland said that she's been just horrible."

Horrible? Fiona? "Horrible in what way?"

"Crying, moping, throwing things, not eating, not talking to anyone, not coming out of her room. Lady Ryland said she'd give Fiona three days to come to her senses on her own and then she was going to take matters in hand herself."

Well, the three days was up. "Do you have any idea of what Lady Ryland intends to do?"

"She said she was going to make Fiona come home this morning and square up to life. The look in her eyes . . ." Charlotte made another O with her mouth and shook her head. "I don't think people tell Lady Ryland 'no' very often. I stayed home today because I didn't want to be in the way in case things went badly."

"Do you think they'd let me in the house if I went over there? Or would they have me shot on the front walk?"

"I don't know, Ian. When Lady Ryland heard that

you were trying to drown your sorrows, she rolled her eyes and muttered something about typical men. Lord Ryland said he was going to have a drink or two in sympathy and Lady Ryland gave him that look of hers."

"They'll let me in," he said on a sigh of utter relief. "They'll let me try."

"If they do, please don't make a mess of your apology, Ian. I adore Fiona."

"As do I," he assured her.

"Then you might want to show her that you do."

That's what he'd been trying to do with all the folderol now crowding his parlor. Apparently in his drunken state he hadn't managed to hit upon anything she really wanted from him. And, sad as it was to say, he didn't think he could do one bit better sober. "Do you have any suggestions? Has she mentioned anything she particularly wants?"

"I can't think of anything, Ian. All I've ever heard her say is that she wants to spend time with you. I'm sorry."

"Thank you, Charlotte." He headed for the door, adding, "If you think of anything else, I'll be here for a while longer. Since I'm still promoting my cause, I might as well take a quick look through the papers that have piled up on my desk in the last couple of days."

"While chewing peppermint leaves."

"I'll go get some right now," he promised, changing

course and heading for the kitchen and the door that led into the small herb garden just outside.

Time with him. Doing what? Other than destroying peignoirs and twisting sheets into knots? He loved her, yes. With all his heart. But dammit, he had people to treat and a hospital to build. He couldn't hover around the house all the time, gazing dreamily into her eyes. She'd be sick of seeing him inside a week. And besides, how the hell was he supposed to put time in a box and wrap it up in a pretty bow?

Ian stopped in the hall, his apparently still impaired brain stumbling over the pure simplicity of the idea. "Lunkhead," he muttered, turning and heading to his study.

Simone paused at the conservatory door to pull on her opera gloves and proclaim, "You can't hide forever."

"Yes, I can," Fiona defiantly called back as she resumed filling the bird feeder. "Watch me."

"Sooner or later," her sister went on, "he's going to sober up and come looking for you."

"No, he's not," Fiona countered. "I wrote him a letter today—when I sent all his gifts back—and told him not to waste his time."

"Oh, really? It would appear that he didn't get it."

Fiona knitted her brows and turned just as her sister said, "Hello, Ian. Lovely night for a reconcilation, isn't it?"

Fiona didn't hear what he said in reply; the only sound in the world was the frantic pounding of her heart. Her foolish, girlishly dreaming heart. She saw his lips move, saw him bow slightly to Simone as she slipped out the door, saw him slowly straighten and bring his gaze to hers.

Just to look at him, just to have him there . . . For all her insistence on respect . . . Despite knowing better in every fiber of her rational being . . . She loved him. God help her, she loved him, heart and soul and forever.

As he made his way toward her, Fiona looked down at the flagstones and drew a ragged breath into her lungs. It did nothing to ease the tightness around her heart or make the truth any less painful. She closed her eyes, took another breath, and willed herself to be strong, to resist the temptation of blind hope and do what was best for both of them. Her love alone wasn't enough for them to build a happy life together.

"Fiona?"

Resolved, she found a smile that she hoped looked serene and confident, lifted her head, and focused her gaze on the second button on his shirt front.

"I'm here," he began, "to apologize for my behavior that afternoon, for the things I said. I was wrong in insisting that you stay in the carriage. And I was most certainly wrong in criticizing your judgment and your abilities."

"Thank you. I should have considered how you might worry about me."

He sighed and then quietly cleared his throat. "And if possible, I'd really appreciate it if you'd forget that I sent you all those ridiculous gifts. If my brain had been working even a little bit, I would have known that I was digging the hole deeper."

That he realized what his blunder was was definitely an unexpected point in his favor. "I got the impression that you were drinking heavily."

"And continuously," he added. "Truth be told, aside from a couple of foggy snippets, I don't remember the last three days. According to my staff, I spent them largely unconscious."

She knew that she needed to keep a distance and formality between them. But . . . She looked up to meet his gaze. "Just how does an unconscious man order flowers?"

"Well," he drawled, one corner of his mouth quirking up in a chagrined smile, "in the hour or so that exists between his mind shutting down and his body falling down, he lets his slightly less inebriated lackwit cousin drag him around to various shops to place ongoing orders."

"So what you sent was Harry's idea of suitable bribes," she observed, wondering why she hadn't considered that possibility the very second Carrie had thrown open the parlor doors.

"I seem to recall that there was one thing I found myself."

"That would be the little box with the only note you *attempted* to write yourself?"

He cocked a brow. "I gather I didn't do all that well with it."

"No, you didn't."

He considered her for a second and then reached inside his coat. "Well, my head's firmly back on my shoulders now," he said, handing her a long, flat, black leather case.

"Ian," she said on a sigh, staring down at it.

"Go ahead," he pressed, seemingly oblivious to her turmoil. "Open it."

Her heart aching, she shook her head. "Didn't you read my note?"

"What note?"

"The one I sent with all the gifts I returned this afternoon."

He shrugged. "I didn't know that you'd sent a note. I didn't even look for one."

Oh, God. "Then let me summarize it, Ian," she said gently, hoping she could get through saying it without the tears she'd shed during the writing. "I don't want jewels or candy or flowers or perfumes from you. I don't want *things*. I didn't call off our engagement because the ring wasn't beautiful enough or because—"

He pressed a fingertip to her lips. "Open it, Fiona," he whispered, his eyes sparkling. "Please."

She didn't want to hurt him, didn't want to make an ugly scene, and so she ignored the little voice of reason and lifted the hinged lid. Fiona blinked, stunned, and then stared in disbelief.

Ian lifted the device from the white satin lining, saying, "Every medical student has to have her own stethoscope."

"They won't let me into a medical school," she pointed out, her heart hammering wildly as she closed the case and blindly placed it on the table beside the bird feeder. "They say that the female mind isn't suited to the profession."

"I don't care what they say. I'll soon have my own teaching hospital. I can let in any student I think is capable of being an excellent doctor."

He thought she . . . She gazed at him in wonder as the warmth of absolute certainty filled every corner of her soul.

"Here," he said, putting the earpieces in place and fitting the amplifier between her trembling fingers.

"Ian?"

"Sssh." Lifting her hand, he pressed the device to the center of his chest and held it there.

She closed her eyes and listened to the steady thrum of the most wonderful, most caring heart in all the world.

"Do you hear the murmur, Fiona?"

"No."

"It's there," he said softly. "In every beat. I love . . . you. I love . . . you. Marry . . . me. Fion . . . a."

She looked up at him and grinned, her joy too boundless to be put into words. But he knew anyway;

she could see her happiness reflected in his own smile, in the delight dancing in the depths of his eyes.

Ian eased his hand away from hers, then reached up to gently remove the earpieces. "Say yes," he murmured, wrapping his arms around her and drawing her close.

"Yes, my love," she whispered as she tipped her head back to offer him her lips. "Forever and always, Ian, yes."